The Daughter of Abraham

Philip Newey

Published by All-read-E
http://philipnewey.com/All-read-E.htm

ISBN: 978-0-646-82190-0

MY NAME IS EMILY AND I'M ALIVE. I PROBABLY SHOULDN'T BE, BUT I AM.

The story I am about to tell is impossible, so pardon me if I take some further liberties in its telling. I was not there for most of the events described here, so forgive me, also, if I put words in mouths and thoughts in minds. Words and thoughts I could not possibly know, except that now and then I have heard them in stories told to me, or read them in letters and journals.

This is the story of my grandfather, Charles Kollock Jr, and his women. His mother Emily and his wife Elaine; Miriam and Tiggi and Sophia, and perhaps many others.

This is the story of how I am alive to tell it.

PART ONE

CHAPTER ONE

Charlie Kollock, my grandfather, was born on February 21, 1940, in the town of Lewes, county Sussex. Not the Sussex (or Lewes) in the United Kingdom, but the county of the same name in the state of Delaware, in those United States of America. His family had lived in and around Lewes since early in the eighteenth century. There had certainly been staunch royalists within the family at the time of the revolution, but I'm not sure on which side of the divide my earliest direct forebears stood. Perhaps both. Without doubt, a certain Anglophilia persisted down the line. It had become a tradition that the eldest son in my grandfather's branch of the family go up to Oxford. Not Oxford, Mississippi, or Oxford, Ohio, or any other Oxford in the USA, but that hallowed institution in the UK. It was also a tradition, though one less firmly adhered to, that this son return to Delaware with a suitable English wife. Charles senior did just that.

Emily Thorburne was the daughter of a lesser baron. Whether by coincidence or design I don't know, but she came from the English county of the same name. The family was not enormously wealthy, although they did own a small estate in Sussex, a small farm in the same county, and a slightly larger farm in Somerset. Emily was not expected to inherit a great deal, but her fortunes changed dramatically when her two brothers were both lost during the war. Emily became the sole heir of the title, the estate and both farms. The family had never shown any interest in farming the land themselves, and both farms were tenanted.

For much of Charlie's early childhood, his father was largely absent, serving in the European theatre of war, initially as a lieutenant, and ultimately as a colonel. His mother helped his father's sister, May, and their elderly father, to run the family business in his absence. That is to say, she occasionally sat in on family discussions and made irrelevant and tangential comments. The family were property developers, with interests up and down the east coast. Emily's interests, however, largely lay elsewhere.

My great-grandmother had a very fair complexion, with ebony hair cascading around her face when she did not tie it back or wear it up. Her eyebrows were similarly dark. She wore little make-up except, occasionally, a scarlet lipstick that contrasted sharply with her skin and hair. I never knew her, but Charlie remembered her from those days as an image in black and white, save for that one slash of scarlet.

Charlie was four years old when his mother received the phone call about her oldest brother, James. Her father broke the news over the telephone. Charlie watched from the corner, where he played with some of his toy soldiers. He watched as what little colour there was in his mother's cheeks faded ... As she slumped sideways in the chair, the receiver falling to the floor.

'Mommy, Mommy!'

He had learned about death. He knew that when people died they stopped moving. His enemies lay dead and unmoving on the carpeted battlefield around him. He approached to within a few feet of his mother, but then called out for Rita, running up the stairs to her room.

'Rita! Rita! It's Mommy.' He pounded on the door.

His young nanny opened the door, yawning and dishevelled. It was late Saturday afternoon, and she was enjoying some time to herself.

'What is it, Charlie?' she snapped.

'Mommy's dead.'

He seized her hand, dragging her along behind him, ignoring her sharp intake of breath, finding unexpected strength when she sought to anchor herself using the rail at the top of the stairs.

They entered the parlour just as his mother was rising unsteadily to her feet.

'Mommy!' He threw his arms around her hips.

'Charlie.' She sat again and pulled him towards her.

'Is it ...? Is it ...?' Rita assumed the worst and stepped hesitantly towards his mother. News of husbands and fathers dying had become commonplace in recent years.

Emily seemed not to notice her at first; then she shook her head and became aware of the fear on the nanny's face.

'No, no ... No, not Charles, Rita. My brother James, in Italy ...' She covered her mouth with her hand and held back the tears.

'I'm so sorry, ma'am.'

'Rita ...' She took in a shuddering breath. 'Rita, could you please do me a favour and call May for me.' But then she became aware of the telephone receiver on the floor beside the chair. 'Oh! I didn't hang up! What must they think? No, no. In a moment.' She waved Rita away, having second thoughts. 'I must first call back Papa. He'll wonder ...' She listened to the receiver for a moment and then replaced it in its cradle. 'Rita, could you please take Charlie away for a while. I need some time.'

'Of course. Come, Charlie. Let's listen to some music! I have a new gramophone record!'

Charlie looked up at his mother. She nodded and kissed his forehead. 'Off you go, Charlie. I'm fine. Everything's fine. Off you go.'

He remembered that day very clearly, because it was the same day that a violent storm, moving down the east coast, struck Lewes, uprooting trees and dislodging roofs. He lay in bed that night listening to the wind, fearing that the rain was coming down so hard that it would shatter his bedroom window.

The awareness had slowly filtered through to him, with the arrival of his Aunt May, and throughout a subdued dinner, that someone important to his mother had been killed in The War. The War, which had been an abstraction, a thing involving toy soldiers, was suddenly something that could come into the house, through the telephone, via the radio, through shattered windows. His own soldiers remained dead and dying in the corner of the parlour.

Among the most well-read and worn books in the library of the three-storey wooden house were the works of Madame Blavatsky. They were among the few possessions, other than her wardrobe and other personal items, that Charlie's mother had insisted on bringing with her from England. Indeed, she seemed to regard them as her *only* truly personal possessions.

Although both the Thorburnes and the Kollocks were Church of England families, neither attended services other than at Christmas and Easter. But his mother would often chatter to him about esoteric matters, not expecting him to understand, but simply because there was no one else to talk to about such things. No one in Charles senior's family was interested, and the nearest meetings of the Theosophical Society took place in Pennsylvania. When she aired these thoughts she was really just thinking aloud.

After the death of her brother, some of these conversations assumed a new intensity.

The day after the storm, a Sunday, Emily, the family's Irish wolfhound—unimaginatively named 'Wolf'—and Charlie went for a walk through town, across the dunes and down to the beach.

'It's as though there's been a war,' she remarked.

This confused Charlie. There *was* a war.

'Look.' She pointed towards the hardware store, where a tree had collapsed and taken half the roof with it.

Small branches littered the streets and sidewalks. It was this general untidiness that drew most of his attention. He had never seen the town looking *untidy* before. People were out and about, tidying yards, making repairs where minor damage had occurred. Several houses had lost shingles from their roofs, and windows were broken here and there. Their own house appeared undamaged, but they were waiting for May's husband to climb up to the roof for a proper inspection.

'What must Europe look like?' she breathed. 'What must London look like?'

The sky was clear and the sun warm and, although the wind still gusted occasionally, it was hard to believe that yesterday's storm had occurred. Standing on a dune, overlooking the bay, his mother held her hat firmly in place. Her chin raised, she stared into the distance. Charlie stared at her. Wolf found something interesting to sniff.

Then she tilted her head, as if listening.

'I sometimes come out here at night,' she said, 'after you're in bed. I listen to the wind and the waves and sometimes I think they speak to me. Sometimes I think I can hear people screaming.'

At that moment a gull screamed nearby. Charlie shivered.

They walked on a little further and found a bench. She sat and patted the seat beside her. He jumped up and swung his legs back and forth. He had picked up one of the small, fallen branches along the way and kicked it, first with one foot, then the other.

'You never had a chance to meet James,' she continued. 'Your Uncle James. You would have liked him.'

'Why?'

'There are forces abroad in the world, Charlie. Forces of darkness and forces of light. James was one of the forces of light.'

Sometimes he liked the darkness. He wasn't afraid of it, the way children were supposed to be. He could hide in the darkness. The light left him exposed. It exposed his mother now. She had removed her hat, and the shadow that had covered her eyes was lifted. But a deeper shadow remained beneath them. Her lips, always narrow, seemed drawn in, and wrinkles radiated from the corners of her mouth. There seemed less of her today. The dim light in the dining room had concealed this from him at breakfast that morning.

'James always made me laugh. Have I shown you a photograph? I must have shown you a photograph.'

He couldn't remember.

'I'll show you when we get back. And Alfie. He's your other uncle. He's more serious. Where are you now, Alfie?'

He followed her gaze out to sea, possibly expecting a reply.

'We should go home, as soon as possible. You must meet Alfie and your grandparents.'

The word 'home' confused him. On the walk back to the house, which was quicker and more purposeful than the outward journey had been, he wasn't sure whether to be excited or anxious at the prospect of meeting his Uncle Alfie and his other grandparents. He was nevertheless disappointed not to find them waiting on the front porch or in the parlour.

'Where are they?' he asked.

'Who?'

'Uncle Alfie and ... and ...'

'A long, long way away, Charlie.'

'But ...'

'Off and wash your hands. Lunch will be ready soon.'

He had been looking forward to meeting his Uncle Alfie.

But Alfie was killed too, a few months later, in the Ardennes.

CHAPTER TWO

IT WASN'T UNTIL AFTER HIS NEW BROTHER, JEREMY, WAS BORN THAT people began describing Charlie's mother as 'delicate'.

The birth of Jeremy had been only one of several events to send tremors through his life during the next two years.

At the end of the summer of 1945, he went to school for the first time. Up to this point, his life had been dominated by the presence of adults. His Auntie May had no children, and the only other children he knew were Ralphie, an older boy who lived two doors down, and Gillie, the young daughter of the cook, who sometimes accompanied her mother on weekends.

Ralphie tended to pick on him when he saw him which, thankfully, was not often. Gillie, a few months younger than him, always had a cold. Or, at least, she sniffled and sneezed constantly.

'Allergies,' her mother reassured him on more than one occasion when he went in search of hot chocolate. As he neither knew what 'allergies' were, nor to what Mrs Harper was referring, it was only many years later that he made the connection. This was when he was re-united with Gillie briefly at college. Mrs Harper and Gillie moved away a year or so after the war. Mr Harper, it seemed, had found a job in construction in Newark.

When Charlie went to college in Pennsylvania, he was very surprised to find Gillie there too. He wouldn't have thought her family had the means. Mr Harper had apparently done very well out of construction. Gillie was still sneezing and sniffling.

'Allergies,' she explained one morning, as they lay together in his narrow, single bed.

In August of 1945, a tall, thin man, with receding hair and a carefully trimmed moustache, came to live with the Kollocks. Within weeks of his father's return, Rita, his nanny of many years, left to marry her sweetheart, who had also returned from the war.

Charlie stood on the porch trembling when Rita came down the stairs, her fiancé carrying her bags. She stooped down and dragged him into her arms. He felt the slight greasiness of her cheek against his own, breathing in again that slightly musty, earthy smell that he associated with her.

'I'll come and visit,' she promised.

She never did.

For a long time, even after the Buick had disappeared around the corner, he could not move. If he moved, the connection would be broken.

Almost exactly nine months after Charlie's father returned, Jeremy was born. From the child's slanted eyes, small chin and enlarged tongue, it was immediately apparent that something was wrong. And it was from that time onwards that Emily Kollock apparently became delicate.

This delicateness manifested itself in several ways. First, Emily was no longer inclined to go on the walks to which she and Charlie had become accustomed, particularly on the weekend. This practice had already been curtailed to some extent by the return of his father. After the birth of Jeremy, the walks ceased completely. At first it had been easy to attribute this to the birth itself and the aftermath. But even after several months, even after a nurse had been employed to help look after the baby, the walks did not resume.

Then there were the occasions when Charlie would pass the library and would know—just know—that his mother was in there, in the darkened room, with perhaps a reading light, one of her favourite books in her lap, but with her eyes closed. He knew because, in trepidation, he had once opened the door a crack. He heard her whispering to herself, almost like an incantation, although the words were unclear. Sometimes she did this at other times too. When working in the garden, for instance.

She had always loved to work in the garden, but now he would spot her from his bedroom window, with gardening gloves on, a trowel in her hand, kneeling before a garden bed, but doing nothing. Her eyes would be closed and her lips moving.

There were also conversations on the telephone, which clearly irritated Charles senior, with someone called Clara. It seemed to be at this Clara's prompting that Emily began to refuse meat. This would cause disagreements between his parents.

'You need to eat. You need to keep up your strength,' his father would insist.

'That's not the kind of strength I need,' his mother would quietly reply.

Since his father had returned, Charlie rarely took his meals with his parents. He would be fed early, sometimes in the kitchen, and his parents would have their meal later, often after eight o'clock. When he was supposed to be in bed, he would hear their disagreements. He would creep onto the landing, and sometimes even downstairs. These disagreements could not be called arguments, because his mother always remained quiet and calm. This, as much as anything, clearly infuriated his father, who would often march from the room with his newspaper under his arm and lock himself away in his study for the remainder of the evening.

His mother's face became thinner, her cheeks slowly receding. With every passing day there seemed to be less and less of her.

Matters reached a critical point one night in March, when Jeremy was just nine months old.

The crisis occurred during the night, although no one became aware of it until early in the morning, when the nurse, Sister Bella, found Jeremy still, cold and unbreathing in his cot. Her scream roused the household.

The doctor could find no immediate cause of death and, within the small community, there were whispers abroad. Some were quick to cast suspicion on the nurse who, after all, came from upstate New York. There were others, though, who were ready to point out that Mrs

Kollock came from England. Wasn't there *inbreeding* among the British aristocracy? This would explain the baby's deficiencies, and perhaps ...

Fortunately, the doctor was a close family friend and questions were taken no further.

After Jeremy's death, Charlie thought his mother might disappear. At times she seemed almost transparent.

He had never been able to understand the fuss about Jeremy. The walks with his mother had been replaced by walks with Sister Bella, with Jeremy in the pram. All babies looked slightly strange to him. And, besides, he had seen few enough to make comparisons. What struck him most about Jeremy was how happy he seemed, usually gurgling and laughing, kicking his feet energetically. He was sad when Jeremy died. He secretly hoped, however, that a lighter mood might now descend upon the household, with the 'problem' out of the way.

It didn't, although, a few weeks after the death, his translucent mother did appear suddenly possessed with a new energy and a feverish excitement.

She had finally organised the long-postponed trip back home. She and Charlie were to leave at the end of August. Passage was booked on the Queen Mary.

'It will only be for two or three months. Perhaps we will stay for Christmas,' she assured him and his father.

On the voyage over, Emily seemed to gain more substance the closer they drew to England.

They were away for a year.

CHAPTER THREE

ELAINE SNUCK UP UNSEEN AND CROUCHED BEHIND A HAY BALE. SHE HAD watched the lambing before, but there seemed to be a problem this time. Her father was there, with her brother Ed, and one of the farm labourers, Jim.

'You need to look see, Ed,' her father was saying. 'It happens once in a while.' Her father spoke with a broad Somerset accent, one not heard so much today. Some would pick him as Mendips born and bred.

Elaine spent many youthful years shucking off any trace of it.

She crept forward a little to see more clearly. No one was looking her way. She had to peer between legs. The head of the lamb was poking out from what she thought of as the ewe's bottom.

'The head's out all right, but not the legs, see?'

Ed nodded.

'So, we need to push the head back in, see. Jim, fetch thee the strips of rope over yonder. Three or four of them. And that tub of grease there.'

Elaine ducked out of the way, but not so quickly that Jim didn't spy her and shoot a wink in her direction. She smiled up at him.

'Right, now. Here we go.' Her father tied a slip knot in one of the ropes and looped it over the lamb's head, behind the ears. Then he began to push the head back in, firmly but gently. The ewe, which had been lying down, rose to her feet in protest.

'Jim, Ed, we have to lay her on her back.'

Between them they subdued the distressed ewe. Now gravity would help as her father pushed the head back in, after coating it with a generous layer of grease.

'Right now.' She was fascinated when her father plunged his hand deep inside the ewe. 'Where's the feet?' The ewe voiced her protest while he felt around. 'Ah.' He carefully manipulated first one foot, and then the other, until they poked out. 'Now, slip a rope around each on um, see?'

This Ed and Jim did.

'Now, stand her up.'

As Ed and Jim set the ewe on her feet, her father pulled on the ropes. The legs came out, and the head followed. Before long, a lamb lay in the hay. The ewe turned and began to lick it.

'He's breathing,' assured Jim.

'Nice big lamb, that. But there's another in there. I felt it when I was poking around.'

Soon, two lambs lay in the enclosure.

'Proper job, lads. I reckon there might be another two ready for lambing tomorrow.'

As he turned to leave, he spotted Elaine. She had forgotten to hide.

'Well now. What have we here? Someone let the swine out?' He wiped his hands on an old blanket that hung nearby. 'Give your old dad a hug, Ellie.'

She squealed with delighted terror as he approached, dirty arms outstretched to grab her. A brief chase ensued. She escaped into the open and made a dash towards the cottage.

Her father shouted after her. 'Tell your mum to put the kettle on. We've worked up a thirst.'

'I heard, girl,' her mother said, as she burst into the kitchen. 'Don't come in here with those wellies on. And look at the mess you are! There'll be a bath for you tonight. Out with thee and get that hay off of thee.'

Elaine sat on the edge of the old bathtub that sometimes served as a water trough, picking hay from her dress. She tugged off her wellington boots and looked with disgust at the mess on her hands, sniffing her fingers. Not just mud.

There was a little water in the bathtub from the overnight rain. She rinsed her hands in that before tackling the hay again.

The visitors would be arriving tomorrow. Her parents had received the request about ten days ago. Her mother read the letter out during supper one night.

'It's the landlord's daughter and her son,' she explained. 'That's this Mrs Kollock. The landlord's daughter. And her boy ... Charlie. Aah, Charlie. They're asking if we'd mind if they stayed in the main wing over Easter. For the three weeks of the school holidays.'

Charlie was eight years old, a few months older than Elaine. And *American*. She was always a little lonely during the school holidays, living way out on the farm. It would be good to have someone to play with. Could she play with him? She wasn't sure. She thought maybe she might not be allowed to play with a landlord's daughter's son. Or an American. They sounded important.

The shadow of the main wing crept towards her across the yard. She looked up at its closed, curtained windows. She had never been in the main wing. Their cottage was actually the original farmhouse, extending at a right angle and forming one side of the yard. She couldn't remember anyone ever living in the main wing, although cleaners came in about once a month from the village.

'I mind,' her father had said. 'But I suppose there's nawt we can do. It's their house, after all. Don't relish the idea of them nosing all over the place. Do we have to feed them?'

'Says here they'll bring some staff. And maybe get in some help from the village.'

'More noses poking around. They might own it, but it's our place. It's our sweat and blood as keeps it running.'

But eventually it was settled. Now Elaine was wondering what Charlie might be like. He could tell her about America.

She knew where America was. She knew about cowboys and Indians. She'd seen a movie. She may even have seen an American soldier one day in the village, during the war. Americans were handsome. And rich. And brave. She began to form a clear image of Charlie in her mind.

When Elaine saw him the next day, he was nowhere near as tall as she had imagined. He was scarcely taller than her. She peered around the corner, towards the front entrance of the main house, where a large car had pulled up. Her mother had gone out to meet them, and managed to keep her head bobbing just short of a bow.

'Welcome to Chetwood, Mrs Kollock. And this must be the young man.' Elaine scarcely recognised her mother's voice. She was 'putting on airs', as she had remarked more than once of others.

'Thank you, Mrs Pierce. This is Charlie.'

'How do you do, Mrs Pierce.' The boy held out his hand in a very grown-up fashion.

'Quite the young gentleman.'

The boy was pale, with a long, narrow face and a prominent, sharply pointed nose. Not handsome, then. Probably rich, though, judging by the car and his clothes. He wore grey shorts, a slightly lighter grey woollen jumper, a white shirt and a blue tie. His black shoes were shiny and his white socks were pulled up neatly to just below his knees. His cap was pushed back a little from his forehead.

It remained to be seen whether he was brave.

The woman, his mother, was as pale and skinny as the boy. Her dress was plain, brown, with a pleated skirt. Her hair was what impressed: almost black, swept up and back from her forehead, and then tumbling down behind her ears to her shoulders in glistening waves.

Snow White.

Two other people, a man and a woman, exited the car. The driver was a short, round man with little hair. He opened the boot of the car and began lifting out suitcases. Elaine's father appeared from inside the big house and offered to help.

'No, no, please,' the boy's mother insisted. 'We're not expecting any help. We're not here to be a bother.'

'No bother at all, ma'am.' Her father touched the brim of his cap, bent down, and picked up a bag.

The other woman was about her mother's age, with grey hair pulled into a tight bun. Mrs Kollock introduced her to her mother.

'This is Mrs Aldershaw. I'm afraid the duties of both cook and housekeeper will fall upon her shoulders this trip. We hope to get some help from the village or hereabouts.'

'How do, Mrs Aldershaw. If there's anything at all we can do to help, just knock on the door.'

'We really plan to keep out of your way as much as possible,' assured Mrs Kollock. 'I just thought it would be nice for Charlie to see the farm while we're here. He'll inherit it one day, after all. But we don't want to be a bother. Although,' she added, 'when you do have a moment I would so *awfully* like to look around. I would have loved to join the Land Army, had I been here. I'm sure Charlie would love to look around, too, wouldn't you, Charlie?'

'Yes, Mommy.'

They passed into the house.

'What are you up to, little eller?'

Elaine squealed. Her oldest brother Jack had snuck up and grabbed her from behind. She loved it when he called her that, because it was almost her name, 'Ellie'. Although she didn't consider herself in the least bit mischievous. 'Put me down! Put me down.' She squirmed and giggled until he did.

'So that's them.' He leaned against the wall and lit a cigarette. 'Come to spy on us.'

'What do you mean?'

'Nawt. Nothing at all.'

'Bist thee staying for lunch?'

'I'm not sure. Not sure Dad would be wanting me around.'

Elaine missed him. When he returned from the war he had remained on the farm for less than a year. He didn't want to be a farmer, he had declared, leaving their father apoplectic.

'What is it you want to be, then?'

'A mechanic, Dad. I learned the trade in the army. There's a job going in Bristol ...'

Bristol could have been the other side of the world as far as Elaine was concerned.

'Let's go see Mum,' suggested Jack.

Her mother had returned to the kitchen after welcoming the Kollocks.

'Jack. I suppose you'll want feeding.'

'Love you too, Mum. How's thee been?

'Fair to middling. And you?'

'Middling to fair.'

'We'd like thee to be coming here every Sunday for lunch, you know.'

Jack didn't answer immediately. Elaine managed to make herself invisible, off to one side, as was her habit.

'I don't want no ... no blather. I know as we don't always see eye to eye and the like.'

'Well, if I was to stay away for fear your dad and I didn't see eye to eye, you'd have never been born. Not a one of thee.'

'There is that.'

Elaine was glad to see Jack laugh. And especially glad to see him and her mother hug. She slipped out of the space in which she had been hiding.

'So is that pork I can smell roasting?' asked Jack.

'Aah. And I mid just be able to shave enough off of it for thee too.'

Sunday lunch was always a special occasion. Elaine was delighted to have the whole family together again. The two farm hands—Jim, with his faded ginger hair and patchy red complexion, and Pete, only a couple of years older than her brother Ed, but with enough teeth in his head for both of them—usually joined the family on Sundays. Her father had taken on Pete after Jack had moved away. Jim was a widower who had been obliged to give up his own tenancy during the war, and Pete was a lad from a nearby village. Both lived on the farm, Jim in an old caravan, and Pete in accommodation above one of the barns.

Her father often joked that neither of them was a patch on the girls who'd helped out during the war. 'And not a fraction as purdy, neither.' He ignored his wife's heavenward glance and her tut-tutting.

'You can talk, Simon Pierce. We've pigs as is better looking than thee.'

'And none of *them* was a patch on thee, Nellie Pierce.' Which would be accompanied by a wink in Elaine's direction.

She would laugh, without being sure why.

It was not long, on this particular Sunday, before talk turned to the visitors.

'They seem nice enough folk. Not too uppity,' observed her mother.

'They could both do with feeding up,' remarked her father. 'And a bit of sun on their faces wouldn't go astray. Pale as corpses, the both of them.'

'It's probably the latest fashion among the landed gentry.' Jack made scarcely any attempt to conceal the contempt in his voice.

Elaine watched her mother and father carefully. A glance was exchanged, and she slipped into hiding again.

'There's no call to be crousty, Jack.' Her mother smoothed her skirts.

For some time there was only the clinking of cutlery against crockery.

'This is a fine piece of pork, Mrs Pierce.'

'Help theeself to seconds, Jim. Leave room for the crumble, though, or thee'll have me begrumpled.'

While her mother served the dessert, there was some talk about the weather and the prospects for the season ahead. Ed and Pete began some side banter about a girl they knew in the village.

Elaine listened only distractedly.

'I'd best be off presently,' said Jack.

'So soon?'

'Aah, I have a meeting this afternoon.'

'A meeting ...' Again her mother glanced surreptitiously at her father.

Jack rose to leave. 'See you, little eller.'

Elaine stepped down from her chair and returned his hug.

'You take care now, Jack,' said her mother. 'Try to drop by a little more often.'

'I will, Mum. Maybe next Sunday.'

'There'll be a place set for thee.'

IT WAS TUESDAY BEFORE ELAINE SAW ANYTHING MORE OF THE VISITORS. The weather turned bad on the Monday, with winter flicking its tail, but Tuesday awoke clear and refreshed.

'Stay out of the mud, Ellie.'

'Yes, Mum.'

'I *mean* it.'

'Yes, Mum.'

'I don't have time ...' Her mother's voice faded when she turned the corner and edged along the wall to the front of the cottage. Neither of her parents had said anything about whether she was allowed to play with Charlie, or interact with the visitors in any way, and she thought it best not to ask. At least this way she hadn't been told not to.

A gravel path led from the front door of the main wing, cutting through the lawn, towards two small stone plinths, guarding the entryway. A low hedge was all that separated the garden from the road beyond. To the right the road came to an end after a few hundred yards, while to the left it led to the nearest village, about half a mile away. The family would go to church there on high days, and Elaine would walk to school there, cutting across the fields when the weather was fine.

Something on the lawn caught her eye. At first she thought it was just the sun reflecting off the dew or raindrops on the lawn, but as she drew closer she saw that it was a small, silver object. She bent down to pick it up.

'You must be the Pierce girl.'

She hadn't heard the door to the main house open. She jerked upright and stared guiltily at the woman's feet.

'It's Elaine ... ma'am,' she muttered.

'Elaine. I'm Mrs Kollock.'

'Aah, I know, Mrs Kollock.'

'What's that you've found there?'

Elaine bent and retrieved the small object, an earring. Inside a circle of silver was a six-pointed star of some kind, made up of two intertwined triangles. And inside that was a small figure that resembled a cross, but with a circle in place of the top part of the cross.

'I don't know. I wasn't going to keep it,' she felt compelled to say.

'Let me see.'

Elaine walked the few steps to the front door and handed it to the woman.

'Ah, I've been looking for this. Well spotted.'

Elaine felt herself being examined from above.

'You have extraordinary hair ... Elaine.'

She considered her own hair to be little but an annoyance that had to be kept out of the way most of the time. Her mother, however, glowed when she brushed it. 'I once had hair like this,' she would remark. Now what hair she did have was usually hidden beneath a head scarf. But coming from a stranger, the compliment made Elaine blush.

'So do you,' she stammered, looking up briefly, but then quickly back down at the ground.

Mrs Kollock laughed, although there was something self-mocking in the tone.

'Would you like to come in for some morning tea, Elaine? I'm sure Charlie would love to meet you.'

'I'm not sure as I should, Mrs Kollock.'

'Why ever not? Do you have something better to do? Do you have *chores*?'

The word never sounded like that when her mother said it. It suddenly seemed shameful to admit that she had already collected the eggs that morning, and that later she would have to peel the potatoes.

'We are having tea with scones, jam and clotted cream. I think there may even be some chocolate.'

Elaine thought about it for a moment, searching for potential ways that this could lead to trouble, but came up with nothing.

'Thank you, Mrs Kollock.'

Mrs Kollock placed a hand on her shoulder and steered her through the door.

'Charlie!' she called. 'He's not far away, I'm sure.'

As Mrs Kollock led Elaine towards a sitting room on the left, Charlie bounded down the narrow staircase from above.

'Mother, have you seen my ...?'

'Ah, Charlie, this is Elaine.'

Charlie halted on the stairs in mid-flight, and Elaine studied him, studying her. When their eyes met, she experienced a strange sensation. For just a fleeting instant there was a peculiar aura around him, and he seemed to flicker in and out of existence. She blinked, and was overcome by a wave of dizziness. It was only when Mrs Kollock spoke to her that she realised she had all but collapsed against her.

'Elaine? Are you all right?'

Something had become dislocated within her, and neither her mouth nor limbs would respond.

'Charlie, fetch a glass of water, please.'

Elaine was aware of being scooped up, aware of the patterned ceiling passing by, aware of the pressure of the sofa against her back. But it was only when Charlie returned with the water and Mrs Kollock raised her head and put the glass to her lips that her body began to respond again to her commands.

'Are you all right?'

'What happened?'

'I suppose you fainted, Elaine. Has that ever happened before?'

'No. I don't reckon so ... T'whirr turbul.' She lapsed into heavy dialect in her confused state. 'It was terrible.'

'We should fetch your mother. And take you to the doctor.'

'No, Mrs Kollock. No, please. I don't want no blather. It's nawt. I'm fine.'

To prove it she sat up on the couch and took the glass into her own hands. She glanced briefly at Charlie, who stood behind the chair in which his mother sat. He seemed substantial enough now, despite his pale, thin form. No strange glows. No dizziness.

'Well ... Stay here awhile, just to be sure.'

She really did feel fine now, and had begun to think about those scones ... and possibly chocolate. 'I'm a little hungry,' she said.

Mrs Kollock smiled. 'That's an excellent sign. I will speak with Mrs Aldershaw. Charlie, sit here with Elaine to keep her company for a moment.'

And sit he did.

Elaine became uncomfortably aware of her hands. There seemed no place to put them. Folded in her lap, they remained still for only a moment before they began performing little movements: rubbing together, fingers weaving together and then coming apart. With them placed palm down on her thighs, it suddenly seemed impossible to move any part of her body at all, even to the extent of taking a breath. Wherever she put her hands, they seemed to demand an extraordinary degree of attention, and require a phenomenal amount of control. Never before had she been so aware of her hands. An awareness that gradually extended to her whole body. What had for her entire life up to this point seemed such an uncomplicated and natural activity—sitting on a sofa— now demanded all her attention. Her body and mind were no longer in complete accord. Whatever she did with her body suddenly required a deliberate, conscious choice.

In an effort to rid herself of this sensation, she turned her focus outwards, towards the boy sitting opposite. It became extremely important to know if the slight wiggling of his fingers—his hands were placed palm down on the arms of the chair—was a conscious movement. His eyes shifted around the room, avoiding hers. He held his upper lip between his teeth. As suddenly conscious as she was of her own body, its movements and its sensations, she seemed to have become equally aware of the minute movements of his. And she began to wonder what it felt like on the inside to be *him*.

'Your mum seems really nice.' All she could do was poke and prod a little around the outside.

'I suppose she's nice to most people, most of the time.'

Elaine hadn't really been thinking of 'nice' in those terms, in terms of being nice *to* people. More in the sense of ... In the sense of ... In the way that chocolate is nice and cod liver oil isn't.

'No. No. I mean'—she had a new thought—'I mean she's nice like vanilla ice-cream.'

For the first time, she heard Charlie laugh. He threw his head back and lifted his feet slightly off the floor. 'That's funny. I'll tell her.'

'No. No. Please don't.' She felt her colour rise.

'Why not? It's funny.'

'Please.'

'All right.' He thought for a moment. 'So what am I?'

'I don't know yet.'

He looked disappointed, but she didn't think he would like it if she said 'salt', which was the first thing to pop into her head. She wasn't sure it made much sense anyway.

'Well, I think you're a ... shepherd's pie.' He laughed heartily, clearly pleased with himself.

Without quite understanding how, Elaine perceived that some kind of connection had been forged between them. They had shared an experience. Shared a joke.

'My dad is a pork pie,' she offered and, amid the slightly hysterical laughter that followed, managed to ask, 'What's your dad?'

Which brought down a curtain of silence, cutting off their laughter.

'I scarcely know my father.' He raised his chin and looked directly into her eyes. 'He was away during most of the war, and he's in America while we are here. I scarcely know him,' he repeated. This was of no concern to him, his tone and demeanour asserted.

While Elaine was struggling to find a response, Mrs Kollock returned, followed by Mrs Aldershaw with a trolley heaped with delicious distractions.

CHAPTER FIVE

DURING THE DAYS AND WEEKS THAT FOLLOWED, ELAINE INTRODUCED Charlie, and sometimes Mrs Kollock, to sheep, cows, goats, pigs, chickens and geese. An angry goose was one of the most terrifying things with which Elaine had so far become acquainted in life. Three of them constituted the stuff of nightmares. Three of them chasing Charlie away from the edge of the pond ... That had her sides splitting from laughter.

Early one morning, when Elaine was collecting the eggs, she saw Mrs Kollock approach the kitchen door of the cottage. It was the first time any of the visitors had ventured that far into her family's personal territory. When she had accompanied the children around the farm, Mrs Kollock had dressed appropriately in dungarees and wellington boots. The latter she had borrowed from Elaine's mother. On this occasion, though, she wore a yellow dress bearing what looked from this distance like a sparse floral design. On her feet were white shoes with a substantial heel, and an ostentatious bow across the top of the foot. She trod carefully across the unpaved yard and then hesitated momentarily at the open door.

Elaine walked over quickly, whether feeling protective, for some reason, of Charlie's mother, or of her own family's territory, she wasn't sure.

'Mrs Kollock!' she called.

'Mrs Pierce!' Charlie's mother called at the same time. 'Ah, Elaine.'

She arrived to see her mother turn from the sink, startled. 'Mrs Kollock.' She wiped her hands on her grubby apron and cast a glance around the kitchen.

'Mrs Pierce, Charlie and I were just about to go for a walk to the village and we wondered if Elaine could come along. I'm sure Charlie would welcome her company.'

Mrs Kollock remained on the threshold.

'I don't mean to intrude, Mrs Pierce,' she continued. 'Would that be all right? Is there anything you need from there?'

'No, no. I mean, yes, I suppose there's no harm in her going. But no, there's nawt we're needing right at the moment. That girl hasn't been making a pest of herself, has she?'

'Not at all, Mrs Pierce.'

'Right. Well ... Ellie, you'd best get out of those rags and put on something half decent. Give me those eggs there.'

After handing over the eggs Elaine made a dash across the kitchen through the dense silence, which her mother broke just as she passed into the hallway.

'Can I fetch you a cup of tea, Mrs Kollock? While we wait.'

There was a prickly discomfort in the pit of Elaine's stomach. Seeing her mother and Mrs Kollock together like that ... She wondered how she appeared in the eyes of Charlie and his mother. She searched among her clothes for something 'half decent', and resorted to an outfit she often wore to school, and her second best pair of shoes.

When she returned to the kitchen, Mrs Kollock had gone.

'The lady said to meet her over in front of the house. She's gone to light a fire under the boy and get him moving. Now, missie ...' She knelt in front of Elaine and took her cheeks between her hands. 'You be sure to be on your best behaviour now, do you hear. Don't be causing any mischief.'

'Yes, Mum.'

'Not like with Mrs Stowe's boy, do you hear?'

'Yes, Mum. That wasn't my fault, Mum.'

'Well let's just hope that nawt else happens that baint your fault. Now, be off with thee.'

It wasn't fair that her mother kept bringing up that incident. It really hadn't been her fault. Plus it had been ages ago. She couldn't have known that the branch they had laid across the creek wouldn't take

Matthew Stowe's weight. It wasn't as if he was going to drown when he fell in. And Elaine knew for a fact that Matthew was always bragging about how many stitches he had to have in his forehead, and was forever showing everyone the scar.

She was just glad her mother hadn't raised the 'Chicken Incident' again. Since the 'Matthew Incident', that seemed to have been forgotten. Perhaps it would be worth a 'Charlie Incident' to erase memory of the 'Matthew Incident'.

Mrs Kollock and Charlie were waiting near the road.

Over the last few days, some of the pallor had left Charlie's cheeks. His mother's cheeks too, perhaps.

'Off you go. Lead the way,' Mrs Kollock ordered.

It was a cool morning but promised to warm up during the day. The first real spring day with any conviction. The roadside was burgeoning with early spring blooms, and birds and insects could be heard springing into life. For a time they walked in silence, enjoying the sun and the gentle susurrus of the breeze in the trees.

'Is your father sowing yet?' Mrs Kollock enquired.

'There's a crop of winter wheat coming up already. Dad'll likely plant oats when the land's dried out some.'

'You like living on a farm, Elaine?'

'I like it well enough. I don't know nawt else.'

As they walked along they passed in and out of the sunshine. Elaine tossed her gaze around, looking for something interesting on which to hang a conversation. Then they passed a barely visible path leading into the forest on the left.

'Mrs Kollock,' Elaine piped up into the growing silence. 'You see that path.'

'Path? Where? There? Is that a path?'

'Yes it is. There's something down there that might ... I thought you might like ...'

'What is it?'

'It's a special place I go to sometimes. In the wood.'

She looked sceptical. 'I'm not sure I'm dressed for ...'

'It's not far. And there's a clear path.'

'Very well. Lead the way.'

It was only as Elaine ducked beneath the occasional low branch that she realised Mrs Kollock's passage might not be so easy. She could hear feet breaking twigs behind her, and the occasional sharp intake of breath.

'Is it much further, Elaine?'

'No, Mrs Kollock.'

The path opened onto a small clearing. The air was still and felt somehow heavier. More stifling, yet cooler. The sunlight slanting through the treetops struck the ground in patches, lighting on the way the mist, or perhaps the dust, which gave the air its weight. There was a silence broken only by the occasional birdcall and, behind Elaine, the final steps of Charlie and his mother as they emerged from the path. The urge to hold her breath was instinctive.

Inside the clearing was a series of large stones, set roughly in a circle. Some remained more or less upright; others had fallen over. All were covered with moss and lichen. Mrs Kollock walked over to the nearest stone and placed her palm on it. 'It's so cold,' she barely whispered.

Then she moved to the centre of the circle and turned around slowly.

Elaine came to this spot quite often, particularly during the summer, when she wanted time alone. She knew that fairies weren't real, but here, sometimes, she would pretend. If there was anywhere that fairies *would* be, it would be there, in that circle of stones. Both Charlie and Elaine watched his mother, as she continued to turn slowly, now with her eyes closed, her head thrown back and her arms extended. It seemed that she might be dancing.

'Your mother is beautiful,' Elaine said suddenly to Charlie.

Charlie had not spoken for some time. She didn't know how to respond to what he said next.

'I think she may be a bit mad,' he said.

As if on cue, Mrs Kollock stopped turning and, with eyes still closed and head tipped slightly to one side, said, 'Almost I can hear voices. Voices from so, so long ago. Do you hear them?'

'No!' Charlie said sharply.

But, for a moment, Elaine wasn't so sure. On other occasions ... But she knew it was only the wind in the trees, or an animal moving furtively through the undergrowth.

Mrs Kollock opened her eyes. 'Charlie, Charlie ... It's probably only the breeze, right? Or something moving through the forest? But how else are the voices from the past going to reach us? Or from the future?'

It seemed to Elaine that Mrs Kollock had read her thoughts, and she shivered.

'What do they say?' she asked past a lump in her throat.

'They say ... They say ...' For a moment her smile faltered, but she quickly restored it. It slipped into place like a curtain. 'They say that it's time to go to the village to buy an ice-cream!'

On the Easter Sunday both households went to St Lawrence's for the morning service. It was a fine morning, and they all walked down to the village, apart from Mrs Aldershaw, who was coordinating a team preparing a late lunch. It was a lunch to which Elaine's family and the farm hands were also invited. Young Pete had declined the invitation, preferring to spend the day with his own family in a neighbouring village. To her mother's shame, her brother Jack had also declined the invitation.

'I neither want to go to church nor to hobnob with those toffs.'

'They're not toffs,' her mother had protested. 'They've been lovely to our Ellie here.'

'All they want is to lord it over us. Show us how much better they are than us.'

There was no point arguing with Jack once he had his mind set in concrete.

Elaine pondered his words, measuring it up against her own experience. Charlie and his mother spoke differently, it was true. Mrs

Kollock sounded posh, speaking the way people did on the radio. Charlie still spoke with an American accent, as far as she could tell. They wore better clothes, owned a better car. More money, clearly. But she didn't think they looked down on her. Perhaps they found her slightly exotic, as she did them.

As they walked along the road towards the village on that Easter morning there was a natural clumping, with the Pierce clump leading the way. Elaine thought this was as much because her family tended to walk faster, as anything else. Charlie and his mother, with their driver—she had never heard his name—alongside, moved at a leisurely pace, whereas her family's progress seemed more purposeful. It occurred to her that Charlie and his mother didn't do anything in a hurry. In fact, they didn't *do* anything. They were under no pressure to get *this* done before *that* happened. They could take their time to do whatever took their fancy. They could change their minds several times a day if it pleased them. Even when she was on school holidays there were certain things Elaine had to do. Charlie and his mother were under no such obligation.

She should probably resent that.

Or envy it.

There was little she understood during the church service. The family went so rarely that there was no time to become accustomed to the rituals. She knew vaguely about Jesus and Moses and ... There were others whose names escaped her. On this Sunday she was more interested in the way the sun shone through the stained-glass windows, lighting patches of the interior, made visible by the dust in the air. She was reminded of that other morning in the clearing.

Her mother and father stood proudly upright during the singing of the hymns, their voices clearly discernible above the background noise. Her brother Ed kept his eyes lowered most of the time, his lips moving, but not really forming words. Occasionally he wiped his nose with the back of his hand. Jim, the older farmhand, was redder than usual, sweat beading his forehead. Once in a while he slipped his finger between his collar and his neck. If Elaine had passed him in the lane, wearing that collar and tie, she may not have recognised him.

Charlie stood on her left, shuffling his feet, not even pretending to sing. His gaze was fixed on a spot somewhere above the vicar's head, where he stood before the altar with his back to them. She wondered what Charlie was thinking. Wondered if he was wondering what she was thinking. Wondered if he thought about her at all, when they weren't actually together. They would be leaving tomorrow. Would she cease to exist for him?

And Mrs Kollock ... Standing with her eyes closed, swaying slightly from side to side, but to her own rhythm. Mouthing words that bore no relationship to those of the hymn.

A bit mad ... A bit mad ... A bit mad ...

On the walk back to the farm there was a little hesitant chatter. Her father made some remarks about the vicar's sermon. She understood neither the sermon nor her father's remarks.

'It's nice to think the country'll climb back to its feet, soon enough,' he remarked. 'Resurrection-like.'

Her mother made agreeable sounds, but added, 'There's whole families what need resurrecting, I reckon. Pity the Good Lord can't see fit to stop the killing in the first place.'

'Now, Mother, it baint the Lord's fault that folks set to killing each other. What we make a mess of, the Lord'll straighten up in good time.'

'Well, let's hope there's good times ahead, starting with a fertile spring and a bountiful summer.'

Elaine was surprised when, following her mother's remark, Mrs Kollock entered the conversation. From the looks on their faces, so were her parents. Perhaps they had all but forgotten they were not alone on the road, as they usually would have been after a Sunday morning at church. It was true that the presence of both Mrs Kollock and Charlie was somehow less solid than that of the Pierce family. Although not shorter in stature than Mrs Kollock, both Elaine's parents and her brother—and Jim—seemed closer to the ground. The boundary between ground and person was not strongly defined.

It would not have surprised Elaine to discover that there was a space between the ground and the soles of Charlie's and Mrs Kollock's shoes. They were tethered only loosely to the earth, if at all. It was easy to overlook their presence, as she might overlook a leaf blown across the path.

'It's to be hoped that something good will come of it,' Mrs Kollock said. 'I would hate to have lost both my brothers for nothing.'

'Oh, Mrs Kollock, dear.' Mrs Pierce halted on the path ahead and half turned towards the other woman. 'We had no idea. It's a terrible thing. We count ourselves very lucky.'

Mrs Kollock may or may not have heard. Her eyes had taken on once more that faraway look that Elaine had come to recognise.

'But I can't think that anything good can be built on the foundation of the wretched past we have left behind,' Mrs Kollock continued, more to herself than the others.

There was a subdued mood during lunch. There were some valiant attempts to maintain a conversation, but subjects of common interest were difficult to come by. Elaine became bored, and even toyed with the idea of kicking Charlie under the table. He sat opposite her, but some tentative exploration indicated that he was beyond her reach.

Perhaps sooner than was entirely polite, the Pierce contingent began to take its leave.

'Mrs Pierce, Charlie has been pestering me for the past few days about a certain matter, and before you leave—before we leave tomorrow—I have a proposal for you.'

Elaine recognised this as one of those moments in life when the adults present apparently forgot she was there. This had been the origin of her conviction that she could become invisible—slip away from the world—at will.

'Charlie—we—would like to return for a week or two in the summer. Assuming we're still in England, that is. We have yet to schedule our return to Delaware.'

'Of course, Mrs Kollock—'

'But that's not the crucial matter,' Mrs Kollock interrupted. 'Charlie would like to invite Elaine to spend two or three weeks with us. In my father's house. Wouldn't you, Charlie? If, of course, that is acceptable to you. And if, of course, we haven't, in fact, left the country.'

'We wouldn't want to impose on you or your family's hospitality, Mrs Kollock.'

'I can assure you it would be no imposition. And if it were, it would only be fair. We have imposed enough on you.'

'Well ... Ellie?'

She was startled into visibility.

She had been listening, but the conversation had an air of unreality. First, she had some difficulty thinking that far ahead. Second, she had no clear conception of where she would be going if she assented. However, she did want to see Charlie again. And she *did* want to see somewhere else. Anywhere else. Although she hadn't realised it until that very instant.

'Yes, Mum, I would like to go.'

'Very well then, Mrs Kollock. There seems no harm in it. Should it come about, that is.'

'Excellent.'

The next morning, Elaine and her parents were there to see the Kollocks on their way. Mrs Kollock sought an opportunity to take Elaine aside.

'Elaine.'

'Yes, Mrs Kollock?'

'Elaine, I have something for you.' She held out a silver chain from which hung a pendant identical to the earrings Mrs Kollock now wore, with the six-pointed star and the strange cross. 'I want you to have this.'

The thread-like quality of the chain and the way the morning sunlight was captured by the edges of the star took Elaine's breath away. 'Mrs Kollock, thanking thee, but I couldn't take it.'

'Nonsense! You can't *not* take it. It came in a set with these earrings, but now it's yours.'

She couldn't say no. She couldn't say anything. Mrs Kollock took her hand, prised open her fingers, and dropped the pendant onto her palm.

'Thank you,' she finally managed.

Mrs Kollock gave a brief nod and returned to the car, where the other adults were busying themselves.

Charlie ran out of the house, dressed in the same clothes he had worn when they arrived, but carrying his cap. He was about to climb into the back seat of the car when he cast a glance over his shoulder. Elaine was standing apart, eyes cast down.

'Bye, Elaine,' he called out to her.

She caught his eye for a moment and smiled, although her mind was far away. She forced her hand to wave. 'Bye, Charlie.'

'See you over summer.' With that he disappeared into the interior.

The car pulled away, and she watched Charlie wave through the rear window. They had gone—he had gone—before she had been able to pull herself back into the world. She raised her arm and waved frantically, jumping up and down.

'See you again, Charlie,' she called.

The car disappeared around the bend. She looked again at the pendant. For the first time in her life the future assumed the quality of something other than a vague abstraction.

CHAPTER SIX

IN THE FIRST WEEK OF SEPTEMBER, 1948, CHARLIE AND HIS MOTHER sailed from Southampton to New York, again aboard the Queen Mary.

The concept of 'home' had lost much of its solidity and structure in Charlie's mind. He wasn't sure, in fact, whether he was leaving it, or returning to it. A year had been long enough for images of the town of Lewes, Delaware, and their house within it, to lose much of their definition.

It was also with a strong but somewhat amorphous dread that he contemplated the prospect of being reunited with his father.

It was difficult to know from where this dread had arisen. There had been overheard conversations ... Occasionally his mother had indulged in soliloquies, on some of which he had unintentionally eavesdropped.

From these fragments, he pieced together an image of his father as a cold, domineering man, with little capacity for affection. He was, as he had overheard his grandfather say one evening, a *businessman*. The tone had suggested that this was an undesirable quality.

'He did serve in the army, Papa,' his mother had said, springing, unpredictably, to her husband's defence.

'A businessman who donned a uniform for a time, but a businessman beneath it all.'

Charlie had scarcely had time to get to know his father. Now he had difficulty even recalling what he looked like. A tall man, he thought. But most men seemed tall to him. Thin, perhaps. With a narrow moustache. This could have been correct. There was his voice, of course. He remembered this as loud and angry. This was probably because—he had to concede—it was at such times that he was most likely to hear it. When he was arguing with Charlie's mother. Their quieter conversations he would not have heard.

He tried to remember when—if—his father had addressed him directly.

'Has the boy been fed?'

'Get the boy off to bed.'

These were phrases he may have heard.

Perhaps, on occasions, his father might have wished him goodnight.

The truth was that he hardly ever saw him, even when he returned from the war. He would leave for the office early and return late, often even on weekends. Charlie registered the impact of his father on the household indirectly for the most part: the departure of his nanny, Rita; the mysterious appearance of his brother, Jeremy. The changes in his mother.

Since being in England his mother had seemed to breathe again, although she was still taken from time to time by a shadow. And often she did not behave the way other adults behaved. Turning slow circles, for instance, among ancient stones in a forest clearing. She seemed to see things that others didn't. Despite this, Charlie felt she came back to him, from wherever she had drifted. They walked together again almost every day when the weather was fine, after he had finished his lessons with his tutor, Mr Ginniver.

He enjoyed those walks enormously. At first this was simply because the countryside was new to him. Then it was the time alone with his mother. Towards the end it was because the fields and woods and hedgerows became his friends. There were several routes they could take on their walks, and he began to measure these out in terms of the important landmarks. Here they walked along a narrow lane, lined on both sides with a tall hedge. Occasionally they would have to press themselves into the hedge when a large tractor or van passed by. Then they would come to The Gap.

The Gap was one of the moments of decision. They could either continue along the lane, or turn left and cross the field which, particularly in summer, was overgrown and abuzz with insects. The path beyond the hedge was only hinted at.

There was The Well. The Well was on the edge of the village, which they sometimes skirted and through which they sometimes passed. The Well was a low, red-brick, circular structure, the opening of which was covered with half-rotted timbers. Overhanging The Well was a crude wooden structure which supported a spindle around which the rope would have coiled. Try as he might, he could not get this spindle to turn. It was obligatory to pause at The Well and drop stones through the gaps in the timbers. He would have liked to remove the timbers and look down, but this was not permitted.

It was not possible to approach The Gap or The Well, or any of several other significant features of the landscape, without pausing for a moment. During this ritual his mother often seemed to be listening, and, if he wasn't distracted, he might listen too. He was usually too timid to ask his mother what she heard—if she heard anything.

Elaine had joined them on their walks in the second week of August. She had grown since Charlie first met her, and now stood slightly taller than him. Over the months and years her face would gradually fade from his memory, but never her hair. Her hair cascaded across her shoulders and down her back in loose, deep-chestnut ringlets. The sun would draw out startling red highlights. It would usually be pulled back into a partial ponytail, but with much still hanging free. As often as not there was a leaf or a twig trapped somewhere in the tresses. How Elaine acquired such embellishments was something of a mystery. At thoughtful moments, or at moments of heightened anxiety, she would take a strand of hair and hold it in her mouth.

Elaine had been staying with them for almost a week and they were taking a walk—on this occasion they had passed through The Gap and across the overgrown field towards a narrow strip of woodland. They had stopped near an ancient elm, more dead than alive, which guarded the path into the woods. It would take five or six men, arms fully extended, to encircle the tree. Knobbed and fissured, it could have housed countless nymphs and fauns. Its outer branches clung stubbornly to life.

It was essential that a pause be made at this station along the way.

The sun was rising towards noon and a slight haze of dust hovered in the air, some of it raised, no doubt, by their passage along the bone-dry path. The small party accepted the shade of the tree and found seats upon its gnarled roots. Spread as they were around the base of the tree none of them could see the others, but Charlie's mother could be heard humming softly to herself. Then she became silent.

'It's so quiet!' Elaine's voice came from somewhere on Charlie's left.

His mother laughed, a sound he would have liked to hear more often.

'Quiet?' She chuckled again. 'No, no, no. It's not quiet at all. It's *never* quiet. Listen!'

Sure enough, Charlie became aware of a riot of sound. Although there was very little breeze, above his head the tree gleefully rubbed its dry, papery leaves together. In a field, somewhere out of sight, a cow lowed mournfully, and sheep protested irritably against the increasing heat of midday. He became aware of tiny chirps and pips and clucks, as birds near and far reminded the world of their continued existence. A chicken chuckled. A rooster crowed. In the distance a train tooted. And, underlying it all, the long, low chord of bees and other insects among the tall grass and wildflowers.

Elaine came into sight, walking from around the tree towards his mother, who sat out of sight on his right.

'Do you hear it, Charlie? Mrs Kollock, I hear it! I almost want to tell everything to shut up and leave us in peace!' She added her own staccato, high-pitched laugh to the chorus.

'Do you hear what it says, Elaine?'

His mother also came into sight. Now they framed his view of the overgrown field, the short figure of Elaine to the left, and the taller figure of his mother to the right. They stood facing each other. Both closed their eyes, but Charlie kept his eyes open, observing them.

'I only hear noise,' he volunteered.

'Elaine, do you hear?'

'I'm not sure. What does it say to thee, Mrs Kollock?'

'Ah, that's for my ears alone.' Some of the lightness left her voice. 'It's a different message for each of us. The world speaks to each of us our own unique, personal message. You must learn to hear that message, beneath the cacophony of the modern world.'

Charlie was surprised to notice that she spoke to *him*.

He couldn't hear it, and he began to suspect some fundamental flaw within. A profound deafness.

'It's just noise,' he said, irritated.

'Ha, yes. Just noise.' And his mother began to walk on.

Somehow the elm tree had managed to hide a leaf in Elaine's hair.

Leaning dangerously out over the railing of the ship, near the bow, Charlie watched the ship cut through the ocean. For some time he had the sense that he was skimming rapidly along the surface of his own life.

CHAPTER SEVEN

CHARLIE'S NEW YOUNGER BROTHER WAS BORN ALMOST EXACTLY ONE year after they returned to Lewes, in Delaware. Charlie was then nine years old and not at all interested.

Life was not easy for him. He had to adapt once more to the idea of *school*. He had grown very comfortable with having a private tutor on his grandfather's estate, if not entirely comfortable with his grandfather. Since the death of his sons in the war, Charlie's mother's father had withdrawn from the world, emerging only occasionally to mutter odd words or phrases that sounded vaguely biblical. Or perhaps Shakespearian. His grandmother, on the other hand, fussed over him terribly. At first the attention was pleasurable, but eventually it became tiresome. He had enjoyed, though, the freedom to wander the grounds; the freedom, virtually, to set his own study schedule. He had enjoyed, also, the time spent with his—if ever-so-slightly-crazy—mother. He preferred her craziness to that of his grandfather, although he could also detect a family resemblance.

Now that they had returned to Lewes, everything seemed to crumble away: his freedom, the attention of others. His mother.

Almost as soon as his father had picked them up from the railway station, he reclaimed Charlie's mother for himself. This did not seem to involve affection. Charlie had recognised affection in the way his grandfather had greeted his mother upon their reunion. A tentative smile. A shy kiss on the cheek. Difficulty maintaining eye contact. What embarrassed his grandfather, Charlie soon realised, was affection.

There was none of this embarrassment when his father met them at the station. He strode towards them and seized Emily in a firm embrace. He greeted her with kind words and with a carefully cultured smile. He attached her to his arm in the same way that he picked up her small suitcase. Later, Charlie would see this behaviour mirrored in his father's interactions with business and political colleagues. Not those precise movements, but others that were similarly orchestrated and controlled.

After greeting his wife, he had bent down slightly towards Charlie, taken his hand and shaken it firmly.

'Welcome back, boy.' This was seconds before he attached the suitcase and Emily to either arm.

Had his father forgotten his name? he wondered. He also wondered if it was significant that his father had said 'welcome back', rather than 'welcome home'. There was not much time to wonder, however. His parents had moved away, clearly expecting him to follow.

During the next few months his mother tried. He could see that. She tried to hold on to him. And to herself. For a time they even walked together.

But his father persuaded Emily that she must become more involved in the community. He was a pillar of the same, as she too must be. In their absence, Charlie's father had become a member of the local city council and deputy mayor. He saw himself as future mayoral material. The wife of the future mayor had certain standards to uphold.

His parents had quickly resumed the custom of eating late, after Charlie was in bed, and there were often strangers present for dinner. Participation in various local charities and community groups ate into the time his mother had for him. Nevertheless, often on weekends she would work in the garden, and encouraged him to help her. She continued this even when swollen with the new baby.

One conversation, on a warm and humid Sunday afternoon in early spring, remained engraved in his mind. Emily was about halfway through the term of her pregnancy and not yet restricted in her movements. She was working in the front garden on this occasion. Along the right-hand fence as one faced the street was a row of rose bushes. Many had been there for years, but one was a recent addition.

'Look,' she said to Charlie, crouched beside her next to the bush. There was not much to see of the bush. It struggled to cast out a few shoots, some of which were already shrivelled and black. 'I don't know what's wrong with it.'

The other bushes in the row were pushing out new and vigorous growth. Some, with precipitous enthusiasm, were already flaunting well-developed buds.

Charlie walked along the row, looking closely at each bush, as if he might have advice to offer. He cherished this time spent with his mother and would do anything to ensure that it continued. Perhaps if he could actually be helpful ...

He *was* helpful, in fact, particularly in the vegetable garden which was in the back yard. About roses, though ...

'This is the bush you brought back with us?'

'Yes it is.' She had wanted to bring with her a token of her family home, and she had carefully dug up a small rose bush, after pruning it back brutally. She had packed the roots in damp moss inside a bag and brought it with her on the voyage across the Atlantic.

Charlie bent down and closely examined the struggling bush.

'It's not happy,' he observed.

'Clearly.'

'It doesn't like being away from home.'

'Apparently not. I've given it everything I can think of to make it "happy".'

He could detect a slight smile in her voice without needing to see her face. Then she sighed and he did look. *She's gone*, he thought. He was used to the unfocused look and the slackening of her facial muscles. When she returned, she would often say things, with great conviction, that he struggled to understand.

'It's homesick,' she said at last.

He waited. There would be more.

'Home—' She suddenly turned a piercing gaze on him; its intensity was startling after the fuzziness of her absence. 'There is a link with home that goes beyond the right drainage and the right minerals and the right pH and the right amount of sunshine. There's a link at a deeper level ... This rose has been uprooted on more than just a physical plane. It can't thrive ...'

Her voice faded away. Or Charlie ceased to listen. He didn't understand. But the word 'home' did resonate in his mind. He glanced at the house. He was back. But was he home?

His father occasionally made some attempts at a *rapprochement* with him. It was clear that he didn't want Charlie drawn to his attention, least of all by Charlie himself. From time to time, though, and quite unexpectedly, he would seek him out.

'There you are, boy,' he might say, as if his son had gone missing or been hiding for days; as if he had spent hours searching for him. He initiated each encounter with this impatient tone. 'And what might you be doing there?'

In all probability, Charlie was sitting at the kitchen table—or on a wicker chair at the wicker table on the back porch—drawing. Or reading. Often copying the images from the book he was reading. He was drawn to English books. *The Famous Five* series and the *Just William* series were among his favourites. He felt comfortable with the landscapes they described.

'Nothing, sir.'

As soon as he said this, he realised his mistake. His father's eyebrows drew down to meet at the centre, and his eyes narrowed. If he was smoking his pipe, he might clench his teeth around it in the corner of his mouth.

'Nonsense, boy. I can see you're drawing there. What is that?'

If his father already knew he was drawing, why had he asked? It seemed unfair that he could ask a meaningless question, but Charlie was expected to give a meaningful reply.

'This is George and Timmy.' *But*, he thought, *he probably already knows that too*. Although Charlie knew George—Georgina—was actually a girl, this was never quite clear from the illustrations in the book. He had tried, in his own drawing, to make her a little more girl-like. He struggled to draw the dog, Timmy, although he generally preferred to draw animals.

'Hmph.' His father shot a glance back over his shoulder towards the door. 'So ... You like drawing then.'

'Yes, sir.'

'I was thinking, you and I ... Perhaps we might go fishing ... Hunting perhaps ... On a weekend soon. What do you think? I was about your age when *my* father took me up north ... the Adirondacks.'

Charlie was not quite happy with the way he had drawn Timmy's legs and wanted to try again, so he said, 'I would like that, sir.'

'A couple of lads from our New York office can arrange something, I'm sure.'

'Yes, sir.'

'Right, then ...'

To Charlie's relief, that was the last he heard of the plan.

While the rose bush didn't survive the summer, James Alfred Kollock, when he made his appearance in the world that September, seemed to be healthy and robust. There was unspoken relief on all sides.

Almost a decade of life separated Charlie from this new brother. It was difficult for him to be interested. I suspect his mother was not terribly interested either. She spent a great deal of time in bed, and very soon a new nurse/nanny was introduced to the household. Charlie saw less and less of his mother, though most evenings she would still come to his room to wish him goodnight. Sometimes, though, his parents were out. The nanny, Sister Babbitch—'call me Elsie, dear'—occasionally thought to offer herself as a substitute, but she was clearly more interested in James Alfred.

In the morning, Charlie would get out of bed, woken usually by the sun streaming through a gap in the curtains, or by the whistling of the cardinal that particularly liked the pear tree which grew just below the window of his bedroom.

He would wash and dress himself—clothes would be laid out for him—and then go downstairs for breakfast in the kitchen. His father had always left the house by then, or was locked away in his study. His mother, although once an early riser, was now rarely out of bed before he left for school.

Mrs Duluth would be in the kitchen to provide him with freshly squeezed orange juice. He might have toast and cereal. Lunch would be prepared for him. Then he would walk to school.

When his mother did come of an evening to say goodnight she sometimes told him a story. He felt he was too old for this but didn't want to discourage her. But the stories rarely made much sense. They were filled with old, twisted gypsy women, incomprehensible druid-like men, and animals with prophetic abilities. One character she called 'the Daughter of Abraham' recurred frequently, but her form and role in the stories was fluid. Charlie had no idea who Abraham was. Sometimes he thought his mother herself might be this Daughter of Abraham, although 'Abraham' wasn't her father's name. He was Geoffrey. Lord Geoffrey. Charlie wondered if he himself was also concealed somewhere in those stories.

Then several nights passed and she did not come. Charlie hadn't seen her at all for days. In the morning, toying with his glass of orange juice before he went to school, he asked Mrs Duluth where she was.

'That's not for me to say. That's not for me to say,' she repeated, turning quickly back to the sink.

That evening—James was just two months old and Thanksgiving was around the corner—Charlie took a bold and unprecedented step. He approached his father, where he sat in the library smoking a cigar and sipping a glass of port, and spoke to him.

'Father.'

'Hmm?'

Charles Sr looked around as if unsure where the voice came from. Charlie was afraid he might have woken him, although he was sure his eyes had been open. He took a step across the threshold.

'Father,' he ventured again.

'What do you want, boy?'

'Where's mother? She ...'

'What? Your mother?' His father's eyes focussed sharply upon him for an instant, and then began to dart around the room, as if searching for something or someone.

A slight haze of cigar smoke hovered around the lamp on the table at Mr Kollock's elbow and spread thinly throughout the room. The pungent yet almost sweet odour threatened to take Charlie's breath away. A cough played around the edges of his throat. He waited for his father to offer more. He couldn't speak again for fear that the cough would bound forth and earn him a reprimand. His father gazed towards the far corner of the room before he spoke again, and Charlie couldn't help looking in that direction.

'Has no one told the boy?' his father asked the corner.

With the haze in the room and the shadows crowding its recesses, Charlie could have been persuaded that someone stood there, listening. But no. No reply came from that direction. He wasn't sure if he was meant to reply himself.

But Charles Sr turned again towards him and brought his gaze to focus some inches to the left of his son's face. 'Your mother's gone away for a week or two. No more than three, for certain. To stay with a friend. Someone should have told you.'

His mother had gone away without so much as a goodbye. Charlie was unable to move for some time. His father seemed not to notice, buried again in the newspaper on his lap.

'Can ...'

His father looked up, surprised again, as if the previous two or three minutes had not occurred.

'Sir, can ... Can I go and visit her?'

'What? No, of course not. You don't need to hang on to her apron strings day in and day out.'

Mr Kollock blinked him out of existence and returned his attention to the newspaper.

For a moment or two Charlie's ghost hovered on the threshold of the library, before accepting its fate and drifting away.

His mother was away for six months.

PART TWO

CHAPTER EIGHT

'YOUR MOTHER HATES IT HERE. SHE'S ALWAYS HATED IT HERE.'

'Sammy's not going. You won't make *him* go.'

'Sammy's eighteen. He can make his own decisions.'

'You can't *make* me. I'll stay with Sammy.'

Miriam felt the mattress sink beneath her father's weight. She resisted the tug of gravity, which would have her slip towards him, into the well he had created.

'You're only eleven, sweetheart.'

The gentle, fleeting touch to her hair almost moved her. Almost. But her body remained tense, rigid.

'She misses her sisters. Her own mother. And now that her father is gone ...'

Miriam had never met any of her grandparents. The only relatives she had in Australia, besides her parents and brother, were her father's brother and his family. And they had moved to Melbourne a year ago. She sometimes wondered what it would be like to have grandparents and aunts and uncles and cousins crowding the house during the holidays. Occasionally they had been invited to someone else's home for Passover or Chanukah. There had been other people's grandparents and aunts and uncles and cousins.

Not that her family was particularly observant. The synagogue terrified her. The bobbing of heads and mumbling of prayers was just creepy.

'I *won't* go.'

'We'll talk again later. Wash your hands for dinner. Five minutes.'

The 'oval' was already very dry and dusty, although it was still only the middle of October. The brown smudge on the northern horizon was not yet ominous.

Debbie and Miriam sat behind the shelter shed in the shade, swapping sandwiches. It made little difference. Both Miriam's cucumber and lettuce and Debbie's ham, cheese and tomato were soggy and wilted. Nevertheless, it was with a guilt-ridden frisson of excitement that Miriam bit down on the ham. Some traditions were difficult to cast aside. Between bites, a sudden gust of wind peppered both food and diners with a dusty condiment. The grittiness set her teeth on edge. She contented herself with the small apple and a shortbread biscuit.

'So, when you going?'

'Don't know. Soon. Maybe two weeks or something.' Miriam had stubbornly refused to retain the date in her memory.

'Wow.'

'We got to go to Sydney, I think. Then we're going on a ship.'

'A ship! Wow!'

'Yeah. It takes weeks. Months.'

'So what's England like?'

'Don't know. There's Buckingham Palace, and the Queen and stuff.'

'I like the Queen. My mum saw her once.'

'I got a magazine with some pictures. I'll bring it tomorrow.'

The wind was gusting stronger. Willy-willies came to life on the oval, dust devils spinning crazily and skirting along the ground briefly, before collapsing from the exertion.

The warning siren signalled that the lunch break would soon be over. To the north the brown stain stretched along the horizon, extending tendrils towards the south. In front of the shelter shed a few boys ignored the siren, continuing to shoot hoops until the second siren sounded, and then making a dash for it, to arrive back in class sweaty and short of breath. The shuffling of feet, the scraping of chairs. And pungent odours. Miriam could not imagine life without those textures.

'Settle down. Quickly now!'

A laugh here. A cough there.

Mr Sutton slammed his hand down on the desktop.

'Thank you. Now ...' He brushed the same hand across his thinning hair, exposing the dark stain under his arm. 'The weather bureau has issued a warning that a severe dust storm is about to hit us from the north.' As one, every eye glanced towards the window. Shufflings and whisperings. 'Quiet, please. It has been decided to close the school for the rest of the day and send you home early, before ...'

The rest of what he had to say went unheard as cheers and conversation erupted throughout the room. The sharp snap of his ruler on the desk restored some order. Knowing it wouldn't hold for long he issued his commands. 'Everything off the desks. Chairs up as usual. Leave in an *orderly* fashion. You still need to have your spelling list ready for tomorrow,' he shouted at the last heels to disappear through the door.

They belonged to Miriam. In her haste to pack up, she had dropped her open pencil case, scattering pencils under scampering feet.

Outside, the brown stain was spreading upwards across the sky.

Debbie was already some distance ahead, and Miriam sprinted to catch up.

'Is your mum home?' she asked breathlessly. 'Mine said she'd be out this arvo. She'd leave the key. Want to come back with me for a bit? I could show you the magazine. With the Queen and stuff.'

'Sure.'

At their dawdling pace the walk took fifteen minutes. Ahead, the stain on the horizon had taken on definition. It was no longer just a discolouration. Quite clear now, beyond the empty paddocks to the north, was a roiling, brown-grey cloud.

'Wow,' said Debbie. 'Is that ...? It looks like a dirty cloud fell out the sky.' Her laugh was a little nervous.

Miriam stooped and collected the key from beneath a pot that had once sustained a geranium.

They let the screen door slam behind them as they scampered across the entry way, into the second room on the right. Miriam jumped onto the bed, springs voicing their jaded protest. Debbie sat more sedately on the edge of the bed, clasping her school bag to her chest.

Miriam leaned over the edge, reached underneath the bed, poised precariously for a few seconds, and then resurfaced with a copy of *Women's Weekly*.

'She's gorgeous.'

The magazine dated from a few months earlier. They admired the young queen but laughed at a picture of Prince Charles wearing a kilt.

'Maybe you'll marry him.'

Miriam scrunched up her nose.

'Don't you think he's handsome?' asked Debbie.

Miriam silently mouthed the word. She knew she was supposed to think certain men, film stars especially, were handsome. Indeed, not thinking so sometimes generated strange looks from her friends, so she had been generally inclined to swim with the tide. But she was leaving in a few weeks. A much bigger tide was sweeping her away.

'No,' she decided, watching Debbie's face closely.

Debbie's attention remained focused on the photograph of Charles. Her fingers fleetingly brushed the page. Then she laughed lightly. 'You're right,' she admitted. 'Those *ears*! But he *is* a prince, and he *is* rich. *I'd* marry him.'

And they laughed together.

They had turned their attention to other stories in the magazine when her mother called from the other room.

'Miriam? You're here? Why are you here? Help me get the washing in before ... Ah, Debbie.' She stood in the doorway to Miriam's room, hat in hand, hair in disarray. 'Come on, both of you. Before it blows away. Before the dust gets here.'

But the dust could already be tasted in the air, and the brown stain now extended to the south.

'Curse this godforsaken land! It'll all have to be re-washed.'

Miriam helped with the washing, but paused from time to time to test the air. It bore a gritty, metallic taste. More than that, it seemed to crackle around her. Her hair lifted, but not from the gusty wind alone. She glanced at Debbie, who half hid in the doorway, whether from the work or the gathering storm Miriam wasn't sure.

'For heaven's sake, Miriam! Stop daydreaming and help me with this. Although why I'm bothering ... Now, inside. Both of you. Inside. Close all the windows. Close everything up.'

'Mrs Levinson, I should go home.'

'Not in this, girl. We'll have to sit it out.' She turned on the radio. Nothing but static emerged.

When Miriam went to close the front door, she jumped back as a jolt of electricity from the doorknob pricked her fingers.

'Debbie!' she called. 'Debbie, come feel this.'

'What is it, girl? Stop messing about and shut the door.'

When Miriam reached forward tentatively to touch the knob again, she was disappointed to feel nothing.

'Shut it, for heaven's sake!' Her mother pushed it closed and moved on quickly to something equally urgent.

Outside had the appearance of dusk. Miriam knelt on the couch, her elbows on the back rest, facing the window. She traced words in the thin layer of dust on the window sill.

Miriam.

Princess, she added before it.

There was surprisingly little wind but, high in the sky now and then, a flash.

'See that, Deb?'

'What?'

'Lightning. Only no thunder.'

'Yeah.'

But Debbie's attention was held by another magazine. The image of an old man, a movie star—someone else Miriam was supposed to consider handsome—graced the cover.

'Look, there's another.'

'It couldn't wait, this weather?' bemoaned her mother. 'Just two weeks it couldn't wait?'

Then came the rain. Huge, muddy globules, spattering against the glass and leaving trails down the window.

'That will help, at least. Settle the dust.' Question marks trailed behind the sentence, though, as mud slewed from the sky.

Later that night Miriam's father explained.

'Static electricity. The plastic soles of your shoes rubbing on the carpet electrified you and then ... *Zap!*' He pounced on her and tousled her hair. 'It came out of you and through the doorknob.'

'I want to do it again.'

'It probably won't work now, princess. The air needs to be dry.'

Her father knew most things.

Her mother only knew that she would be spending days, now, re-washing clothes and sheets, wiping dust from every surface, and cleaning windows. She made sure everyone else knew that, too.

CHAPTER NINE

IN 1960, AUNTIE MIRIAM—SHE WASN'T MY AUNTIE, BUT I GREW UP calling her that—had seen little beyond the flat, open, northern suburbs of Adelaide, in South Australia, during her eleven and a half years of life. She had been to the city perhaps four times. Once had been in the back of her uncle's old van, with her parents, brother and three cousins. The journey seemed to take hours, and probably had. The van crawled southward along the highway, halting every twenty minutes or so, while Uncle David went in search of water for the radiator, which held water no better than a colander. Having rocked back and forth and bounced up and down on a rough, wooden bench in the airless, windowless rear of the van, Miriam had vomited during two of those halts.

She recalled a sweltering train journey at the beginning of the year, with all the windows and doors open, the hot wind tying her hair in knots before they arrived in the city. It was January, during the school holidays. They had been to see *Sleeping Beauty*, she and her mother. It was one of only three movies she had seen. She had sat through *Auntie Mame* the year before. And perhaps two years before that, but less clear in her memory, had been *Tammy ... Tammy* something. The title escaped her. On that occasion it had been just she and her father on a rare Saturday afternoon outing. Her life before that was little more than a haze, with the occasional face or incident emerging from the mist.

Three times she could recall a trip to the beach, to Glenelg, catching the train into the city and the tram out west. Glenelg, she had overheard her father saying to Sammy, was a palindrome, and she had looked forward to seeing a palindrome, having never seen one before. It was only later, when she was expressing her disappointment on the homeward trip, that he had explained what he meant. 'No, no, princess, the word ... The name "Glenelg" is a palindrome. The same backwards as forwards, you see?'

She saw, when he wrote it down. Her father knew everything.

There was a week's holiday in Victor Harbor, at a caravan park. It had seemed a long journey on the bus, but nothing like this. As the family travelled across to Sydney on the train the country opened up before her, and she vowed to return one day, if only to see Sammy again. Sammy had a girl. Sammy had a job. Sammy had a future here. He had no interest in returning to the country he had left when he was no more than four years old. He had no memory of it.

Saying goodbye to Debbie and Sharon and Rita had been heartbreaking. At the end of her final day at school there had been hugs and tears, and heartfelt avowals to stay in touch. She had yet to say goodbye to Sammy. He was travelling with them to Sydney to say his goodbyes there. When she thought of that her throat closed.

Time ticked by beneath her feet—with the *clackety-clack* of the wheels—and through the windows—with the regular passing of telephone poles. The sameness of the countryside and the numbing rhythms found her struggling to stay awake. *Charlotte's Web* lay open on her lap at the same page as an hour or more ago. This was the second day of their journey. They would arrive in Sydney late the next day.

Miriam's mother clung to Sammy, her father standing apart, pretending to check their passports and tickets. Miriam hovered somewhere in between. What appeared to be happening couldn't *actually* be happening. During the train journey, the overnight stay in the motel, and the taxi ride to the harbour, Miriam had been in a state of suspension. She went through all the required motions, eating, sleeping, walking ... at times even talking. She was pretty sure she had laughed occasionally. That was because she knew deep down that this wasn't real. Or, if it was real, that very soon something would intervene and prevent this sequence of events from continuing. Her mother would suddenly realise that she had forgotten to lock the house, and they would have to return. The tickets would prove to be invalid.

'We can't go,' her mother would suddenly say, 'because Marjorie Hollingworth has invited us over for a barbeque next weekend.'

The regular pattern of life would reassert itself. Or Miriam would wake up in her own bed. When she had woken during the second night on the train she had convinced herself that they had turned around during the night and were heading back to Adelaide.

Even as Sammy dragged her to him and hugged her, the tears didn't flow. Even as they climbed the gangway to board the ship ... Even as she stood between her father and mother, waving feverishly to her brother below ... There was still time, she was convinced. The ocean liner's engines would fail. A terrible storm would prevent their departure. They would sail away but have to return because the ship was in danger of sinking.

As the SS *Oriana* skirted around Bennelong Point, she became convinced that this *had* happened, and that even as she stood there, feeling the deck rise and fall beneath her feet, her *real* self had descended from the ship. She was even now running back towards the terminal building, her mother and father struggling behind her with the bags and trunks. Her brother swept her up into his arms and they laughed.

For part of her, that was always what had really happened.

CHAPTER TEN

THE FIRST TIME MIRIAM SAW BRIGHTON 'BEACH', SHE WOULD HAVE laughed, if she hadn't been struggling to hold back tears. It was the middle of summer, eight months after their arrival in England, and it was cold, windy and starting to drizzle. On the pebbles. Where was the sand between her toes? She would need thick-soled boots just to walk down to the water.

Upon arriving in England, the family had moved into a tiny, two-bedroom flat in Spitalfields, located in a Georgian townhouse owned by one of her father's cousins. She thought she must have shifted not only in space, but also in time. The flat contained a pre-historic bathroom with no shower, and only occasional hot water. The oil-filled heater in the front room—the only room with any kind of built-in heating—also worked only occasionally, as she was to discover during the obscenely cold winter. At first she thought the coin-operated electricity meter was a sick joke. The tiny windows and steep, narrow stairways made her claustrophobic. Fortunately, this was to be only a temporary arrangement.

In Australia, her father had risen to a middle-management position within the state public service. Upon arriving in the UK, the plan was for him to work for a time in his cousin's furniture factory, while searching for a similar position in the civil service. After eight months he was finally successful.

Where they had lived in Spitalfields there seemed to be not a sprig of greenery nor a square foot of open space. Narrow, dirty streets and alleys. The road surfaces, often laid with brick rather than bitumen, always seemed to be wet, even when it hadn't rained for days. It could have been the previous century. The only redeeming feature—and Miriam often thought of this as she walked to and from her temporary school—was that Jack the Ripper had allegedly walked streets just like these, not very far away, almost a century earlier. Her fellow students were quick to inform her of this. Apparently it was meant to frighten her.

Thankfully, when her father scored the position as bursar at the Brighton College of Arts, Miriam thought she might be able to breathe again. Brighton, she knew, was by the seaside. The word 'seaside' still sounded odd to her ears. In Australia no one ever talked about going to the seaside. They went to the beach. So she had wondered, a little, about this term, and why people didn't go to the beach. Now she knew.

The wind whipped her hair about her face as she leaned against the low railing, staring out to sea.

It had been three days now. Enough time helping her mother unpack and arrange the furniture, put up curtains and clean the cupboards.

'They're clean! They were clean before we got here. Before they left, there was someone *just like you* cleaning everything. And now you want to do it again!'

'You never know—'

'I want to go out. Pu-leeeease!'

'You don't know the area. You don't know your way around.'

'I never *will* if I don't go out!' There were few sentences these days that she didn't end with an exclamation mark and pepper with italics, especially when talking with her mother. Her father wasn't there. He had gone to the college for the first time. She was stuck in the house with her mother. Cleaning cupboards. Moving furniture that had been moved a hundred times. Throwing out stuff that could have been thrown out before they left Australia.

'All right, all right. But don't go far. And be back by lunchtime.'

'Yeah, yeah.'

The sun had been shining, with the promise of a nice day. But she had not walked far before clouds rolled in again and it began to drizzle, as it had for the previous two days. She didn't care. She was out of the house. And out of Spitalfields and the nineteenth century.

It was only with the fourth match, shielding it carefully with her hands, that she finally managed to light the cigarette she had stolen from her mother's purse. She had only begun smoking when she started school in Spitalfields, stealing one or two cigarettes at a time from her parents, lest they notice. She rarely had enough money to buy her own.

Before her parents had broken the terrible news that they would be moving to England, she had been looking forward to starting high school in the new year. But she had been horrified to discover that the new school year in England didn't start until after summer and, of course, that summer was in the middle of *next year*.

'But that means I'll be in grade seven for *ages*! It's not fair!'

Furthermore, she would have to sit her eleven plus exams.

'The eleven *whats*?'

She found herself a year older than most others in her class. She turned twelve in the April of 1961, while most of her classmates would only turn eleven that year. It was humiliating. However, she soon realised that the age difference gave her some advantages. She was taller than most other students, especially the boys, and there were also other ... changes. She began to stuff tissues into the bra she now became accustomed to wearing.

It seemed appropriate that she behave older, so she began smoking. She also increased the frequency and amplitude of her use of colourful language. Smoking and swearing she understood to be signs maturity, although her parents never swore. Her brother Sammy had sworn liberally, at least out of their parents' hearing. Her new posture became a tribute to him. She exaggerated her Australian accent and vocabulary, turning what might have been a disadvantage into an advantage. Over the months she achieved something close to celebrity status, and even became a figure to be feared.

Now they had moved again. She was glad to be out of the archaic, claustrophobic apartment. Even *this*—she cast her glance at the pebbly beach again—was better than that. But she would have to start again at a new school, after summer. After the eleven plus exams. Most of the advantages she had gained would be lost.

To her left, about half a mile away, stood the Pier. It tugged at her, but she checked the time: 11.45. She would be in trouble again if she was late. And she was hungry.

The walk back was uphill. She pretended not to hurry.

She was pleased to see her father's car parked in the street. The car was a new acquisition. Not *new*, but new to the family. A light blue Austin A40 with a white roof.

The new house was also a Georgian townhouse, with steps leading up from the street. There were three storeys above street level and one storey below, with steps leading down to a separate entrance. Beyond a railing the window and door of the lower room could be seen, fronted by a very small courtyard. Miriam had wanted that room, but her parents had insisted on leaving it empty for the moment. The freshly painted white façade of the south-facing house caught the midday sun, which chose that moment to appear. A small, narrow garden at the rear never saw the sun.

As she climbed the steps the front door opened.

'Just in time.'

Her mother must have been watching from a window.

Miriam pushed past her and started up the stairs, towards the top floor, where her room overlooked narrow back gardens and other buildings like theirs. The rears of buildings never look as attractive as their public façades. Rusty pipes. Wires that seem to emerge randomly at one point only to vanish again, just as randomly, a little farther down. Window frames with paint peeling. Stains streaking the walls below leaking gutters and downpipes.

'Lunch is practically on the table.'

'All *right*. I'll be down in a minute.'

There were some mints in her room. She had forgotten to take them with her. She only hoped her mother hadn't already smelt the smoke on her breath.

'Remind me again why we came to this miserable little country?' she asked, sitting at the table. She didn't really expect an answer. It was a question she asked most days. 'And have you seen that beach?'

'You're going to have to get used to it.'

Her father was always very tolerant and understanding, but the edge in his voice warned that his patience was not without its limits.

'We came out here to see family, and we hardly ever see them anyway,' Miriam complained.

'That's about to change,' her father proposed mysteriously. With a glance he passed the baton to his wife.

'I spoke to your grandmother on the telephone earlier.'

They had a telephone, for the first time ever. Miriam was a little excited by the idea. Except that she had no one to call.

'Now that your grandfather's estate has been settled,' her mother continued, 'she's going to move down here to live with us, in a week or two. She can't afford the rent on her own. Besides, there's word that they're planning to demolish the entire street.'

Miriam had met her grandmother when they had spent two weeks at the house in Manchester. Nothing in Australia could have prepared her for Manchester. She lacked the words and context for comprehending, let alone describing, the grim conditions in which her grandmother lived. She would have avoided breathing, if she could. As much as possible she tried not to touch anything. And this was before she even entered the house. The external walls looked diseased, suppurating, dissolving.

Her grandmother was a small, slug-like woman, with odd bulges showing through clothes that were too tight. Below the edge of her dress, pale, puffy ankles emerged from shoes that must have sheltered tiny feet. Wisps of grey hair escaped from the faded floral scarf that surrounded her sagging face.

The inside walls of the house seemed perpetually damp. Miriam thought at night that she could hear the *drip drip* of water and imagined herself in a cave, deep underground. She awoke expecting to find stalactites descending from the mottled ceiling.

Babcia Lansky herself gave off a slightly rancid odour. She showed little interest in Miriam. She was, after all, only one of some fifteen or so grandchildren.

'And which one's this again?' she would ask from time to time, in her heavily accented English.

'She'll be staying in the downstairs rooms,' Miriam's mother was saying.

Now she understood why she had been relegated to the top floor.

There was, in the pit of her stomach, an absence, a hole, a nothingness. It seemed that her life had become like the external walls of her grandmother's house. But she was determined not to cry. There had to be another way.

Chapter Eleven

MIRIAM WOULD BE FOURTEEN YEARS OLD BEFORE SHE REALISED THAT she didn't really wish her parents were dead, but by then it was too late.

During the preceding two years she often wished it, and even made the air vibrate with the actual words. There were times when she wished everyone was dead, including herself. *Babcia* Lansky alone provided ample reason for supposing that life was God's biggest mistake.

Babcia Lansky did not wear black for mourning, but she seemed shrouded in black nevertheless. She seemed to cast a shadow, even in a darkened room.

It was with some horror that Miriam saw her own mother ageing into *her* mother, and feared the same fate for herself.

Babcia Lansky would generally eat her meals with the family, unless one of her physical ailments kept her downstairs. There was an abundance of these: gout, arthritis, heartburn; headaches of various intensity. She would suffer from sudden and intense bouts of itching for no apparent reason. On more than one occasion she claimed to be unable to come upstairs for a meal because her leg 'felt funny'. Or her arm. Or her back was giving her trouble.

'When you get to my age …' was something she said frequently. Except that she seemed able to insert the letter R anywhere in a sentence. 'Vern urrr get to myr age …'

Then there was the smell.

It was difficult to define, but eventually it lodged itself up Miriam's nose and she began to wonder if *she* smelt that way. In the bus on the way to school she would suddenly catch a whiff, and was sure others must smell it too: it was … cheesy. She would wash herself obsessively, even trying to wash up her nose. Anything to be rid of the smell. But sometime during the day it would surface again and she would try to keep her distance from others. She began to suspect that others were keeping their distance from her.

She did reasonably well in her eleven plus exams and found herself in a respectable grammar school. 'Respectable' people looked down on her Australian (and Jewish) heritage. Emphasising her Australian-ness did not have the same effect as in primary school. Furthermore, she felt it slipping away, slowly being sloughed off like last year's skin. Her advantage in age was no longer any advantage at all, as many of the girls seemed to have reached and even surpassed her level of maturity. The growth of her breasts had 'peaked' early, and she was no longer even slightly impressed with what she saw in the mirror. She was beginning to look slender, and even slightly bony, her angular form edging towards that of her father, rather than the more rounded form of her mother. That, at least, gave her some relief.

Even her father, often her only ally within the family—within the world—at times turned against her. That Christmas of 1962, even he would not agree to the transistor radio she so desperately wanted, so that she could listen to the music *she* liked in her room. It would distract her from her homework, he claimed.

'That music, that music …' her mother almost said.

It was only after Miriam met Charlie that she finally owned one.

There was no reason to consider the slender, rather pale young man particularly handsome. Miriam wouldn't have spoken to him at all had she not sneezed all over his chips. She felt the sneeze coming on and tried to find a tissue in her bag, but it was too late. Instinctively she turned to the left, bringing her hand up to smother some of the impact.

The rest of the impact was absorbed by the sleeve of the young man standing beside her … and his chips.

It was an early spring Saturday afternoon, and the sun was actually shining. It had been a bitterly cold winter. Miriam's geography teacher informed the class that it had been the coldest January of the century, the coldest, in fact, since 1814. Miriam only cared that it was at last warm enough to go about without a heavy coat and gloves. Today, she even wore a short-sleeved dress beneath her cardigan.

She was fighting the tail end of a cold, and her chip-spraying sneeze was one of the cold's last hurrahs. She had awoken that morning with her nose clear at last. There had been only a little nasal drizzle during the morning, and she had faced the afternoon with some confidence. This final sneeze had taken her by surprise.

It had taken her neighbour by surprise too.

'Ah,' he said. 'Bless you,' he added belatedly.

'I'm sorry!'

He pulled out a clean, carefully ironed and folded handkerchief.

'Thank you. I'm sorry.' Miriam only noticed the embroidered crest after she had applied the handkerchief to her nose in what she hoped was a delicate manner. She dared not actually blow.

'Keep it,' he suggested when she tried to return it to him. 'The name's Charlie,' he added, extending a narrow, long-fingered hand.

'Miriam.' No one had ever shaken her hand before, and the gesture was brief and awkward. Particularly as she still clung to the handkerchief in the same hand.

All in all, she decided her best course of action was to leave.

'Wait.' He caught hold of her elbow. 'You can't just leave. You can't sneeze all over a fellow's chips and then just leave.'

Miriam wondered if she should be offering to replace them.

'I'll buy some more and we shall share them,' he suggested.

She raised her head briefly and caught the mischievous smile playing around his lips and eyes.

No, not handsome. His face was too long and thin, his nose and chin too pointed. His eyes, though, sparkled, and there was something about his voice …

'You're American,' she half queried.

'Somewhat. I permit myself the luxury of being more American down here than up at college. It's not considered good form to be too American up at Balliol.'

'Balliol?'

'Ha! Delightful.'

She was still struggling to understand his amusement when Charlie, leaning casually against the railing, sprang upright. 'Ah, there you are. Anthony, Tiggi … meet my new best friend, Miriam. She and I were just about to get some more chips. These are only fit for the seagulls now.' He dumped the contents over the side.

A man and a woman about Charlie's age—which she guessed to be the early twenties—strolled towards them arm in arm.

'Miriam? How very … biblical.'

'Now, Anthony, don't start. Pay no attention to him, Miriam dear. It's a lovely name.' Tiggi laid a hand intimately upon her forearm.

Miriam was not quite sure what she was not supposed to pay attention to. Anthony looked very much like someone who wanted people to pay attention. He wore Tiggi as an accessory. She didn't seem to mind. And what kind of name was 'Tiggi'?

'Come on then, let's get those chips.' Charlie hooked his arm through Miriam's and propelled her forward. She wondered if she was now an accessory too. She wasn't sure she minded. She was slightly more startled when Tiggi took her other arm and leaned in towards her.

'How old are you, Miriam dear?'

'Sixteen,' she lied.

'Of course you are. Delightful!'

As the afternoon wore on, Miriam began to relax. At first she could think of little to say and held herself stiffly, her head darting back and forth like that of a vigilant sparrow. Little of what these people considered conversation was intelligible to her—or very interesting. She blushed when they sought her opinion on a matter of law, politics or society. She was not oblivious to the laughter behind their eyes. She was an afternoon's amusement for them.

Except that occasionally Charlie's eyes would soften and he would lower his voice and speak to her, and her alone, while Anthony and Tiggi were sharing some joke, or engaged in private bickering.

'You're not English,' he said at one point.

'No. We're from Australia.'

'And how long have you been here?'

'Two and a half years.'

'You're not sixteen, are you, Miriam. You were telling porky pies.'

She blushed but didn't answer. She would be fourteen in a month or two.

'It doesn't matter,' he said. 'I like your nose.'

Her nose? She had never really considered her nose. Why her nose? Was there something different about her nose? Her hand came up before she could stop it.

'Charlie,' Tiggi broke in, 'it's getting late and it's getting cold. We should be going.'

'You're right, Tiggi, as always.'

They had been lounging on deck chairs and rose to leave.

'We plan to pop down here quite often—don't we?—some of us chaps, on a Saturday or Sunday afternoon if the weather's fine. Keep an eye out for us, Miriam.' Charlie brushed her forehead with the sketch of a kiss.

Tiggi did the same. 'Lovely to meet you, Miriam. And I'm eager to spend the afternoon with you again.'

'I shall buy more chips for you to sneeze on. Indeed, you must come up to the house one weekend and sneeze on everyone's supper.'

'Now, now, Charlie, you know you can't keep her.' Tiggi offered Miriam one last smile and a squeeze on the arm. Anthony waved vaguely in her direction.

They walked away, laughter drifting back on the breeze. Tiggi now hung on Charlie's arm while Anthony brought up the rear, head down, kicking pebbles as he went.

Later that day, Miriam spent a long time standing before the mirror, examining her nose from every angle.

CHAPTER TWELVE

'I KNEW IT WAS YOUR BIRTHDAY, SO ...'

The interior of the coffee shop above the shoe store was dim and smoky, the music from the jukebox a little too loud. Charlie flicked his wrist to slide a cigarette partway from the packet—a skill he had mastered—and offered it to Miriam. He took one for himself and lit both.

She had been startled to find Charlie waiting for her when she stepped down from the bus.

'What are you doing here?' That might not have sounded very polite, but it was Friday afternoon.

'Waiting for you, of course.'

'But how did you know ...?'

'It doesn't matter. I have my ways.'

'But ...'

'Why don't you shut that pretty little mouth of yours for a moment. Let's grab some coffee.'

Over the weeks, Miriam had caught up with Charlie and his friends several times on a Saturday or Sunday afternoon. Sometimes Tiggi and Anthony were with him; sometimes others. After that first meeting, she had not tried very hard to remember names. Charlie had a lot of friends. She was aware that they tolerated her presence as a favour to him. They talked about all kinds of thing—politics, religion, philosophy, history, food—much of which she scarcely understood. She knew who John Kennedy was, but had only the vaguest notion where Cuba might be. Anthony seemed to think she should know someone called 'Spinoza' too. 'He was a Jew,' he said. And who knew that wine, chocolate and cheese could create such controversy?

She didn't care. It was Charlie she came to see. Charlie in his shiny, collarless jacket. Charlie with his black hair tumbling around his ears and down his forehead. Charlie in his winklepickers.

During their second cup of coffee, he reached into the canvas bag he often carried and pulled out a package.

'Here. Happy birthday.'

Smoke—it must have been the smoke—was making her eyes water. She was glad that in the dim light and smoky haze Charlie could not see this. Her own vision was seriously obscured.

That morning she had fought back tears when her brother Sammy called from Australia. He had sent a package, he said. It had not yet arrived.

Over breakfast her parents had given her some books and some clothes. Tonight, her mother had promised, they would have a special dinner. A while ago they had offered to host a party for some of her friends on the Saturday, but there was no one she wanted to invite. Her parents would not understand Charlie and his entourage. And why would they come anyway?

Now Charlie was handing her, across the table, a gift-wrapped box.

The tears that threatened to spill ... It was only the smoke in her eyes.

'Charlie ...'

'Open it.'

She did. Inside the box was a transistor radio.

'I knew you didn't have one.'

'Oh, Charlie! I can't ... You shouldn't ...'

'And this.'

He handed her an envelope containing a birthday card. When she opened it two tickets fell out. Tickets to a concert in June at the Hippodrome to see a new group from Liverpool that was taking the country by storm.

'Oh, Charlie.'

She stood, walked around the table, crouched beside him and kissed his cheek. So close to him, feeling the dark stubble rough against her lips, her hand on his shoulder, her stomach fluttered, turned somersaults.

With a will of their own her lips sought his, but with a sharp intake of breath he turned away, holding up his hand.

He may as well have slapped her face.

She stood with difficulty. The smoke, the thrumming of the jukebox ... The world spun around her.

'You can take a friend,' he was saying.

A friend? She almost laughed. She did laugh, but no one could hear her.

Love, love me do, sang the jukebox.

Then she was moving. For a moment she struggled to find the exit, but then made her way carefully down the steep staircase.

I'll always be true.

At the door to the street she paused. It had been warm upstairs. Her cheeks were flushed. When she finally pushed open the door the cool outside air *did* slap her in the face.

So plee-e-e-ease, love me do-o, drifted from above.

She was well down the street before she realised she had forgotten the radio and the concert tickets. She couldn't go back. She dared not even look back in case Charlie chose to follow her.

At the corner of her street she hesitated. What must she look like? What must she smell like? Cigarettes and coffee, neither of which was permitted. She would have to try to sneak in unnoticed.

Not a chance. The door was locked and she had no key. Her mother had done this before when she'd been late home, no doubt at the urging of *Babcia*.

Sometimes she thought it might be easier just to stay away.

'Miriam!'

A voice behind her.

'What are *you* doing here?'

Hoping neither her mother nor *Babcia* was watching through the window—a quick glance proved inconclusive—she turned back down the street, ushering Charlie before her.

'You forgot these.'

There was a narrow alley a short way down into which she ducked, pulling him after her.

'I don't want them.'

'Of course you do.'

'No I *don't*. Go away, Charlie. If my mum sees me with you she'll kill me.'

'Take them anyway.'

She wouldn't look at him. It was safer to watch the pigeons on the eaves opposite. She could imagine faces in the pigeon shit that stained the walls below them.

'Go away, Charlie.'

There was a moment of silence during which she closed her eyes.

'Don't cry, Miriam.'

'I'm not crying,' she snapped. 'Go *away*.'

For a few more seconds her eyes remained closed. When she opened them, he was gone. On the ground before her was the box containing the radio, with the envelope tucked beneath it. She picked them up and put them in her bag.

The wind gusted briefly as she climbed the steps to the front door. She hated having to knock on the door of her own home to be let in. 'I'll steal a key and get a copy made,' she muttered, before knocking and waiting.

When the door opened she pushed through, her mother's voice in pursuit. 'Where have you been? What's that smell? Have you been smoking again?'

'With friends,' she muttered.

'And these friends ... When do we get to meet these friends? Your father will kill you when he finds out you've been smoking again.'

She turned back and spoke from the third step. 'Then if you tell him, that will make you an accessory to murder, won't it. And what are you looking at?' Her grandmother looked on from the dim sitting room.

'Don't speak like that to *Babcia*!'

'Drop dead. You too,' she added to the shadow lurking among the shadows.

CHAPTER THIRTEEN

WHO ARE THESE PEOPLE? WHAT ARE THEY SAYING? WHY AM I SITTING ON the pavement?

The pavement was hard beneath her buttocks and warm to the touch of her hand. Miriam became aware of the sun shining in her eyes, obscuring her vision. For a moment she thought about raising her hand to provide some shade, but then realised she didn't really want to see anything. It was simpler just to close her eyes, and perhaps let herself sink backwards onto the concrete. Something—someone—prevented her, supporting her from behind.

'Do you know those people?' It was a woman's voice, vaguely familiar.

Miriam didn't really understand the question. *What people?* She had intended to say this out loud, but the words stuck somewhere in her throat. It was then that she vomited up ... something, if not the words. Donuts. She vomited up partially digested donuts.

The day had started out so well. It made a pleasant change after the previous few weeks. The morning was sunny and promised some genuine warmth. It was the first Saturday for some time that she actually considered going out for the afternoon. It was not only the late and prolonged cold snap and accompanying rain that had kept her locked away in her room. She didn't want to go down to the Pier and meet Charlie. She didn't want to go down to the Pier and *not* meet Charlie. But this was the fourth Sunday after her birthday and, despite herself, the memory of her pain and humiliation had begun to fade.

There was more to life than Charlie and his friends, she decided. In her imagination she ran through various scenarios, should she encounter them today or in the future. She would walk up to them as if nothing had happened. She would turn around and walk away. She would avoid the places they were likely to be. She would walk right past them as if she didn't see them. She would ignore Charlie if he called out to her.

She would run into his arms. He would run into hers.

The truth was, she suspected, that he would have forgotten all about her by now, found a new pet. So she would forget all about him.

Her parents looked relieved when she came downstairs and announced that she was going out to the Pier for the afternoon. Had they actually been concerned for her welfare, locked away as she was in her room for hour after hour? She hadn't told them about the radio. It would have been too difficult to explain how she came by it. She had spent hours listening to it through the earpiece. She listened, even though every time they played a Beatles' song she felt an exquisite ache somewhere in the pit of her stomach. Even that had faded over time. But she had no intention of going to the concert.

'We were thinking of doing the same thing,' they offered.

'Well,' she was quick to assert, 'I'm going right now. Don't expect me to hang around with you guys.' She had to pause for a moment, though. 'Dad, can I have some money?'

'What have you spent your pocket money on?' asked her mother.

'I'm saving up to buy you both birthday presents,' she lied. 'Just a couple of shillings, Dad?'

Then, suddenly, for no apparent reason, she thought of her nose. Her father moved over to the sideboard, reaching for his wallet. He had a full head of dark, curly hair ... and her nose. He had her eyes, too—startlingly green—although she supposed she really had his. He was tall and angular, and she feared she would be too. Though at the moment only the angularity applied. On the other hand, the roundness, the *bulginess*, of her mother repelled her.

What she actually spent her money on, apart from occasional cigarettes, was magazines. In them the young women wore plaid—skirts and jackets—with fur trim here and there, and high boots. Pillbox hats and gloves were everywhere. Her parents looked out at her from somewhere in the early part of the last decade.

'Here,' her father was saying. 'Stay out of trouble.'

'What trouble? What do you think I'm going to *do*, Dad? Don't you trust me?'

She didn't know why her father went on so. What trouble had she ever been in, really? Twice she had skipped school, but had been caught only once. The first time she had failed to do her homework and just couldn't face Mr Caldwell, her maths teacher. The second time she had awoken with a red volcano ready to erupt in the centre of her forehead. That day she had hidden in the cinema, sneaking past the usher when he was distracted. She couldn't recall what movie was showing, although she had sat through it three or four times. She was caught when, in desperation, she needed the toilet. The police were called and escorted her home. Her mother had exploded while *Babcia* smirked and muttered words with too many Rs in them. At least, she thought it was a smirk. If clay, badly moulded to resemble a face, could be said to smirk.

Later that evening, her father had been less concerned. While frowning and speaking sternly, she thought he might have been suppressing a smile. That was even worse, in some ways. That her crime was not taken seriously.

'Just stay out of trouble,' her father re-iterated, holding back a half-crown piece.

'All right. *All right!*' She was wise enough not to snatch the money from his hand. 'Thanks,' she muttered.

'We might see you down there,' her mother's voice followed her out the door.

She made some kind of sound that could have been interpreted as a response.

Donuts were the first order of business when she reached the Pier. The Palace Pier had the best donuts in the world, according to Charlie.

'Which means,' Anthony had added, 'that they are scarcely edible.'

'You British just don't appreciate fine cuisine.'

'You Yanks ...'

She preferred not to have memories of Charlie running around inside her head, so she sought to distract herself in the amusement arcade. The noise was almost enough to drown her thoughts; the flashing lights and chaotic activity were enough to obscure her vision.

But Charlie would not be here, in any case. This would not interest him. It didn't really interest Miriam. On that first day when she had skipped school—when she hadn't completed her homework—she had come down here and spent the day among the amusements. It had been much quieter then, of course. Honestly, though, she had been bored. She just couldn't feel the same excitement, playing the arcade games, that others obviously felt. She had watched one young man operating a pinball machine for hour after hour, gesticulating when things went badly. Sometimes bringing his fist down hard on the machine. Punching the air when he scored a great win, calling out and looking around for a reaction from the disinterested people around him. Most were totally engrossed in their own battles.

It had been the most interesting part of the day, watching that young man, observing as discreetly as possible the rainbow of emotions that traversed his blotched features. When he glanced in her direction the third time she became uncomfortable and wandered back towards the beach.

Today the crowds and noise threatened her with another headache. *Why am I here?*

She bought a bottle of Coke and sat at a small, round, sticky table. It was scarcely two o'clock and she was tempted to go home. There was nothing for her here.

Deck chairs lined the edge of the Pier, mostly burdened with older people. The younger people were among the amusements, on the beach or in the water. One older couple, older even than her parents, caught her attention as she sauntered back towards the road. The woman's legs were spread in a rather unladylike fashion, and her head tilted back. Miriam would have liked to drop something—a spider perhaps—into the woman's wide-open mouth. The man beside her was slumped down in his chair, his head tilted uncomfortably forward and to one side. *They could be dead*, she thought. *We would all just walk by and never know.* But then the woman emitted something between a cough, a snort and a snore. Her eyes opened briefly, unseeingly, before closing again. Her mouth, having snapped closed at the moment of waking, gradually slackened and fell open again.

How utterly repulsive it is to be human. Miriam became conscious of herself as a kind of balloon made of skin, filled with water and worse. She saw herself burst, and splatter the world around her with gore.

Indecisiveness slowed her steps. She could think of no reason to stay here. She could think of no reason to go home. For the first time that day she truly raised her eyes and surveyed the crowd. If she caught a glimpse of Charlie ...

But a commotion in the road beyond the Pier drew her attention. Something was happening. There were shouts and screams. A crowd began to converge on a point to the west. It was inevitable that she gravitate towards it.

It was difficult to see through the crowd exactly what was happening. She could see, though, the body of a car, the front of which disappeared into the crumpled remains of one of the shellfish stalls scattered along the path.

'I saw it,' someone said to her right. A woman in her mid to late twenties. 'I saw it,' she repeated. Miriam couldn't tell who she was talking to. She was a pretty woman, with red hair hanging in wisps below a straw bonnet. One gloved hand was held to her mouth, and she may have suppressed a sob. Bright red lipstick stained the white material of the glove.

'What? What did you see?'

'It came out of nowhere, you see.' It was a Welsh accent, Miriam decided. 'The car, it just came right across the street there. Slammed straight into the stall.'

The woman began to take quick, heaving breaths. Sirens sounded in the distance. Miriam pushed through the crowd. Voices arose here and there, offering advice, opinions, warnings.

'It could have hit me.'

'Did you see ...?'

'I think ...'

'Don't ...'

The police car was first to arrive. An officer was quick to leap from the car and begin moving people away.

'Step back, please.'

The crowd thinned in front of her.

'There were two people ...' It was little more than a whisper from the woman in the straw hat, who had followed Miriam forward.

An ambulance had arrived, with a fire truck not far behind. Two policemen were now holding the crowd back. The seafood smell was strong. Here and there on the ground, among broken glass and twisted plastic, were whelks and cockles and mussels.

Miriam averted her eyes from a shoe. A quite unremarkable, sensible, comfortable brown shoe. It was still attached to a foot and leg which disappeared somewhere beneath the carnage. It could have been any woman's shoe. Just a glance around the crowd and she could see several others like it.

But the handbag was a different matter.

It lay on the path near the rear passenger side of the car. She knew that handbag. Many times she had surreptitiously rummaged through it in search of a cigarette, or spare change that wouldn't be missed. It was unusual. The handle was bamboo, and the bag itself was embossed with pairs of bright red cherries.

That was when Miriam sank to the pavement.

It was some time before anyone made a connection between the girl, and the middle-aged couple sprawled dead among the whelk juice.

PART THREE

CHAPTER FOURTEEN

15 November 1949

My dear, darling Charlie,

You must think that I have abandoned you, slipping away that day while you were at school. That wasn't my intention. Your father did not want a scene. I certainly intended to make one. But in the end my will deserted me.

So much seems to have deserted me. I can't quite find myself, it seems. Where did I go?

Well, in one sense, of course, I came to this place, so quaintly named Emerald Hill. I think of Oz, of course. There are many wizards and scarecrows here. I can't seem to find my ruby slippers. But there you are, you see: something else that has deserted me.

I'm rambling, I know.

I can't seem to ... I don't know, sometimes. Is it darkness? Or is it a light so bright that it blinds? I don't know, but in that light or darkness I see things. Or no, that's not quite right. I just know things. There are people, sometimes names, occasional glimpses. I know there's something important but it slips away again.

Is that baby really mine? Did it really come from me?

But you, dear Charlie, I know you are mine. I see it in you though you fight it. You deny it.

Don't you see the signs? Sometimes I can read the script and glance ahead. Sometimes I hear the whispers.

Oh but it's so heavy sometimes. I'm like Dorothy in the field of poppies. I feel sleepy. But I don't want to fight it. I would love to sleep a dreamless sleep. But my sleep is never dreamless, of course.

But you, Charlie, are my hope. Somehow I have fired from my body an arrow. I see it arcing into the future. I believe it will be good. I have to believe that.

I will write to you again soon, my darling boy.

From your loving mother.

This was one of many letters that Charlie did not receive from his mother during that absence of six months, when he was eleven or twelve years old.

Many years later, when he came home for the summer holidays from college in Pennsylvania, he found them, locked in the drawer of his father's desk.

It was a strange set of circumstances that found him breaking into the desk. His father the congressman was away, and his mother was in a panic.

'We have to find them! We have to find them!'

'Them' referred to her tarot cards, not the letters. The letters were wholly unexpected.

Charlie stood calmly before his mother as she paced the length of the study. Growing up with someone, seeing them day after day, it was easy to miss the inevitable signs of ageing. Seeing someone only every few months—as was now the case with his mother—it was usually easy to spot those changes. It could be a shock to see the grey hairs, the deeper wrinkles around the eyes and mouth, the slight stooping of the shoulders, the sagging of the flesh. But his mother remained a mystery.

She could traverse the decades in a matter of seconds. One instant she might sparkle and glow with the energy and enthusiasm of youth; then she could ease into the quiet tranquillity of the middle years; but then, within the blink of an eye, she might collapse in upon herself, assuming the age and wisdom of the universe. There were those other times, though, when nothing seemed to hold her together. Fragments of her would bounce around the room, as they did now, leaving bloody trails.

'I have to read them before you go,' she pleaded.

Several days before Charlie arrived home his father had taken the cards and hidden them away. He did this from time to time, fearing that his wife might be heading for another of her 'episodes'. Usually, of course, this triggered one. As strong as Charlie's disdain was for those arcane cards, his desire to prevent such an episode was stronger.

The drawers of his father's desk were the last place he thought to look. Actually, that wasn't true. They were almost the first place he thought of, but a superstitious awe held him back. The broad chisel shook in his hand. He sensed his mother pause behind him. A quick glance revealed that a deep calm had descended upon her in anticipation. Her features were smoother, her back straighter. Her eyes were sharply focussed. Charlie would enjoy the company of his playful, youthful mother—at least for a time. The old woman she sometimes became would fill him with a mixture of sorrow and awe. But the woman who stood behind him now was someone to be feared. Despite himself he would listen to what she said. This woman was a queen, an empress.

'Do it!'

The tarot cards were not in the first drawer, but the letters were. His father had never shown them to him. Until that day he had no idea they existed. When he read them later he thought perhaps his father had been wise. What would an eleven-year-old have made of these? What did a nineteen-year-old make of them?

He didn't read them immediately. At first, he didn't realise what they were. He pushed them aside, looking for the cards. Then he forced open the second draw; and finally the third down on the left-hand side of the desk. There they were, his mother's elaborate, Russian tarot cards. Beautiful really, he had to admit. Hand painted in the previous century.

But when he turned to hand them to her, her gaze was directed elsewhere, towards the half-closed top draw, and the letters within.

'What?'

She turned and left the room without answering.

Only a few of the letters had been opened. He opened them all now. They were all dated, and, with enforced calm and patience, he sat in the leather chair behind his father's desk, laid out all fifteen and sorted them into chronological order. It might have bothered him once—perhaps even fifteen minutes earlier—to be sitting in his father's chair. That chair with shiny patches here, and minute surface cracks there. The slightly musty odour of his father was strongest around that chair. He could almost taste it. But he barely gave it a thought as he slid into it. What did it matter now? He had already violated his father's inner sanctum.

Monday, 21 November 1949

My precious boy,

When will you visit? I don't really expect you to write ... Although, perhaps one of your beautiful drawings ... I wonder if that will be your way, your way of seeing.

Your father promised to bring you here to see me. I thought perhaps the weekend past. But it's probably too soon. I know he is very busy. Very. Busy.

Perhaps you will draw your future. Our future. *The* future. You are the future. I see you shooting forth ahead of us all.

The air here is full of portents. There are people here who mutter and moan, and sometimes I think there is meaning in what they say. They laugh at things no one else can hear or see. Sometimes I laugh with them. Sometimes I laugh without them too. I hardly know why. One man ... He stopped me in the corridor on the way to the evening meal. He is a well-dressed man. His family takes good care of him. At least, they clearly provide for him. He reminds me of Benjamin Franklin as I saw him once in a portrait. He wears his hair long but is balding at the front. His mouth is small and his lips narrow; his eyes droop above and below, like those of a bloodhound. He stopped me in the corridor and looked directly up into my eyes—he is a man of no great height—and he said to me: 'Who are you? Why are you here? You shouldn't be here. You know that.'

And I do know that, don't I, that I shouldn't be here. And yet I am. I don't know where else I *should* be, or if there is anywhere else. And now that I'm here I so seldom know what to do.

Still, here I don't have to worry too much about anything, which I suppose is a good thing. But ...

Oh, I'm suddenly so very tired, so I think I'd better say goodbye now. Come visit soon.

All my love,

Your Mother.

The next letter was a little surprising.

... I don't think I ever told you that my grandmother on my mother's side was Jewish. Which I suppose makes my mother and me Jewish. And you. We never made much of it though. My mother brought us up Church of England—baptism, confirmation—the whole lot. She only told me all this when we were over there.

I suppose that explains why I hurt so badly during the war, when we began to understand ... And then I was so excited—proud even—when Israel became a state. I never understood at the time why I ...

This was just the kind of thing that annoyed him about his mother, the way she had of twisting things. She hurt during the war because ... Well, because everyone hurt. And she lost both her brothers. And as for Israel ... He couldn't remember a word from her about it at the time. She would always find explanations for things that didn't need explaining. Or that hadn't happened.

And Jewish? What did that mean? Did it mean anything to him? Was it even true?

The letter ended abruptly: 'They're coming for me—' The next letter clarified this.

> I ache all over. My head hurts sometimes. Dreadful headaches sometimes. Thankfully, I don't remember the actual sessions. Every second day. I sometimes forget other things too. But they say it helps. The room is terrifying. I always notice first the bright yellow tiles on the wall, like some badly decorated bathroom. Then the narrow bed with the thin mattress laid on top. I never look at the trolley with that strange device, and the electrodes. There is a lovely nurse. I always look at her when she is on duty. She has lovely green eyes.
>
> Each time I go in there I feel sure I'll never come out. It's like being sent to the electric chair. Or so I imagine.
>
> That nurse. I wonder what her name is. She probably tells me every time I see her and I forget again. She is what I imagine the Daughter of Abraham will look like. At least, occasionally in my dreams I see those green eyes looking back at me.
>
> It is Christmas very soon. Surely you will come and see me then.

The Daughter of Abraham. There she was again. It was the first he'd heard of her green eyes. His mother's eyes were so brown as to be almost black at times, as were his own.

She had referred to this figure more than once during her letters while he was at college. At some stage he had grown too old for his mother's bedtime stories, and some years passed before he heard again of the Daughter of Abraham. What was it she had written once? Something she had 'seen' in a dream or vision.

He shook his head to bring himself back to the present. Why was he wasting his time and effort thinking about this kind of nonsense? And what on earth had his mother been thinking, writing to him about her shock treatment?

They hadn't visited at Christmas, nor ever once in the months that followed. At least, Charlie hadn't. Perhaps his father had.

It wasn't his fault. Nor was it his fault that he had gradually begun to forget how to miss her.

In another letter, written some weeks later:

I realise now that I'm not allowed to die yet. Not for many, many years ... I don't know whether to be grateful.

It was not until his mother returned that he discovered she had *not* simply being staying with friends. By that time—was it March? April?—he had more or less convinced himself that she was dead. People died.

The woman who returned was much quieter than the one who left. And not so tall. Or so it seemed to him. Her hair had been cut short at some point and was only just beginning to gain some length. She didn't seem to quite fill her body.

Charlie didn't know how to ask the questions he wanted to ask. She hugged him. When she whispered an apology in his ear, he felt he should reciprocate.

Gathering up the letters, he rose slowly from his father's chair. A glance at his watch told him that James—Jimmy—would be home from school soon. Jimmy was now about the age Charlie had been back then. He scarcely knew him.

He found his mother in the conservatory that had been added to the back of the house.

'I didn't know about these.' He waved the letters in front of her.

'I didn't know that you didn't know.'

'What were you thinking, writing this stuff to me!'

'I wasn't in my right mind, clearly. Everyone was agreed on that point.'

'There's not much I'm grateful to Father for, but not letting me read these is one thing I should probably thank him for.'

'Don't talk about—'

'I'll talk about him however I wish!'

His mother returned her attention to the plants she was re-potting.

'You won't have seen these. They're from Hawaii. The big island. They call it the Orchid Isle. Did you know that? I didn't know that.'

Her sudden serenity infuriated him. He waved the letters again, unsure what point he was trying to make before her silent indifference. He sat in a tattered director's chair and read part of the last letter again.

> I think I understand now. Part of it anyway. I am fixed, apparently. I suppose I do feel better. When I carried you and those other babies, I was weighed down from the inside. But for months—perhaps years—I have felt weighed down from the outside. I have been pregnant on the outside, carrying some heavy weight, some kind of almost life. Perhaps now it has been born, having been borne for so long ...

She didn't sound 'fixed' to him. He doubted the doctors would have thought so either if they had read this. Was she fixed now, this woman who bent down to kiss the blossom as she might have been expected to kiss the forehead of her baby?

She removed her garden gloves and the stained apron she always wore on such occasions and turned to him.

'I must read for you.'

'No you mustn't.'

'You leave in less than two weeks. This is important.'

'I'm leaving tomorrow.' He was pleased to see that the announcement cracked her composure. 'I'm going to New York to spend the last few days with Gillie and her family.' It made sense, as the ship sailed from there. Gillie would be somewhat surprised, though, when he rang to tell her in a few minutes.

CHAPTER FIFTEEN

IF THE WORLD WAS CHANGING AROUND IT, OXFORD DID NOT DEIGN TO notice. Arrogantly self-assured, it sneered at the world racing by, which thought it knew where it was heading. Oxford knew better. It would preserve what was important and true within the ark.

Despite this, Charlie found the cloistered, old-world atmosphere of Oxford amusing rather than stifling. In fact, this old-world feel was not unlike the old-world feel of much of 'New' England. While within Oxford's cloisters, he could be its harshest critic. Beyond its confines, he would blast the superficiality and transience of the 'modern' world. It became something of a habit, this contrariness, and he did not always like it within himself, but could do little to quieten it.

He also did not like the way he had treated Gillie. She was a good kid, and he would miss her. But his attention was forever drawn to the horizon. It had been a mistake to spend those last two weeks with Gillie and her family. It raised Gillie's hopes unnecessarily. The goodbyes were only that much more difficult.

Over the next few years, Charlie set himself the task of becoming as British as possible. It was rarely British enough for the other denizens of Balliol. Even the English were rarely British enough. Nevertheless, the fact that conversations were frequently peppered with japes, jests and gibes did not stand in the way of his forming many genuine friendships.

'Hey, Bollocks.' It had been too much of a temptation for Anthony, one of his best friends, not to coin this term of affection for him, although he generally only used it when they were alone or among their closest friends.

'What is it, my noble friend Ward?'

'I was chatting to Hawkins earlier today,' said Anthony.

'And what did Dickie have to say?'

'He has invited us to a party this weekend and apparently there will be some sort of Russian countess present.'

'I envisage some enormous, upholstered, couch-like woman, bedecked in jewels. I fail to see the attraction.'

'Well, she's not exactly a countess yet, although her father lays claim to some sort of noble heritage. She's nineteen years old and more in the form of a *chaise longue* than a sofa, if we must use furnitorial imagery.'

'When and where is this *soirée* to take place?'

'*Chez* Hawkins senior—the ancestral home in Reading. I only mention it because you happen to have independent means of transport. Saturday next.'

'And does the *chaise longue* have a name?'

'Sophia Abramovna Batiashvili. I have been practising that for hours. I think I'm in love with her already.'

Charlie was slow to respond. His Russian was limited to the point of non-existent, but it did not take a scholar to recognise the meaning of the *chaise longue*'s patronymic.

'Yes. Yes of course,' he said into the growing silence and under Anthony's puzzled gaze. 'I would be delighted to meet Sofa—I mean, Sophia.'

Of course he would have to meet Sophia, daughter of Abraham.

'But it seems to me that Cicero leaves no room at all in the world for friendship.'

'How so?' Charlie peered keenly at the road ahead, searching for the turnoff to Oakedown Manor, only half attending to what Anthony was saying.

'Because he asserts that only *good* men can be friends, and I am yet to be convinced that any such exist.'

'Hear, hear,' chimed Tiggi from the back seat.

'Nor good women, either.' Anthony twisted in his seat to look at the third passenger. 'Nor ... What is it that you are exactly, Trots?'

Arnold Yallop became Trots by a circuitous route. 'Gallop' was bounced around for a while but wasn't considered very clever or amusing. Then someone came up with Trots because, as some witty wag had asserted, 'Arnold never gallops anywhere.' Arnold also liked to pretend occasionally that he was a Trotskyite. Finally, there was that unfortunate occasion when he came down with a gastric bug and ... That clinched it.

'We *Übermenschen*,' observed Trots laconically, 'are beyond good and evil.'

'Here's the turn.'

Charlie realised how silly and irrational his excitement was, but could do little to slow his heart rate or dry his increasingly sweaty palms. He eased his grip on the steering wheel as the large Elizabethan country house came into view.

Several vehicles were parked to the left of the house and he pulled in alongside them. On the immaculate lawn a large marquee had been erected, and dozens of people moved back and forth between it and the house. The dust raised by the passage of vehicles along the unsealed driveway gave substance to the early evening light. There was insufficient breeze to shift the dust along.

'What was the occasion again?' Tiggi slipped on her heels and straightened her skirt.

Anthony extended his arm for Tiggi. 'Oh, some kind of last hurrah for summer. Possibly sacrificing to the gods. Or it might have something to do with the fact that Hawkins' old man has just announced that he will stand for parliament in the by-election.'

'What side of the fence?' asked Trots.

'I thought it indelicate to ask,' replied Anthony. 'But I'm sure you'll adopt your usual subtle methods and find out for us.'

'The red bunting hanging from those oak trees might be a hint,' observed Tiggi.

'Oh God, another wealthy armchair socialist.'

'Try to keep Trotsky on a leash tonight, there's a good chap.' Anthony extended his other arm towards Trots.

He ignored it and slouched towards the marquee. 'I need a drink.'

'Your own backside looks fairly armchair-shaped from this angle,' Anthony called after him. Trots responded with a V-sign over his shoulder.

Charlie hung back, surveying the scene. The house was larger than that of his grandparents, and perhaps even older. He had spent some of the past summer there, with his ageing grandparents, and part of it back in the States.

He had been surprised by his father's attention. Charlie was now a 'man', apparently, and more interesting. Still, he couldn't warm to his father. They could never become the friends his father now wanted them to be. The family business was of no interest at all to Charlie. He was passionate about the ancient Greek and Roman philosophers he was currently studying. There was something solid and eternal in the ...

'Wake up, Charlie.' Tiggi held out her other arm for him and their linked chain followed Trots towards the marquee.

Hawkins had already draped his arm across Trots's shoulder and, catching sight of the others, signalled them over.

'We're here to meet genuine royalty, Dickie, not tired old queens like you. Show us the way.'

'She denies it of course, Ward, but that only proves it's true. Walk this way.'

'Couldn't possibly.'

'I'm getting a drink first.'

'Of course you are, Trots. And probably last too,' observed Hawkins.

The rest of them followed Hawkins towards the north-eastern corner of the marquee, where a string quartet was playing. 'She's cello.'

'Wouldn't mind being that cello myself,' Anthony whispered to Charlie.

The cellist looked neither Russian nor Jewish. She wore her red hair long and straight. Her pale, freckled face was intense. Wrapped around the cello, the shape of her legs was clear beneath her long, black, sheer gown. Her body swayed, her head jerked back and forth. She slashed the bow across the strings like a crazy woman.

When the performance came to an end, performers and audience alike needed to catch their breath. Then Hawkins introduced Charlie and the others.

'Sophia, these are the miscreants I was talking about. This is Anthony. This is Tiggi who, astonishingly, is still vertical although it's past eight. And this is Charlie, who we call Bollocks for reasons you would probably never understand. Trots is already leaning against a bar somewhere.'

'Hey, guys. So you're the other American.' She homed in on Charlie.

'You're from New York? Hawkins here told us you were a Russian countess. Sophia Something-Unpronounceable.'

'Dickie's been spinning tales. Queens born and bred. But, to be fair, my grandfather arrived on Ellis from Russia in 1905.'

'And I suppose the whole countess thing ...'

'Ha! There weren't too many Jewish Russian aristocrats on the boat.'

'But your father's name *is* Abraham, isn't it?'

'Well, yeah, but er ...'

'Sophia,' interrupted Anthony, 'do you have time to join us for a drink before you have to play again?'

'Half an hour or so. Anyway, Charlie, ain't you the lord or something? And your father's a congressman, am I right?'

'I suppose one day I'll be a baron, but I don't think about it much. I imagine the world will end first.'

'You're an optimist then.'

'And fortunately, being a congressman isn't yet hereditary.'

They steered between chairs, tables and people towards the bar in the opposite corner.

'What can I get you, Sophia?' asked Anthony.

'Nothing for me, thank you. I still have to play. My father's here actually,' Sophia resumed in Charlie's direction.

'So, your father is who exactly?'

She frowned slightly. 'Professor of physics at Columbia. He *says* he came over here to visit me, but I think Cambridge is courting him.'

'Don't use the "C" word in polite company, Sophia.' Anthony pulled out a chair for her and they settled around a table with their drinks.

'And what are you studying, Charlie?'

'Classics.'

'Those of us who may actually have to earn a living one day,' injected Anthony, 'are studying more relevant things. I'm reading Law. I look forward to a long life of defending the interests of bloated global corporations. Tiggi here is the real brains. Organic chemistry, isn't it, dear? She has her mind set on inventing new ways to poison the planet. Never leave your drink unguarded around Tiggi.'

'There you are. Lost you chaps.'

'And this is Trots, our token revolutionary, reading ...'

'Palaeontology, actually.' He borrowed another chair while the rest of them made room for him.

'Which explains why he's more than half fossilised himself,' continued Anthony with scarcely a pause. 'And Hawkins here—as I'm sure you already know—is our medical man.'

'Just shut up for a moment would you, Anthony dear, and let others get a word in?'

'Tiggi'—Anthony ignored the barb—'is my second cousin once removed. Always looking for a way to remove her again. No luck so far.'

'And always looking for a way to slip that line in. I take it you live here in England, Sophia?' Tiggi offered her a cigarette—which she declined—and lit one for herself.

'Yes. I'm studying the cello at The Royal College—as I'm sure you're all stunned to discover.'

'Splendid.'

'And I need to resume my place.' Indeed, there was movement in the opposite corner. 'Are you hanging around awhile, Charlie?'

'I have nowhere better to be.'

'Later then.'

Charlie watched her retreating figure, neatly silhouetted against the sun setting beyond her. Some of the ridiculous phrases his mother had used over the years when referring to the 'Daughter of Abraham' refused to be silenced.

'The sons of Abraham have failed,' she had said one day. 'It's up to the Daughter of Abraham now.'

Or had she said 'daughters'? He had been very young at the time.

'She has remained hidden through the ages, the Daughter of Abraham, but one day soon she will be revealed.'

Esoteric nonsense, all of it!

'You must be there for the Daughter of Abraham when she needs you.'

Then Tiggi's voice broke into his reverie.

'I must say, I love that whole wan, pale vampire look she has going there. And the teeth. I guess that's why she has her eye on you, Charlie.'

The string quartet completed its final set at around 10 pm. His friends had dispersed, but Charlie hovered around the marquee, trying to catch Sophia during her free moments.

'I'll have that drink now.'

He could feel the heat rising from her body and detect the slight hint of body odour as she sat beside him.

A tall, thin, angular man approached Sophia, who rose to greet him. Charlie rose with her.

'Daddy, this is Charlie. Charlie, this is my father.'

'Nice to meet you, sir.'

The man's narrow face made his nose appear disproportionately large. His eyes, close together behind thick lenses, appeared to move independently of his face as he peered closely at Charlie. Unruly hair tumbled about his ears.

'Charlie. I've been hearing about you. Sophia tells me you're from Delaware, and that your father is a congressman. Is that right?'

'Yes, sir, that's correct.'

'And you're heir to some title or other on your mother's side.'

'Yes, sir.' Charlie didn't enjoy discussing these aspects of his life, and the professor's intense gaze was disconcerting.

'Kollock. Your father's Charles Kollock.'

'Dad, what's with the third degree already?'

'Sophia, I've heard this boy's father speak on occasions. Private conversations. Nothing public. Nothing written. Yet. It's led me to believe the man might be both racist and an anti-Semite.'

'Dad!'

Charlie didn't believe that about his father. But ... How would he know?

The professor pushed his glasses further up his nose and leaned in closer. 'How much of the father is in the son, I wonder?'

'Dad! I'm sorry, Charlie.'

'There's much more of my mother in me than my father'—the admission surprised Charlie himself—'and my mother is Jewish.'

'Your father married a Jewish woman?'

'He probably doesn't know.'

'How could he not know?'

'She didn't know until ... It's a long story.'

'You have not received the *aliyeh*?' At Charlie's blank look, the professor continued, 'Clearly not. The call to chant the blessing. What you would call *bar mitzvah*.'

'No.'

Professor Abraham Batiashvili sat down, and Sophia and Charlie followed suit. The professor looked thoughtful. 'Your father, he could become a powerful man. I would not welcome that.'

'Sir, I scarcely know my father. I know nothing at all about his work or his convictions.'

'I need to think about this.'

After he had left, Charlie spoke, more or less to himself. 'Think about what?'

'Don't worry about him, Charlie. Why don't we go for a walk? I have to work off some of this energy. I always get hyped up after performing.'

Out in the gardens, beneath an arbour through which Charlie could see the figure of Orion marching across the sky, Sophia enlisted his assistance to work off some energy.

CHAPTER SIXTEEN

25 October 1962
Dear Mother,

Granddad seems to be rallying. Of course I would like you to come over for a visit, but I don't think you need feel pressured. Anyway, these days with a phone call from me you can hop on a plane and be here in no time. I doubt that I can be home for Christmas. Is there any chance that you could come here? Perhaps Jimmy could come. How old was he at his last birthday? Thirteen? I would hardly recognise him, I'm sure.

I hope Father is well. There is someone over here who knows him a little. Well, her father knows him a little. Do you know a Professor Abraham Batiashvili of Columbia? His father was a Russian Jew; crossed the Atlantic during one of those terrible Russian pogroms. Does his name ring any bells with you?

His daughter Sophia is a very talented cellist studying at the Royal Academy in London. We have been seeing each other a little. I think you would like her. That's another reason I thought you might consider coming over here at Christmas. That and Granddad's poor health. As I said, he is rallying, but one never knows ...

We have never talked about the letters you sent me while you were away, when I was a boy. Perhaps there's nothing much to say. But one of them left me wondering a great deal, the one in which you discuss your mother's heritage. Your heritage. My heritage. Perhaps this *is* something we need to talk about.

Well, that's about it for now. Back to tackling Plato's *Republic*.

All my love,

Charlie.

It was a very cold and early winter, and two-metre-deep snow drifts hugged the house on Christmas morning.

Charlie's grandfather, never a robust man, looked pale and frail in his tartan dressing gown, seated in the over-large armchair which was his nest most days. Behind him, in the corner, an impressively tall, once-living pine tree almost brushed the ceiling. Its scent pervaded the room, sweeping aside the smells of breakfast. And old age.

Charlie's brother, Jimmy, thirteen years old, was the only one who appeared animated. His grandmother had already dozed off, and his mother was a statue by the window, staring at the snow, the pale, reflected light washing any remaining hint of colour from her features.

'It really is quite beautiful,' she remarked unnecessarily.

She had arrived late yesterday, and Charlie was still wondering how he was going to broach the topic that had been bothering him since his conversation with his grandmother at breakfast two days earlier.

'Grandma,' he had begun tentatively. 'Grandma?'

There was a little of his mother in his grandmother's features, although her hair was now grey and her skin mottled here and there. It took a moment for her eyes to focus on him—as it did, sometimes, those of his mother.

'What is it, Charles?'

'There's something I've been meaning to raise with you, but ... Well, I don't wish to appear indelicate.'

A sudden smile brought warmth to her features. 'Good heavens, Charles, I don't give a fig about delicacy! What is it?'

'I wondered why ... I wondered why you never discuss your heritage.'

'My heritage?'

'Your Jewish heritage.'

'My what?'

'Your ...' Charlie could tell, however, that her mystification was not the result of her sometimes poor hearing. 'My mother ... There seems to be some misunderstanding here.' He felt the colour rising in his cheeks.

He lowered his eyes and dabbed at his lips with his napkin. *Such assertive white cotton*, he observed. The family crest embroidered in gold in the corner.

'What nonsense has that daughter of mine been feeding you?'

'Perhaps I misunderstood. It was many years ago that she—that I thought she mentioned it.' That was only a partial lie. It was true that the letter in which she mentioned it was written when he was only a child, though he had first read it only two or three years ago. She had written it when she was in a mental hospital, and he wondered why he had never given more weight to this.

'The most I can be accused of,' Lady Thorburne declared, 'is of concealing my non-conformist background. My mother, God bless her, was staunchly Presbyterian before she married my father, after which she converted to the true faith.'

A tiny smile tugged at her lips as she said this and her eyes twinkled. Charlie did not need reminding that this referred to the Church of England.

'Not that there would be anything to be ashamed of ...'

'Of course.'

'Look, Charlie'—he liked it when she used the less formal designation—'your mother ... I'm sure you realise that she has ... episodes. Yes, yes, I see you know this. But I also see that she has a way about her that can ... affect you. I know. I understand. She knows how to reach deeply into your soul. Even when you resist it most fiercely. Perhaps especially then.'

Now Christmas morning was slipping away; then, after a demanding Christmas lunch, the afternoon struggled to stay awake. In the end he decided to postpone any serious conversation with his mother until after the arrival of Sophia—which would, in any case, certainly provoke further discussion. Or perhaps he wouldn't raise the issue at all.

On the second day of the new year—the snow having eased some days earlier and the roads having been cleared—he drove to the railway station to pick up Sophia. She had been away over Christmas, performing with an RCM orchestra at Carnegie Hall.

The train was on time, and he was a little late, so by the time he arrived a figure that he took to be Sophia was waiting by the kerb. Little could be seen of her, wrapped as she was in a red, hooded coat and scarf. A gloved hand waved at his approach.

Once out of the car he found the tip of a nose, between sunglasses and a scarf, on which to bestow a kiss, before loading Sophia's bag into the boot. At least, he hoped it was Sophia's bag. Hoped it was the tip of Sophia's nose. There was little supporting evidence until a muffled voice said, 'Give me a balmy Noo Yawk winter any day! Screw this shit.'

'You may need to keep all this on in the house. It's not what you'd call centrally heated.'

'We'll have to stay snuggled up together all week in bed.'

'Ah, about that ...'

'Separate rooms, right?'

Her face slowly emerged as she pushed back her hood, removed her sunglasses and unwound several layers of wool. High cheek bones, narrowing quickly to a sharp chin, forcing her lips into an almost permanent pout. Charlie wondered sometimes if he actually found her attractive. It was hard to tell after a while.

'We have to at least maintain the illusion of virtue, for the oldies.'

'Thank God for the invention of darkness and doors.'

'How were your concerts?'

'We're performing at the Royal Albert in about two weeks. You'll be able to see for yourself.'

'I ...'

'Oh, it's all right. You'd probably be bored.'

'No, I ...'

'No, seriously. It would be like me going to a lecture about Plato or Socrates, or whoever.'

'No, of course I'll come.'

'That would be nice. But if you don't, I'll understand.'

'Welcome to Fernlea House.'

The driveway swept around a circle of snow-covered lawn, at the centre of which a large fountain remained iced over. Ivy climbed halfway up the walls of the Georgian façade, framing the windows—a green surprise in the stark landscape.

'There's something Tudor hiding beneath the surface,' he said, surprised by a sudden surge of pride. 'An ancestor buried it back in the mid-eighteenth century.'

'It's charming.'

'And cold.'

Their arrival prompted the emergence of staff and family members. Blundell took Sophia's bag and Humphreys took the car.

'Mother, Grandma, this is Sophia. Sophia, this is Lady Thorburne.'

'Lovely to meet you, dear.'

'And this is my mother,'

'Sophia.'

'Sophia's father is Professor Abraham Batiashvili of Columbia. Soon to be of Cambridge. I thought you might know him.'

'I don't think so. Come along, Sophia dear. Blundell will show you to your room.'

Charlie observed his mother's reaction closely, but saw nothing of note. He wasn't sure what he had expected. A lifting of the eyebrows? An inflection in her voice? A faltering step? Nothing. Again he recalled some of the things she had said over the years. On more than one occasion she had turned his face so that she could hold his eyes with her own. 'You must be there to protect her when the time comes, Charlie.' Now, as then, he shivered.

'It's so damn cold in here,' he muttered.

'It's many years since I visited New York,' his mother was saying, 'although my husband spends much time there, I believe.'

'I understand that he and my father have crossed paths on occasions, if not quite swords.'

'Politics? I don't care much for politics.'

'Nor I, particularly, Mrs Kollock.'

'Emily, please. Music, I believe?'

'Yes. It's where my soul is.'

'Soul. Yes.'

Sophia glanced over her shoulder at Charlie, trailing up the broad stairway behind her and his mother, who, in turn, trailed behind Blundell. His grandmother seemed to have melted away. He thought he read in Sophia's glance a plea for assurance. He gave what he could in a quick smile.

'I must leave you here,' said his mother suddenly. 'We'll see you down at dinner at eight. You must tell us about your concerts. No formalities, please.'

'Did I say anything wrong?' Sophia whispered as Charlie drew alongside.

'No, no. Not at all. Mother's like a feather on the breeze: you never know in which direction she's likely to drift.' They paused outside her room while Blundell placed her bag on the ottoman. 'Shall I come in?'

'I'd like to rest for a while, and then freshen up before dinner.'

'Of course. My room is two doors down.'

A little later he found his mother in the library. Tripped over her, in fact. The library was the warmest room in the house, with a large fire burning, and he would spend many evenings there reading. The only light in the room at the moment was from the fire, which cast living shadows across the room. One of those shadows, it turned out, was his mother's legs, stretched out before her.

'Uh!' His mother, clearly asleep, was startled awake. 'I didn't ... when there was ...' Her words were fragmented and unclear.

He prevented himself from falling only by bracing himself against the adjacent chair.

'Mother?'

'Charlie, is that you?'

'Yes. Let me turn the lamp on.'

'No, no. I prefer the dark. I hadn't realised I was so tired.'

He sat in the other armchair, turning it slightly to face her. Her own chair faced away from the fire, and her features were shrouded.

'So ... What did you think of Sophia?'

'Lovely. Charming. I'm sure.'

'Yes, but I ...'

'What, darling?'

He was unable to suppress the sigh that escaped as he sank more deeply into the chair. 'Mom, I've been meaning to ask ... In one of the letters you sent to me all those years ago—'

'I scarcely remember what I said to you, sweetheart. I wasn't ... well.'

'In one of them you said you were Jewish, that Grandma was Jewish.' Her response was a long time coming, and he thought she may have fallen asleep again. 'Mom?'

'Yes. Yes, I think I remember that.'

'But it's not true, is it?'

'True? What does that mean exactly?'

'You're not Jewish.'

'Who can say? Perhaps somewhere back in our ancestry ... Is being Jewish really about descent? I sometimes felt Jewish in those days. It felt important to be Jewish.'

'Mother, could you try to talk sense for once?'

'Oh, Charlie, sometimes sense isn't really very important.' As he fought to contain his frustration, she continued, 'I once thought you might be an artist, a painter. Does art make sense?' He maintained his silence. 'Life,' she concluded, 'is much more like art than science. We are works of art, and sometimes I wanted to paint myself as Jewish.'

'But *why?* Why Jewish and not ... I don't know ... Hindu?'

'I don't entirely know.'

'There are other things you've said ... I'm not sure what I'm supposed to do with them.'

'Feel them.'

'What?'

'Don't try to *understand* them; *feel* them; experience them. What's important is whatever process my words—*anything*—provokes in you. That's really all there is, after all.'

He was slightly astonished to hear, in his mother's words, an echo of one strand of pre-Socratic thought. *Nothing exists. Even if something exists, nothing can be known about it. Even if something could be known about it, knowledge about it can't be communicated to others.* All that is left is the experience, or the self, experiencing. There is no *it*. Where would that line of thought ultimately lead? Descartes believed he could battle his way back up to a form of dualistic realism, but Charlie wasn't so sure. He sensed an abyss. The hairs on the back of his neck rose.

He was in no hurry to break the silence. His mother's next whispered words barely did so. 'We are wind harps.'

Then she slept again.

CHAPTER SEVENTEEN

'A FEW OF US ARE GOING DOWN TO BRIGHTON ON SATURDAY AFTERNOON. Would you like to join us, Sophe?'

'It's still a bit cold, I'm thinking. Oh, and I have rehearsals. Maybe when the weather warms up. If it ever really does again.'

'Sure. I'll see you Sunday then, maybe?'

'You can stop by here after your excursion, if you like.'

'Sounds good. See you then.'

Charlie sometimes wondered if he should add 'I love you' before these phone calls came to a conclusion, but once again the faint *click* beat him to it.

And that afternoon his chips were sneezed upon by a young Jewish girl with unruly hair and surprising green eyes; and a nose prepared to make a statement, whether sneezing or not.

She was only, what ... fourteen? But his heart had quickened in a strange way the first time he saw Miriam. It wasn't love; it wasn't infatuation; it wasn't lust ...

That was it! It was the same feeling he had experienced the first time he saw film footage of an atomic bomb being detonated. *Awe*, with all the connotations that word had borne across the centuries. *Mysterium tremendum et fascinans*. He was the harp of which his mother had spoken, but he was confused by the 'tune' Miriam played upon him. It was ridiculous.

Then she disappeared.

He had been dividing his time between his room at Balliol, his grandparent's estate, and Sophia's flat in Paddington. More and more often, the last.

He and Sophia had drifted into a relationship that others, at least, were beginning to regard as 'serious'. He wasn't sure if he shared that view. Or if Sophia did. There was no telling where their paths would lead them. Sophia dreamed of gaining a place with a major orchestra upon graduation. Where? Who knew?

He was increasingly uncertain about his own path.

He had tentatively agreed to spend part of the summer in New York, to meet Sophia's mother and wider family.

With some embarrassment he had explained to Sophia that his mother and grandmother were not, apparently, Jewish after all, but she seemed unconcerned.

'She's an interesting woman, your mother. We had some fascinating chats about you.'

'You realise nothing she says can be relied upon, right?'

'Fascinating, though.' She refused to expand on this and he suspected she was only teasing.

So the Jewish stuff was nonsense. The 'Daughter of Abraham' stuff was surely nonsense. It had nothing to do with his involvement with Sophia.

But then he met Miriam.

And then she disappeared.

Following the misunderstanding on the occasion of Miriam's birthday, he had returned to Brighton almost every Saturday, and some Sundays, sometimes with company, sometimes alone. But it was almost two months before he found himself outside the Georgian house in St Michael's Place.

He had never mentioned Miriam to Sophia. What, exactly, would he say? As the weather grew warmer, Sophia did occasionally accompany him—with or without his other friends—to the seaside. He wondered what he would say if they actually met Miriam, and was torn between wanting and not wanting to see her.

'I really can't figure the attraction, you know.'

'What?'

'It ain't Coney Island. And Brighton Beach *back home*, it's, you know, an actual beach, with sand and all.'

On this particular Saturday afternoon they were alone, but the crowds were out in force, drawn forth by the sunshine. Sometimes the sounds from the Pier grated against his nerves; and today the mixture of food smells—cooking fat, syrupy sugar, fried onions, shell fish—threatened to empty the contents of his stomach.

'Yeah, well, maybe this is the last time. For a while at least. I was thinking we could maybe pop out to the farm—Chetwood—once in a while. You might like it there ... the quiet. How are you with country smells?'

'You mean like cows and sheep and stuff?'

'And pigs. Especially the pigs.'

'Sounds divine.'

'Seriously, though ...'

A disturbance out near the road snatched their attention. 'Looks like some kind of accident.'

'Want to go take a closer look?'

'No, Sophe, I don't think so. There's plenty of people there already.'

Police cars and ambulances arrived. Whatever it was didn't look good for someone. Later, on the way up to the railway station, they walked past police barriers placed around a car and a demolished food stall. There were unsettling stains on the pavement.

'Yeah, I think we'll find another place to hang out. What do you say? Time to introduce you to Chetwood.'

Yet, only three weeks later, he stood on the pavement outside Miriam's house, gazing up at the sun-drenched façade. He was there because of a dream. His mother's dream.

She had telephoned two days earlier, leaving a message at the Porter's Lodge for him to call back as soon as possible. It was urgent, she insisted. He returned the call late Friday afternoon. He was disinclined to lend the 'urgency' much weight.

'Something's wrong,' she said, after accepting the reverse-charges call.'

He waited for her to say more, but she didn't.

'I suppose something's always wrong somewhere, for someone,' he replied eventually.

'Don't be facetious. Is Sophia all right?'

'As far as I know—'

'Call her.'

'I—'

'Call her.'

'I'm going to see her tomorrow anyway. I'm not going to call her because of some—'

'It's the green eyes. I'm being haunted by those damn green eyes.' His mother rarely swore, but when she did it was with great conviction.

'Green eyes? Sophia doesn't have green eyes. What's this about, Mom?'

'There's a dream ...'

'Of course there is.'

'I'm in a forest, although I have a sense that I'm not really me. I'm someone else. It's night time and very still. Far too still, I think. Aren't forests noisy places at night? Or is that jungles? Anyway, I find myself in a clearing, at the centre of which is a tarn. Actually, it's probably not a tarn. I'm not entirely sure what a tarn is ... Some very specific body of water, I should think. It's such a lovely word, though. Anyway, this small body of water, this lake, is very still, and in it I see the full moon reflected. I hadn't noticed the moon before. It had seemed too dark for there to be a moon.

'So I kneel down at the side of this lake—the dream's so vivid! I catch a strong scent of garlic and realise that I've crushed a plant—garlic chive I suppose it is, or some such. And that's when I realise that I'm naked.'

'Naturally.'

His mother, on the other end of the line, seemed not to register the interruption.

'I lean over the water and see my own reflection. Only it's not me at all. I think it's Sophia, but the image shifts and quivers as a slight breeze disturbs the surface of the lake. But then I realise it's not a reflection at all. There's someone in the water looking back up at me with green eyes, bright green eyes. But then—and here is the terrifying part—*I* am under the water ... Or, rather, I am the one under the water, but looking back up at me looking down. And I can't breathe, and I start to struggle and thrash around. And then I wake up.'

'So what would make you think this was Sophia?'

'As I was waking ... I heard a cello playing. Mendelssohn, I think.'

It was perhaps these irrelevant details that most frustrated Charlie when his mother was surging full steam ahead like this. Mendelssohn? What did it matter?

He wanted to say, 'So you had a dream. So what?' But once again she had said just enough to unsettle him.

'Does this have something to do with "the Daughter of Abraham"? In your mind at least.' This was the first time since childhood—and perhaps not even then—that he had asked such a direct question about this aspect of his mother's ... *delusions*!

'You remember that? You don't! *I* don't.'

'Mom, tell me right out: do you think Sophia is the Daughter of Abraham, and, if she is, what does that *mean*?'

'That was all just silliness, when I was unwell.'

'Right. Then what makes you think this ... this dream isn't just more silliness?'

'It never feels silly at the time.'

'Right.' He took a deep breath. 'Look, Mom, I'm really tired of all this. I don't want to hear anything more about it, any of it. I'm sure Sophia's fine. I'll see her tomorrow. I'm going to hang up now.'

There may have been more words travelling down the line towards him, passing deep beneath the Atlantic, when he did so.

The next day Sophia was, indeed, fine.

'I've never noticed, before,' he said. 'The green highlights in your eyes.' Her brown eyes.

'Are there?'

'Yes, particularly in a certain light and from a certain angle.'

But, no matter how hard he tried, it was not those eyes that occupied his mind; and the following afternoon he prepared to knock on the door in St Michael's Place.

He needed to knock three times, and was about to give up, when the door finally opened to reveal a man about his age.

'Yeah? What can I do for you?'

Charlie recognised the broad Australian accent. Miriam's brother? She had mentioned a brother, still living in Australia.

'Er, my name's Kollock, Charlie Kollock. I was looking for Miriam. Is she home?'

The man looked slightly askance at him. 'What's she to you?'

'Nothing. A friend.'

'What would Miriam be doing with a friend like you?' Then something in his expression changed. Whatever he had been about to say seemed to stick in his throat. He cleared it, as if that might help, glancing down at his shoes. Charlie could smell the pomade in his hair, even at this distance.

'Is everything OK? Is Miriam OK?' Charlie took half a step closer to the door.

'How the fuck do *you* know Miriam? Where is she?' The man stepped forward and grabbed him by the lapel of his jacket. '*Charlie*, was it? Charlie what? I'm calling the cops. If ...'

'She's just a friend. I haven't seen her for weeks.'

'What's a bloke like you doing with a fourteen-year-old girl for a friend? Eh?'

'No. We just—'

Charlie didn't see the fist. He scarcely even felt it. He just knew that his backward trajectory down the steps to the street probably wouldn't end well.

❧

Clearly, this was a hospital. Where the hospital was, how he came to be there, and how long he had been there eluded his grasp for the moment. He was alert enough to press the call button and summon a nurse.

'Ah, Mr Kollock, you've returned to us, I see.'

Trying not to sound like a character in a corny melodrama, he asked, 'Where am I?'

'Well, at least it's not "who am I",' the nurse responded in a musical, Irish lilt and with a cheeky smile. 'You're in the Royal Sussex County Hospital, Mr Kollock. You came in yesterday with a severe concussion. And a nasty shiner.'

He began to remember.

'There are a few people waiting to see you. Your grandmother has been in to see you. I'll give her a call presently. The doctor will call in shortly. And then there is ...'

'Who?'

'We'll have to notify the police that you have regained consciousness. They want to talk to you.'

He supposed they would. He didn't feel inclined to press charges against Miriam's brother, though.

'How did I get here?'

'Someone called an ambulance, following your ... fall.'

He surmised it might have been his assailant.

The doctor's visit was brief. They wanted him to stay in for one more night.

Charlie was slightly embarrassed, shortly after, to let his grandmother see him under these circumstances.

'Grandma, about what happened ...'

'Oh, Charles, I don't need to know that. I've no interest in what young men get up to when my back is turned. That's what backs are for. You're all right, and that's what matters.'

He hesitated before posing his next question. 'Grandma, was Mom always ...?'

'A little doolally? I suppose I should say "sensitive". Yes, I suppose she was, but in a quite harmless way. I blame it on your grandfather's side, of course. One or more too many marriages between cousins over the years, I suspect.'

'I never understood how she came to marry my father.'

'Well, she is quite beautiful, your mother. *That* she gets from my side.' His grandmother patted his hand. 'What has she done this time?'

He shook his head. 'Nothing.'

'She does a great deal of that.'

'Harrumph. Excuse us.' Two large figures, one in uniform, filled the doorway. 'Mr Kollock?'

'I'll leave you to it for a moment.' His grandmother seemed unperturbed by the appearance of the constabulary.

The man who had spoken nodded at her and stepped aside to let her pass. Both men entered the room and remained standing at the foot of the bed. 'I'm Detective Sergeant Mansfield. I have a few questions to ask you.'

'Of course, but I don't want to press charges.'

'Charges? Right. There is that I suppose, but that's not why we're here. We're here to ascertain exactly what your relationship was with Miss Levinson.'

'Miriam? We're just friends.'

'Pardon me, sir, but it seems a little odd, a gentleman like yourself being friends with the young lady.'

The man remained at the foot of the bed, his trilby under one arm, leaning his weight casually on the hand that grasped the bedrail. The uniformed officer stood silently beside him, almost at attention. His unwavering gaze unnerved Charlie.

'Look, Sergeant ... Mansfield? What's all this about? Miriam's brother—I assume it was her brother who ...' His hand drifted towards his partly closed eye. 'He asked me where Miriam was. Has something happened?'

The detective held Charlie's gaze for a moment or two before answering. 'Mind if I sit down?'

'Not at all.'

Mansfield jerked his head towards the uniformed officer, who promptly took up a position outside the room.

'About two weeks ago, after the death of her parents—'

'The death of her parents?'

'You didn't know? About three weeks ago both her parents were killed in a dreadful vehicle accident. The driver lost control and mowed them down on the pavement—together with the owner-operator of a seafood stall. Miriam witnessed the aftermath.'

'Jesus!'

'A week later, she disappeared. We assume she ran away. She packed a few things ...'

'I had no idea.'

'If she ran away with *you*, Mr Kollock ...'

'Good grief, no! I haven't seen her for about six weeks.'

Again the detective took his time before speaking again, watching him closely. 'Mr Kollock, she is underage. If we have reason to believe that anything untoward—'

'No, I tell you! We're just friends. It was a chance meeting, and we occasionally bumped into each other down at the Pier. Myself and some of my friends.'

Charlie could see how it might look.

'Do you have any idea where she may have gone?'

He had been about to ask the detective the same question. 'No.'

'Well ...' The detective rose, placing his hat on his head as he did so. He took a card from his wallet and placed it on the bedside table. 'If you think of anything, or if she contacts you ...'

'Of course.'

'Good afternoon, Mr Kollock. I hope you're feeling better soon.'

It was not only the smell of stale cigarette smoke that lingered in the room after the detective left.

CHAPTER EIGHTEEN

NOVEMBER 22, 1963, HAD MADE IT VERY DIFFICULT FOR CHARLIE TO imagine ever returning to live in the US. Sophia's family had known the Kennedys personally. They had a summer house in Cape Cod.

'Daddy never liked Joe, but Jack ... He had a lot of time for Jack.'

America's idyllic childhood, it seemed, was well and truly over. Charlie didn't like what the cracks in American society were revealing. England was stuffy, still weary from the war and shuddering on its shaky foundations; but somehow its decrepitude seemed more honest than the corruption across the Atlantic. If he had harboured any doubts, the events of Bloody Sunday in Selma, Alabama, had put paid to those. Add to that the growing conflict in some corner of Indochina, and the possibility of conscription ... No, he had no desire to return.

He and Sophia had argued about this. She would apply first for jobs in the US. New York was her first choice.

"Charlie, you know ... It's New York. Who wouldn't want to live in New York, for chrissake?'

There had been talk of getting married after she graduated. Sophia would graduate at the end of this year, and Charlie ...

Well, he was in the midst of producing a potentially interminable dissertation on 'The Influence of Pre-Socratic Philosophy on the Philosophical Writings of Alfred North Whitehead.'

'You can finish that anywhere, right?'

What exactly he would do after he did finish remained comfortably vague. He had imagined drifting into a teaching position at Oxford, or some other suitably time-honoured—but English—institution if necessary.

Or possibly retiring to the country and producing academic tomes that would rock the establishment. He was almost ready to be seduced by the writings of Tolstoy and Gandhi. When his grandfather had died in March, his mother had inherited the estate. She sold the smaller farm in Sussex to help pay for some much-needed repairs to Fernlea House, and then signed Chetwood Farm over to Charlie. 'I have no interest in it,' she insisted.

He had not yet reported the gist of his most recent conversation with his father to Sophia. A conversation that had taken place after his grandfather's funeral, just three months earlier.

'My father ...' he began. 'My father has made it clear that his financial support for me is not without its temporal limitations.'

'Which means?'

'He will only support me until the end of next year, after which he expects me to return and take a responsible role in the business, or ...'

'Or?'

'Or I'm on my own.'

'Well, Charlie, what's the problem with that? If we have a future together ...'

'Do we have a future together, Sophia?'

She was taken aback by the question. 'Well, I ... I suppose I'd begun to think so, after all this time. I mean, what have we been doing here if not ...?'

Charlie didn't like to think that they had simply drifted into this arrangement over the last two years. Some time ago he had actually decided that he loved Sophia. Everyone agreed that it was a good match. Except, perhaps, his father, who expressed his disapproval by being very guarded with his approval.

The last time Charlie had visited his parents' home—he no longer thought of it as *his* home—in Delaware, his father had been more reserved than ever. The gate that had briefly opened on the possibility of friendship between them was now firmly secured.

'The mother is formidable,' had been his father's most decisive comment to date on Sophia's family.

The families had met at a dinner in New York. Congressman Kollock gave no indication of having met Professor Batiashvili before, though the latter was adamant they had met—on several occasions. The meeting was cool, at best, but Mrs Batiashvili had earned his grudging admiration.

While her husband divided his time between New York and Cambridge, Mrs Batiashvili was currently teaching at Rutgers School of Law in Newark. She made few concessions to the fashions of the day, wearing her hair pulled straight back in a ponytail, revealing a slightly darkened complexion and a strong underlying bone structure. She wore little or no make-up, and had what Charlie regarded as 'honest' eyebrows. When he first met her, he had been slightly intimidated— most people were, Sophia assured him. Her rather stern and severe appearance, however, concealed a wicked if not dark sense of humour. During the dinner, he had overheard her 'whispered' comment to Sophia, with reference to his father: 'That man's going to get a nasty surprise one day, when he finally realises he doesn't actually control his world.'

Shortly after that dinner Charlie had observed to Sophia that she seemed to take after neither of her parents in appearance. It was then that she told him something that would send tremors through his world. It wasn't until she said this that he realised how important it had been to him at a visceral level.

'I'm told I look like my father. My biological father, that is.'

'You're biological father?'

'He was my mother's first husband. He died before I was born.'

'I never knew ...'

She shrugged. 'I don't think about it. Daddy's ... Daddy.'

So Sophia *wasn't* the Daughter of Abraham Batiashvili? But he loved her, right? He loved *her*.

He squeezed next to her on the narrow couch. Just a few weeks earlier he had moved out of his room at Balliol and taken a small flat not far from the college. He had a little independent income from some tutoring he did at the college, and from some translation work he carried out for a local publisher—Greek and Latin. There was also a small income now in the form of rent from Chetwood; but none of this would be sufficient without the allowance from his father.

'No no, Sophe, it's all right. I think so too. I *know* so. I love you, and ... I want to marry you. Will you marry me?'

'I'm swept off my feet here.'

'Sorry, I didn't intend it to come out like that.'

'C'mere. Of course I'll marry you, Chawlie.' She sometimes exaggerated her accent, which he found adorable.

It was probably time he became a grown-up.

Charlie caught the train to Paddington, but it was early in the day. Sophia wouldn't be at her apartment yet. He disliked driving in London, so he had driven back from Chetwood early that morning and left the car in Oxford.

He had taken to spending some time at the farm, playing at rural living, and the past three days there had left him in a pensive mood. More pensive than usual. It was a beautiful summer's day. The more oppressive heat that could assault the city at the height of summer was still some weeks away. From Paddington he wandered south toward Hyde Park.

He wasn't sure why he felt so drawn to Chetwood Farm. He didn't believe in such things as being 'drawn', yet drawn he was.

What *did* he believe in?

The busyness of Hyde Park—the sounds, the colours—assaulted his senses. He found a bench at which only one other person sat, and placed himself at the end, as far from her as possible.

What was happening—had happened—to the world? It seemed not so long ago that the world was simply black and white—the fifties, the early years of this decade. He was reminded of the The *Wizard of Oz*. The opening scenes were filmed in black and white and set in Kansas. Then, suddenly, there was colour and jangly music. *We're not in Kansas anymore.*

Where are we?

He was reminded, too, of those early photographs, black and white but hand painted in colour. All around him in the park were hand-painted young people; but it wasn't enough to cover an underlying melancholy: black and white or, at best, sepia. But perhaps the melancholy was his alone.

And Oz? Oz was based on a fraud, wasn't it? Not that he was in any position to judge. He was quite at home in Carnaby Street, despite his publicly expressed opinions.

'It's all still black and white below the surface.'

A movement to his left caught his eye, and he realised he had spoken out loud. He prepared a smile and turned towards the young woman with whom he shared the bench. 'Sorry,' he began, and then froze.

Green eyes stared back at him. The hair was short and the face pale and gaunt. But the eyes were the same. And the nose. That emphatic nose. Even more emphatic in that thin face.

'Miriam?'

But there was no recognition in those eyes. Worse still, there was no light. He would usually become impatient with verbal expressions like that. How could there be light in anyone's eyes other than what was reflected back? But there it was. Her eyes were matt rather than glossy.

'Do I know you?' she said eventually.

'Miriam? It's Charlie.'

'I'm Millie. And who the fuck's Charlie?'

'Sorry, I thought for a moment ...'

'Fuck you.' She stood abruptly and walked away.

He had stopped looking for Miriam over a year ago. Not that he had ever looked consciously or with any purpose. Just once in a while he would wonder ... And then he would cast about, as if she might be there, at that bus stop, or crossing that street. He had never returned to her house since that day. He had never returned to Brighton since that day. He had forgotten Miriam. Except ...

For just a moment he could have sworn that the girl was Miriam. Then it struck him as odd that she had asked 'Who's Charlie?' but not 'Who's Miriam?' Miriam. Millie. Was it a stretch?

He didn't believe in moments like this. Yet he followed her carefully at a distance. She exited Hyde Park onto Kensington High Street, and eventually turned left into Abingdon Road. Partway down she stepped into a small grocery store, and Charlie stopped to gaze in the window of a second-hand shop. As the moments passed he became aware of an old man staring out at him and moved a little further down the street. He ducked into a doorway just past the grocery store and waited for the young woman to emerge. When she finally did, she was carrying two bags of groceries.

She walked back a little way and turned into a narrow, one-way side street. Many of the houses looked derelict. It was near one of these that she paused, put down the bags, and opened the gate. She picked up the bags, passed through, and kicked the gate closed behind her.

Charlie paused across the street from the gate, no more than ten feet away. He lit a cigarette, smoked half and then crushed it under foot. Lit another.

What if it wasn't Miriam? But it surely was.

What if it wasn't?

He destroyed the second cigarette on the wall behind him.

What if it was?

Charlie had been slowly preparing the large house on the farm so that it could serve as a retreat or a holiday home for him and Sophia. He occasionally arranged for this to be cleaned or that repaired. Some things he tried to do himself, with middling success. The lawns, at least, he could mow, and the gardens he could tend. This was something he had absorbed from his mother over the years. He savoured the toughening of the skin on the edges of his fingers and the pads of his hands. The operation of most tools, however, remained beyond his grasp. He brought in tradesmen from the village. Occasionally, for small or urgent jobs, he called on one of the farmhands. He hated to intrude, though.

Sometimes Sophia would accompany him on a weekend. The sound of her cello flowed out across the landscape, smoothing the edges of the sharper sounds: a lamb bleating, a rooster crowing, a tractor in the distance; the sound of his hammer as he sought to repair the trellis. He would sometimes just stop and listen. The contours of the music followed the contours of the hills.

Until, suddenly, the more strident and staccato tones of Shostakovich might burst forth and fragment the afternoon. From time to time the music would stop abruptly and Sophia's colourful repertoire of curses would pepper the air. It was a risky time, but worth it. He would climb upstairs to the bedroom where she practised and take the place of the cello between her legs.

He rarely came away unscathed.

Sometimes he cornered Mr Pierce for a chat. Occasionally they wandered down to the Castle 'n' Crow. The years had not been kind to the old man. Gout forced him to walk with a limp and his shoulders were stooped beneath an invisible weight. They'd been fortunate during the war, he had confided to Charlie, not to lose a son, as so many had. Yet somehow Charlie sensed that he had lost his sons anyway. The younger had moved to Canada some years ago, and the older was now ... Mr Pierce was vague about this. Up north somewhere. They scarcely saw him. He didn't like to talk about whatever it was his son—Jack—was mixed up in. But his eyes lit up when he talked about his daughter, and his voice became almost musical.

'Our girl now, our Ellie ...'

Elaine. Charlie hadn't thought of Elaine for many years.

'Got herself a place in one of them colleges way over Birmingham way. Smart girl our Ellie. Worked her way into the *Royal Mail* she has since. The *Royal Mail*, mind thee.'

It was clear that this dusted Elaine herself with a hint of royalty in his mind.

On a later visit Mr Pierce was all aglow with the news that Elaine would be returning to the area later in the year.

'Over Coxton Sudbury way, mind. To be *postmistress* no less, when old Miss Harrowood retires.'

Charlie wondered what it would be like to see Elaine again. Would she remember him? He scarcely remembered her face, but the majesty of her unruly hair had stayed with him. During the intervening years, his memory of it had acquired a mythological aura.

Sometimes the conversations between Charlie and Elaine's father drifted into more dangerous territory, regarding the future of the farm. At such times Mr Pierce's features would collapse on themselves. Charlie reassured him that he and his wife would always have a home on the farm, no matter what.

'I would love to learn more about farming,' he suggested one day, but Mr Pierce had looked at him slightly askance.

'It baint something you can learn, Charlie.' He still stumbled a little when addressing him as 'Charlie'. 'It's in the blood.'

Charlie thought this a rather quaint and old-fashioned idea. He had been reading up on modern farming techniques. But he kept his opinion to himself.

In truth, he could never really see himself as a farmer. But he sensed—or imagined he sensed—within himself a desire to connect with the earth in a more sensual way. This was, as Sophia would no doubt inform him, also a 'quaint and old-fashioned idea'. Another manifestation of his ill-defined romanticism.

There was little of romance in the street where Charlie watched the gate through which 'Miriam' had passed. There was, however, something dangerously romantic in his growing urge to rescue her. Anyone living in a house like that surely needed rescuing. Anyone with such sunken, emaciated features.

The house itself ... He could not see the windows on the ground floor, but those on the floors above were mostly boarded up. Only a few on the second floor retained some intact panes of glass. Crude graffiti adorned the wall that lined the street, behind which there might once have been a garden. Further down the street the wall had partly collapsed, and thistles could be seen, pushing up through discarded furniture.

Beyond that the carcass of a car left little room for traffic to pass by.

The decision was made. He stubbed out the third—no, fourth—cigarette and approached the gate. A simple latch, accessed through a hole in the wood, was all that held it closed.

The garden was worse than he had imagined: sheets of tin, some chicken wire; a refrigerator on its side, gaping open. Something scurried away through the jungle of thistles and clumps of burdock.

The ground-floor windows were all boarded up. The front door, up three steps, was slightly ajar. On closer inspection it appeared to be held closed only by a piece of wire looped over the interior door handle and a hook nailed into the doorframe on the right. It would be a simple matter to undo it, but he chose not to forego the usual conventions. He knocked sharply on the solid panels of the door.

No sound came from within.

He knocked again, at the same time calling out, 'Hello! Anyone home?' He couldn't help thinking that the scene required something more imaginative, but his imagination failed him. 'HELLO!' he called again, with slightly more volume, if not conviction.

Having made the decision to come this far, it seemed that additional decisions were required. Several of his inner voices were advising against proceeding any further. One of the wiliest among them was reminding him that he could come back tomorrow, or the next day, perhaps with a friend. He was well acquainted with the voice he termed the Procrastinator. There were the usual voices advising him that the situation was dangerous, that the girl was not his concern, or that she would have no interest in him. One of the loudest proclaimed that she couldn't possibly be Miriam anyway.

Inevitably, though, there was the quiet but firm voice. The one that still said to him occasionally in his dreams, 'You must be there for the Daughter of Abraham when she needs you.' This voice, he knew, was not to be relied upon. This voice, he knew, would only lead him astray.

He reached through the gap between the door and the doorjamb and slipped the wire off the nail.

CHAPTER NINETEEN

ONCE THROUGH THE DOOR, CHARLIE FOUND A BUILDING THAT HAD BEEN divided into apartments, probably between the wars. Now the door opened onto a long, dim corridor, with doors either side. Doors, or at least doorways. Many of the doors were gone, or hanging off their frames. Very little light came in through the boarded-up windows, but he could see that the ground-floor apartments, at least, had long since been stripped to the bones. Even the bones were missing in places. Stumbling in the near darkness, he found a stairway at the end of the corridor, leading to the levels above.

He called up the stairs but there was no reply. There were faint sounds of movement, perhaps scurrying feet, and he dreaded to think what might have taken up residence there. Taking care on the stairs, he mounted slowly to the floor above. Some light came through from a window on the landing, where one of the timbers had been dislodged.

The entire building smelt of rot and decay, but, through that, as he climbed higher, he detected a more mundane smell. It took a moment to identify the smell of a burning candle. Then something else, something more pungent.

'Miriam?'

The arrangement on the first floor was the same as that on the ground floor: a long corridor with doors on either side. More of these doors were in place, and several were closed. About halfway along, faint light flickered through one open door.

'Miriam?' This now came out as little more than a whisper. Perhaps this had not been a great idea.

He approached the door with caution, peering around the casing to determine what faced him within.

A candle burned on the floor near the corner, mounted on a saucer. The flame was steady for a moment, but then flickered back and forth in unseen air currents. Next to the candle was a bare mattress. And on the mattress, her back propped up against the wall, her eyes closed, smoking a small pipe, sat the girl who might or might not have been ...

'Miriam?

'Miriam,' he said with a little more volume and confidence.

With a quick glance towards both ends of the corridor he stepped through the doorway, knelt beside the girl and shook her shoulder gently.

Her eyes flickered open slowly, and her lips moved. Perhaps she whispered a word or two, but he couldn't make out what she said.

Then, 'Who the fuck are you?'

'Jesus!' Charlie leapt to his feet and spun around.

This other voice came from behind him, near the door. In the opposite corner, where the open door had kept it from sight, another figure struggled to its feet.

Charlie took a step or two to the side, towards the door. 'My name's Charlie. The girl ... Miriam ... I've come to see Miriam.'

'Millie, you mean? Who the fuck are you?'

'Charlie,' he repeated, edging closer to the door. But, much to his relief, the figure subsided back into the tatty armchair in which it had lain hidden. He turned back to Miriam. 'Miriam. Millie. Can you hear me?'

Miriam's eyes—surely it was her, although the shadows moving across her face obscured her features—became more focussed, and something like a laugh escaped her.

'Can you stand?' He placed a hand beneath her elbow and tried to lift her.

'Are we going somewhere?' Her words were clear this time.

'Yes, that's right. You're coming with me.'

'I am?' She made a feeble effort to rise, but fell back almost immediately.

'Miriam. Millie. Can you stand up?'

'Why would I want to do that?'

'I'd like you to come with me.'

'I think we must be in some kind of time loop, man. Do I have to say "Why would I want to do that?" again?' Her laugh came out as a snort and developed into a hacking cough.

'Can I sit with you for a minute, then?'

'Whatever. Want a toke? It's strong shit.'

Some mumbled words sputtered from the far corner.

'Don't worry about Nick there. He's well and truly out of it.'

'Why are you here, Miriam?'

'Millie. Who's this Miriam chick? I live here. Where else would I be? And who are you again? Maybe you told me already.'

'It's Charlie.'

'It is? Cool, but who are you?' Again she snorted her amusement into the air around them. 'Oh, wait a minute,' she added, when she had caught her breath. 'The bench guy. You're Charlie, the bench guy. Are you following me, Bench Guy?' She glanced up at him coquettishly, holding the pipe towards him. 'Sure you don't want some?' She shrugged when he refused, and then picked up the candle and drew the flame down into the pipe, drawing deeply on the smoke. Again she coughed. 'Strong shit,' she re-affirmed.

'Why don't I take you out and buy you a coffee?' he suggested.

'Why don't you buy *me* and a coffee?' This time her look was openly suggestive.

'Oh, Miriam.'

'Stop calling me that!' The dream in which the dope had wrapped her shuddered for a moment.

In the corner, the other figure stirred. Rose. Took some steps towards them.

'Millie, 'sevrythin' OK?'

'I'm fine, Nick. Don't worry. Great shit, by the way. Thanks. I owe you.'

'Yeah, you do. What about this bloke?'

'Bench Guy's just leaving, aren't you, Bench Guy.'

She seemed to have sobered up.

'Meet me tomorrow morning. Ten o'clock. At Kenco's in Sloane Street.'

'Yeah, sure. I'll be there. Now leave a girl in peace.'
'Please.'
'Get the fuck out of here, pal.' The shadowy figure loomed closer.
'Kenco's,' Charlie called back, beating a hasty retreat.

She wouldn't come. She probably wouldn't even remember he'd invited her. Since nine thirty Charlie had been sitting at a table under an awning on the pavement. He was already on his second coffee. From time to time he wondered what he was doing and why. He had wondered this acutely when he had arrived at Sophia's flat the previous evening, later than expected. He wondered what—if—he should tell Sophia. What, indeed, would he tell her?

'I spent the afternoon with a young pothead, and possibly a prostitute, who I think might be someone I knew a couple of years ago. Oh, and I think she might be the "Daughter of Abraham" ... Unless you are.'

Instead he had muttered something lame about losing track of time in Hyde Park, watching the world go by.

She wouldn't turn up, and that would be the end of it.

He was still thinking this when a shadow to his right shifted and formed into someone taking the seat opposite.

'Well, where's this coffee, Bench Guy?'

'Miriam!'

'Millie. Coffee. Now!' She lit a cigarette.

This was the first opportunity he had to observe her closely and in full daylight. She wore a short, woollen skirt, revealing a few inches of animal-print tights above knee-high boots that probably weren't leather. An open-weave sweater hung loosely from her shoulders, with sleeves extending only about three inches below her elbows. It slipped off her left shoulder, revealing a prominent clavicle. Her blond hair was very short at the back, with a long fringe combed over from the right. Her eyes seemed preternaturally large above high cheekbones and a prominent nose. The shadows around them made them sink more deeply into her face; whether the shadows were the result of make-up or not, they looked like bruises. Her mouth was wide between sunken cheeks.

What had made him so sure the day before, when he had seen her so briefly on the bench, that this was Miriam? The prominent nose? The bump across its bridge? The last traces, he wondered, of an Australian accent?

He called the waitress over and ordered coffee, one for Miriam and another for himself. He was already wired.

'So, you're Millie,' he finally said.

'Yeah, what of it?'

'Not Miriam.'

She puffed quickly on her cigarette and flicked the ash aggressively towards the ground. He heard her finger tapping the paper. She uncrossed her legs and crossed them the opposite way.

'It's just that I knew a girl a few years ago. Her name was Miriam ...'

'Yeah, no shit.' She flicked her fringe out of her eyes.

'So why did you come? I didn't think you would.'

'Free coffee.'

Her eyes darted all around, avoiding his face, never stopping to rest.

'What did you say your name was, Bench Guy?'

'Charlie. Charlie Kollock.'

He held out his hand across the table. For several seconds she just stared at it, and then, reluctantly, let him take her fingers in his hand and shake them. She pulled back abruptly, as if from an electric shock. The sudden movement sent her handbag to the pavement, spilling the contents towards his feet. He reached down to pick up an envelope.

'Don't ...'

He had it in his hand before he registered her objection, but it was only as he moved to hand it over that he noticed the writing on the back. The words: To Miriam; the hand, his own.

'Give it here, you bastard.'

But he withheld it. Withdrew the contents. A birthday card. And from inside the card fell two tickets. Tickets to a Beatles concert that had taken place in Brighton two years ago.

'Miriam ...' He could scarcely get the words out past the lump in his throat. 'I'm so ...'

Across from him, the girl's face crumpled. Her body caved in on itself. From somewhere deep within, a groan, a heaving sob, erupted. She seemed unable to breathe.

Then the tears came.

The scene later that afternoon with Sophia was unreal, dreamlike. Charlie had paced back and forth in the apartment, rehearsing words and gestures. She came in with some groceries, and, while helping her unpack and put them away, he repeatedly drew in a short breath, as if about to speak, and then exhaled wordlessly.

'What's with the heavy breathing? Something on your mind?'

'Let's sit for a moment.'

We act as if we're safe in the world, he reflected, seeing the sudden furrowing of her brow. He imagined the quickening of her pulse, the tightening of her gut. *But we're on a tightrope, struggling to keep our balance. A drop—we have no idea how far—below us.* He patted the other seat of the couch beside him. *A nothing, a zephyr, a falling petal, a momentary distraction, upsets our balance.* He drew in another breath.

'There's someone I need to help,' he began, 'and I need your help to help her.'

'Her?'

'Yes. It's ... It's a long story.'

'I ain't going nowhere.'

He told her about meeting Miriam all those years earlier, and of how she became a friend; about what happened to her parents and how she disappeared.

He didn't mention 'the Daughter of Abraham'. It had nothing to do with that anyway.

'I found her yesterday. Quite by accident. She's living in terrible conditions. She's a mess. She needs our … She needs my help.'

There was a long silence. At some point, Sophia had stood and begun retracing his earlier path back and forth across the apartment.

'And did you sleep with this girl? The truth now, Charlie.'

'No no. It's nothing like that. It was never anything like that. She was—is—just a kid.'

'A kid with a pussy though, right?'

'It was never like that, Sophe.'

He stood and took a step or two towards her. She stopped him with her eyes.

'I dunno, Charlie. It sounds kind of weird, you know? You and some kid? What's that about, Charlie?'

'There's nothing between us. I swear.'

'Wanting to rescue some stray kid you scarcely knew years ago … A drug addict? A hooker? That's some big fat *nothing*, Charlie. Does she *want* to be rescued?'

'I'm meeting with her again tomorrow. I thought maybe she could come here.'

'Here?'

'If it's all right with you. She can sleep on the couch for a few days.'

'No way, Charlie.'

'I think …'

'*No!*'

'My plan is … She has a brother. Probably in Australia. I want to connect them. At least meet her.'

'This is just too weird, Charlie.'

'Meet her. *Please.*'

One step closer. She held her ground.

'I'm not promising anything.'

PART FOUR

CHAPTER TWENTY

I'LL USE HIM TO GET OUT OF HERE. I'LL USE HIM AND THAT'S THE END OF it.

As for getting out of there, Millie knew the 'from' but remained fuzzy about the 'to'.

Charlie had told her to be ready the next morning. He would pick her up in a taxi at 10 am and they would catch the train to Oxford. From there they would drive to ... She had no idea where. All she knew was some farm. Somewhere west. Millie, on a farm? He asked if she had much stuff. A suitcase. That was the sum total of her life. That, and the meagre contents of her handbag.

The encounter the day before had been ... tense.

Millie hadn't expected to see his woman. One of his women. Sophia. With that voice. She could have injured someone with that pointy chin.

She did most of the talking. Asking endless questions.

Was she a drug user?

Was she a hooker?

She looked sick. Was she sick?

She didn't pull any punches.

I don't use the hard stuff, Millie had said.

No one paid her for sex. Why? Was she afraid of a little competition? If someone occasionally wanted to give her a little gift …

Before they could come to blows, Charlie took his woman aside. Millie couldn't hear what they said, but their gestures spoke volumes. Eventually Sophia stormed off.

Charlie walked back towards Millie. They were again in Hyde Park, not far from the new restaurant. He wore a lopsided smile and shrugged.

'Plan B,' he said.

'Your hair is longer,' Millie remarked as he stepped out of the taxi to help with her bag. He was right on time.

'And yours is shorter.'

'You sound more English.'

'So do you. Do you have everything?' Charlie looked sceptically at the single suitcase.

It wasn't until they were on the train that Charlie spoke again. 'Are you … well?'

'I'm just peachy.'

'I … I was really sorry to hear about your parents.'

'My parents? What about my parents?'

'The accident … The way they were killed. You saw … It must have been—'

'What are you talking about?'

'The accident …'

'What accident? My parents went back to Australia. I had no intention of joining them in that shithole.'

'Australia? I thought—'

'You thought wrong.'

That silenced Charlie again, and Millie watched the countryside pass by beyond the window.

Yesterday doesn't exist.

'How have you managed during the last two years?' Charlie prodded again at her silence.

'I would like to be Audrey Hepburn.'

'What?'

'If I could be anyone in the world, I would like to be Audrey Hepburn.'

'You're skinny enough.'

'Did you see *My Fair Lady*? I could do that. And *Breakfast at Tiffany's*. Holly Golightly. What a wonderful name.'

'Miriam—'

'Millie. Millie Lewis is my name, Bench Guy. I don't know any Miriam.'

'The guy who was with you the other day, in the squat—'

'What is it with all the questions, already? You and your woman. How is she, by the way? Look! Look at the sunflowers!'

And Millie didn't know a Nick anymore, either. A Nick who was in a band—had been in a band—would be in a band. Who knew other guys who were in bands—had been in bands—would be in bands. Pete, Jack, Eric and whoever else he said he knew.

Yesterday doesn't exist.

'I'm hungry.'

'We'll be at Oxford in half an hour. We can get some lunch there.'

From her handbag Millie took out a small tin and a cigarette paper. She began to construct a cigarette using the greenish material from the tin.

Charlie leaned towards her. 'You can't smoke that in here!' he whispered, casting an eye towards the other two passengers sharing the compartment with them.

Millie had scarcely noticed them. One—a man dressed in a dark suit and wearing a fedora—hid behind a newspaper. An elderly woman stared at her, edging further away along the seat. Millie tilted her head and smiled up at her, batting her eyelashes and flicking her tongue across her lips. The woman turned towards the door of the compartment.

'Why not? It's a smoking compartment isn't it?' She licked the gum on the paper and then blew noisily at a small piece of green, leafy material that had stuck to her upper lip.

'*Miriam!*' Charlie turned the whisper into as much of a shout as was possible.

'All right, Bench Guy. Don't go ape on me. And it's Millie, for fuck's sake.'

'OK, "Millie". How about you call me Charlie, then.'

'Deal.'

She put the joint away for later consumption.

'If you want to wait here I'll fetch the car—it's not far. Then get something to eat. I know a nice café ...'

'Is your place nearby? We could go there.'

'After we eat. I have a few things to pack. You will wait here?'

'Why wouldn't I?'

'Right.' Charlie shrugged off his concern and set off at a brisk pace, with one quick glance over his shoulder.

It had started to drizzle. Millie sat on the platform, on a bench undercover, her suitcase in front of her as a footstool. She gazed admiringly at her olive, suede, kitten-heel shoes. They had been very expensive. She wore the knee-high socks that were so fashionable— these in a bright-orange chequered pattern—although she personally favoured sheer stockings or bare legs. Socks hid the shape of her calves, which she thought by far her best feature. From the knees down she could almost believe herself attractive.

The station was rather grim, as were most railway stations. Weeds grew vigorously between the tracks, despite the oil staining the ballast. They grew, also, within the cracks in the platform. She wondered with some distaste what had caused the stains here and there on the platform. She began to suspect the air of harbouring unpleasant odours.

She had considered, for a moment, slipping away. Perhaps catching the next train back to London. Or heading in the other direction, to wherever that led. It had probably been a mistake to leave with Charlie. He hinted at the past.

After a while, though, she began to worry that it was Charlie who had slipped away. Why was he taking so long?

Time for that joint.

The dope began to ease away her rising anxiety and, as if in complicity, the drizzle eased to the lightest of mists, the sun came out, and a rainbow appeared opposite her. Here and their droplets of water clinging to the weeds caught the sun. Suddenly the dreary station was jewel bedecked.

'Mi-Millie?'

'Ch-Charlie.'

'Are you ready?' He gazed up and down the platform, looking worried.

'Just a minute. Let me finish this. Want a toke?'

'You know, I think I do.'

'Here. Finish it off.'

He sat beside her on the bench and she watched him closely. Her Bench Guy. After a moment or two a smile eased its way onto his face. Only the second she had seen since meeting up with him again. The strength of her scrutiny drew his gaze and she mirrored his smile.

'Right. Let's go. There's a café just around the corner. Let's put this in the car.' He struggled with her suitcase and walked away lopsidedly. Her eyes followed his narrow hips and skinny legs. Nick had been taller ... Except that she didn't know anyone called Nick.

'Nice wheels.' She ran her fingers lightly along the metallic-blue bonnet of the Ford Cortina. White roof. White-walled tyres.

'A twenty-first birthday present from the old man. Before he realised I was a loser.'

'What's there to win?'

'You're a philosopher too, I see.'

The café was not much to look at from the outside: down a step from the street and through a strip curtain of red, yellow and blue. The faint smell of incense lingered in the air, and foreign-sounding music played in the background.

'Cool joint.'

'It's vegetarian. Do you mind?'

'Nah. That's cool.'

A few tables were occupied by young people she took to be students. Charlie steered her towards a table near the back, beneath a large tapestry depicting two elephants facing each other, in pink and black. The right half was the mirrored negative of the left half.

The only light came from a candle on the table.

'So is this place, like, Indian or something?'

'Yeah, more or less. A bit of this. A bit of that. Do you want me to order?'

She glanced at the menu, angling it towards the light of the candle. 'Yeah.'

'Spicy or not so?'

'Not so. For lunch anyway.'

He gestured for the waitress. 'Mini idli and sambar please, for two. And some chapatti. My mother loves this place,' he added to Miriam. 'And that's her favourite.'

'I remember ... You talked about your mother before. She's into all that ...' She slipped her shoes off under the table.

'Well, yeah. Theosophy. Mysticism and whatever. She used to be weird. Now everyone's starting to get into it.'

'And are you into it?' She flexed her toes, enjoying the freedom.

'No, not really. Well some of it ... I like the food here. But I still like donuts too.' He smiled at the memory. Millie didn't.

'So what are you *into*, Charlie?' She brushed her foot again his shin, enjoying his sudden intake of breath. She sank down into her chair, slid her foot along his thigh and rested it in his crotch.

'What are you doing?'

'What you want me to do, Charlie.' She felt his response and lightly brushed her toes against his growing interest.

'Stop it!' He shoved her foot aside and pushed back his chair. The legs screeched across the slate floor and drew eyes towards them. 'I don't want that from you.'

'If you say so.' She knew what men wanted. She knew what *she* wanted.

Charlie avoided eye contact with her throughout the meal, and they ate in silence. The silence continued as they walked back to the car. He opened the door for her and climbed into the driver's seat, but did not start the car immediately.

'This was a mistake,' he said. 'I'm taking you back to London.'

'No. I can't go back, Charlie.' Her heartbeat was amplified like the ticking of a clock in the stillness of the night.

'Why not? Why shouldn't I just take you back?'

'There has to be a reason that you found me, doesn't there, Charlie? Like it was meant to be, or something?'

'I don't believe ...' His heart was clearly not in his words.

'Don't take me back. Please.' The ticking of her heart ... What was it counting down towards?

He started the car without answering. After just a few minutes he pulled up outside an apartment building. The road divided around an imposing willow.

'Is this your place?' she asked quietly.

'No. Wait here a minute.'

She wound down the window and lit a cigarette. Then she stepped out and leaned against the car, searching the windows of the apartments above. She'd become used to living without windows. A copy of the sky and clouds was all she saw.

She wore no watch, but minutes were surely passing. She climbed back into the car and went through Charlie's glove box. She found some gum and popped a stick. Some receipts.

'What are you doing?'

She almost bumped her head on the roof of the car, but managed to shine a crooked smile in Charlie's direction. 'Snooping.'

'Come up with me.' He held out his hand, but quickly withdrew it.

'You *can* touch me, Charlie. I'm not contagious.'

'This way.'

They climbed to the first floor, and Charlie knocked and opened the first door on the left.

'Tiggi, you remember Miriam, as she was? Now Millie.'

'Of course.'

'You remember Tiggi?'

'No.'

'Well, this is she. Tiggi is coming away with us for a while. I'm just going to get some of my stuff. Won't be long.'

Tiggi and Miriam watched each other as Charlie left.

'So, are you the reason he won't shag me?'

'Oh.' Tiggi's laugh was not entirely natural. 'He will eventually, I'm sure. He's a man after all.'

'So he *has* shagged you, then?'

'Tea?'

'Sure. Why not?'

'A long time ago. Once or twice. Before Sophia.' Tiggi occupied herself at the small kitchenette.

'So this Sophia ... *She's* the reason he won't shag me?'

'Probably. Maybe not any longer. Who knows? Milk? Sugar?'

'Yeah. Both. One sugar. So, what's the story with this Sophia then?'

'What's your game, "Millie"?'

'You think I dragged him away from this Sophia? Maybe you should be asking Charlie what his game is. He came after me.'

'Oh, I did.'

'And?'

Tiggi carried a tray with the makings of tea and placed it on a coffee table in front of the couch. For the first time, Millie took in the room. It was small: a sitting room and the kitchenette, with a door off to the right. The furnishings looked ... Posh was all she could think of. What she imagined antiques might look like. There was a small TV in the corner. Miriam's family had never owned a TV, before ... And there had not been a working TV in the squat, although Idris was always trying to repair one he had found. She pushed the thoughts aside.

'Well? What's Charlie's game?'

'Charlie ...' Tiggi let escape a long breath. 'Charlie doesn't always think things through. He probably sees himself as your Sir Galahad. Or your Henry Higgins.'

'Oi ain't no flaar lady, missus!'

Tiggi smiled, and it seemed genuine. 'Do you need rescuing, Millie? I'm not so sure.'

'Do you have any biscuits?'

'Somewhere.'

'Mind if I smoke?'

'No.' Tiggi searched the top shelf of the cupboard over the sink. 'These will have to do, I'm afraid. Normally I might have some cake that my grandmother baked, but I ate the last piece this morning.' She spread some Cheddars on a plate.

'Taa.' She offered a cigarette to Tiggi.

'Thank you.'

'So why did you agree to come with us?'

'Which reminds me. I should be packing.' She went to the door, which opened onto a bedroom.

'So why?' Millie followed partway and leaned against the kitchen bench top.

'I think Charlie might need protecting from you. Or from himself.'

'Do you always do that? Protect Charlie?'

Tiggi paused in the process of folding a sweater. 'You know, I think I do.'

'You love him.'

She thought about this for a while. 'No. No, not exactly. Maybe I did once.'

'So what then?'

'You like to ask questions, but you're not so keen on answering them.'

Millie just shrugged and blew smoke from the side of her mouth.

'Charlie ... Charlie doesn't quite *get* the world.' Tiggi had placed her cigarette in an ashtray on the bedside table, next to an open book. She picked it up now and took a long drag. Like all the other furniture, the table, the bed—everything looked posh to Millie. She'd never seen so many pillows in her life.

Tiggi stepped into the *en suite* and returned with some toiletries, which she tossed into the suitcase. 'That will do.'

They returned to the sitting room and Millie took another biscuit.

'I remember one time,' Tiggi resumed. 'It was a couple of years ago. Charlie befriended this young fourteen-year-old girl. He even went to her home one day looking for her, and was flattened by her brother. Charlie had no idea how his friendship with this girl might look to the world.'

Millie swallowed the last of her biscuit with difficulty.

'Or maybe he did. He never told Sophia about her. I have no idea how he explained his injuries to her.'

Charlie had been with Sophia for more than two years? And now he wasn't? Or was he?

'I didn't know about Sophia.'

'No. I didn't think you did, then or now. And what's he doing now? Who knows?'

Millie didn't realise at first that these words were addressed over her shoulder, towards the door. She turned to see Charlie standing there, looking sheepish.

'Well, Charlie,' repeated Tiggi, 'what are you doing?'

ELAINE LOOKED UP FROM THE DISPLAY SHE WAS PREPARING WHEN THE door opened. Was it another curious villager coming to check out the new young postmistress? Some thought much too young: too young to be postmistress; too old to be single. The latest postcards of the village and the surrounding area had arrived late the previous afternoon and she was keen to have them in place. They were mostly of the churches, outside and in. There was a new image of Cheddar Gorge that she particularly liked. She resented the intrusion on her work.

The bright morning sun framed a figure that at first she didn't recognise.

'We're not ... Jack!' She greeted her brother with surprise. 'You're back in town too?'

'For a spell.' His swarthy, stocky form cast a long shadow across the floor and counter. 'You're looking fine, Elaine.'

She wasn't so sure about that. Her time in Birmingham had wrought some changes.

'And what brings you home?' Even as she asked, she wasn't sure she wanted to know.

'A spot of business to sort in Bristol.'

Party or union business, no doubt. The stuff that had been dividing the family for years.

'Will you be here very long? Sunday lunch?'

'Aah. Most likely. Heading back north on Wednesday.'

It was odd watching Jack stand there, cap in hand, as though he were addressing a stranger. How long had it been? Nearly two years. The Christmas before last. She walked around the counter and pulled him into a hug.

'Good to see you, Jack.'

'Likewise, Elaine. Likewise. Look I'm sorry ...'

'There'll be none of that. You're my brother and I love thee.' She felt some of the years and the superficial veneer of city life fall away. 'Why not let's go to the pub later for lunch. I can shut up shop here for an hour or so. No one'd know the difference.'

Her memories of that Christmas, when she'd last seen Jack, were mostly pleasant. The food, as usual, was splendid. She was always delighted to find herself eating the pink, glistening meat from the breast of one of the detestable geese that roamed the farm. Her mother had a way of roasting the vegetables—potatoes, turnips, carrots—that left them sticky and sweet. The heavy, rich pudding would sit at the base of her stomach for days. Christmas was one of the few occasions she allowed herself a little alcohol. It took no more than a glass and a half of wine before her head began to float away.

That year, 1963, it had felt as though the planet had tilted further on its axis. By Christmas, the world was battered and bruised, tottering on its feet. No one around the table during Christmas lunch was unaffected by it; and no amount of forced jollity could dispel the sense that there had been a shift; that something fundamental had changed.

After enough ale had entered Jack's system he began to radiate a kind of gloomy optimism. She could think of no other way to describe it. The mood made her want to disappear, but her body felt too bulky, heavy and cumbersome to slip into the tiny spaces of her childhood.

'It's going to blow soon. Can thee feel it? It's a powder keg, and it's going to blow.'

'Well, don't you be putting no match to it,' observed their father.

It was quiet after lunch. Everyone's stomach was uncomfortably full and eyes were closing. Observing her father, Elaine was acutely aware of how old he had become. He had never been a young man during her lifetime. He was already forty years old when she was born, the last of three children spread over two decades. He was now approaching sixty-five. How long could he go on working the farm? And who would take over when he retired ... or died? Ed, her other brother, had married and left the farm some years ago and moved to Canada. They had little contact with him these days.

'Someone has to do it,' her brother observed.

'Dinnuz have enough trouble in the world, boy!'

'Not near, I reckon. The wind's a-changing and those who stand in the way'll get blown away.'

'Dang I!' Her father looked ready to jump to his feet, but sank back in defeat. 'If I could I'd give thee a drubbin.'

'Aah well ...'

A silence descended, but Jack's eyes were black coals in the failing light.

Now almost two years had gone by and little had changed in the world that she could see. Except that her father was older and her brother harder.

That was her impression over lunch in the pub: that something inside him had turned brittle.

She had only a vague understanding of Jack's political activities. She knew he was very active in some big engineering union. She was also reasonably certain that he was a member of the Communist Party, although he had never said so openly. Ostensibly he worked for an engineering firm in Leeds, but she suspected he did little engineering work these days. He spent most of his time hopping around the country sorting out 'business' of the kind that had brought him home. She doubted it was engineering business. He had become more emotionally distant over time.

It saddened her that both she and Jack had to hide important parts of their lives from each other, under the bed and on the top shelf of the closet. He, his political activities; Elaine, her humiliating love life. She had spoken to no one in the family about her relationship with Maurice.

'You've been to the farm?' she asked.

'Aah.'

'Dad's not too well.' Since Ed left the farm some years back, her father had relied more and more on hired help. He did what he could himself, but she could tell his heart wasn't in it. And it was his heart that was giving him trouble.

'I could see that right enough.'

'I worry what'll happen to the farm.'

'I'm reckoning that toff Charlie might be harbouring plans.'

'Charlie?'

'Aah, Charlie. You know, that grandson of Lord Wassisname. The owner.'

Charlie? She hadn't seen Charlie since that summer all those years ago. Scarcely remembered him.

'What makes thee say that?'

'Well, why else would he have moved into the big house?'

She fought off a slight dizziness and fingered the pendant around her neck.

Charlie.

She remembered that summer more as a fairy tale she had been told as a child than as something that had actually happened. The restlessness that had been born during those weeks had never quite been extinguished, either by Birmingham or Maurice. Even while her stomach had warmed at the idea of returning to her place of birth, a worm gnawed away at her contentment.

Charlie.

'When ... Have thee spoken to him?' She didn't know why she asked this. It was the last thing she could imagine Jack doing. But she had to say something.

Jack replied with a grunt.

They finished their drinks in silence and parted with another hug.

'See you on Sunday then,' she said.

'Aah, that thee will.'

From behind he looked much like their father. They could have been brothers rather than father and son.

It was a half-mile walk back to the post office, and she welcomed the thinking time. Everything from that summer appeared in a hazy light, and it was silly to yearn after it. She didn't want to be one of those who believed that 'before' was always somehow better than 'now'. She sometimes heard that in her father's voice and saw it in his eyes. Although, to be fair, 'before' for his generation meant 'before the War', and that was understandable.

What was 'now' for her? It was recovering from that foolishness with Maurice. It was settling into a new job. It was breathing the fresh country air. *Love that cow manure!* It was being a young, successful woman. It was trying to fit into a smaller dress size. It was ...

... remembering the promise of that summer.

She glimpsed her segmented reflection in the window of the post office, following her to the door. The slightly warped glass made her appear slimmer. Without thinking, she ran her hands down her body, measuring it, becoming reacquainted with it.

Later, after a quiet afternoon during which her mind remained out of focus, she cycled out to the farm.

CHAPTER TWENTY-TWO

'I'M BORED.'

'Of course you are, dear. Your life is normally so busy and fulfilling.' Tiggi didn't even glance up from the book she was reading, and Millie cast around for something to throw at her.

'I'm not going to stay here forever.'

'You're free to leave any time you like. Pete will drive you to the station.'

Pete was a tall, gangly man with protruding teeth and one eye lower than the other. He had been on the farm for many years and was now more or less the manager. He had never married. Unless, Millie thought unkindly, it was to one of the pigs. She didn't want to be in the confined space of a car with him again. She had made that mistake last week, offering to go into town with him to pick up some supplies. Anything to break the monotony. No matter how many baths she had taken after that trip, she couldn't rid herself of the smell. Even now ...

It had been two weeks now, and Charlie had been there for a total of perhaps one. Tiggi was always there.

'Don't you have better things to do?'

'Than babysit you? Certainly.'

'Then *you* go. I don't need a babysitter.'

'Millie, Millie.' Tiggi finally laid her book aside. 'What is it that you really *want*?'

I want never to have left Australia. I want my parents to be alive. I want not to have wished them dead.

'What difference does it make? I won't get it.'

'You won't without trying.'

In her casting around earlier, her hand had lighted upon an art deco, Bakelite ashtray that she actually quite admired. Without thinking, she launched it towards Tiggi. It clipped her left shoulder—

'Jesus!'

—before bouncing off the back of the chair and careening into a vase on the table behind her. The vase tottered and then crashed to the floor, spilling water and scattering pink peonies and green hydrangeas.

'What is *wrong* with you?'

Millie surged from her chair. 'What's wrong with me? What's wrong with *me*? *You*, prattling on about *wanting* and *trying* and calling me *dear* in your piping, sarcastic, snotty-nosed voice! As if what you are now is actually your own doing. Where would you be without Daddy's money and Mummy's Mothers' Union friends?'

'Fuck you. I'm leaving today. Clean up the mess.'

The doorbell rang.

Elaine had called on her parents first.

'Hello, Mum.'

'Hello, Ellie dear. Are you here for dinner?'

'I might stay, if it's no bother.'

'No bother at all. I can make it go further if needs be.'

'Is Dad home?'

'No, he's gone up to Bristol for the day with Pete, looking for some fencing materials. He'll be in a right state when he gets back. You know how he gets.'

'Maybe I'll give dinner a miss, then,' she said, laughing. She sat at the table, chewing on a strand of hair.

'Tea, pet?'

'Yes, thank thee.'

'Settling in?'

'Well enough.'

'Is something bothering thee, pet?'

'Not exactly. Well, I worry about Dad ...'

'Aah well, baint no point worrying, though as we all do.'

'And the farm.'

'We'll be all right, pet. Mr Charlie has promised us a place here long as we like.'

'Well, let's hope he's as good as his word. He's here, so Jack tells me.'

'You've seen our Jack, then?'

'Aah, this morning. We had lunch together.'

They worried about him, too, silently.

'Mr Charlie's in and out.'

'Doing what?'

'Well … I'm not right sure. Fixing a bit of this and that.'

'I must drop in on him. Do you think he would mind?'

'If he does then he's puggle 'eaded for certain.' Her mother hesitated. 'He baint on his own in the house, mind.'

'Who else is there?'

'Well ...'

'What?'

'There's two young ladies staying there with him. Giving um the benefit of the doubt.'

'Who are they? Relatives? Friends?'

'Don't rightly know and it baint my place to ask.'

'Well, I shall make it my place.'

'I don't doubt it, pet. You be careful now,' she added, as Elaine stepped out the back door.

'I'm sure you won't want to learn anything I find out.'

'I'm not one for judging folk or gossiping ... unless it's over a good meal.'

'Better make it a good one then, hadn't thee.' She laughed.

'Get on with thee.'

'Now who the fuck's that?' Tiggi pulled her top down over her left shoulder and poked gently at a reddening patch. 'Bitch,' she muttered. 'Well, answer it!'

'You answer it.' Millie didn't rise from the couch.

Tiggi marched out of the drawing room but continued past the front door and directly up the stairs. The doorbell rang a second time.

'All right! Coming!' Millie rose and stretched, tugging down her skirt and pushing her fingers through her hair. 'Something to break the boredom,' she muttered. Passing the broken vase and scattered flowers, she sniggered. 'Breaking things; now *that* I can do.'

The light outlined a female figure through the elaborate stained glass of the front door.

'Yeah?' she said, opening it a notch and looking the figure up and down. Who was this? Did she drop in from the fifties? Sensible shoes. Thick brown tights. A woollen skirt. Short, narrow-waisted cardigan. Millie once would have envied the hair, but it wasn't at all stylish now.

'Is Charlie in, please?'

'No.'

'Right. Do you know when he'll be back?'

'Tomorrow morning.'

'OK. Could you tell him Elaine called. Elaine Pierce.'

'Sure.' Millie shrugged.

'If he wants he can catch me at the post office in Coxton Sudbury.'

'Pfffffff. Is that a *place*?'

'Yes about four miles ... Never mind. I'm sure he'll know. Do you want me to write it down?'

'Cock something.'

'Coxton Sudbury.' Elaine took a biro and notebook from her bag and wrote down the name. To be on the safe side she added her own name, tore out the page and gave it to Millie. 'You'll make sure he gets that?'

'I said I would, didn't I?'

'OK. And ... What was your name?'

'It was and still is Millie.'

'Thanks, Millie.'

The woman remained standing there. 'Well?' Millie asked.

'Um, your Charlie's ...'

Into the space left by the woman's hesitation Millie slipped in, 'Yes,' and quickly closed the door, stifling a laugh.

'Did you see that?' she said to Tiggi, who stood on the first floor landing.

'From the window. Pretty.'

'Fat.'

'Lovely hair.'

'Scarecrow.'

'I'm going over to see if Pete's available to run me to the station.'

'Sorry,' Millie muttered.

'You could have really hurt me this time, Millie.'

'I said I was sorry, OK?'

'That's as may be, but I'm leaving anyway. Believe it or not, I *do* have other things to do.'

'Can we talk with Charlie first?'

Tiggi hesitated and came down the stairs. 'At least clean up the mess.'

'I will.'

'We'll talk to Charlie tomorrow. I won't change my mind, but maybe we can come up with a plan.'

Two days later on the Friday afternoon, when Elaine was closing the post office, a thin, pale young man crossed the threshold.

'What is it with you and the women in your life that you're all so pale and thin?' Elaine spoke with barely a glance in his direction.

'The women in my life?'

'I remember your mother ... And now there's that waif ... What was it? Millie.'

'Hardly a woman!'

'I totally agree.'

Charlie smiled broadly. 'It's lovely to see you, Elaine.'

'What is it? Almost twenty years?'

'Seventeen, I think.'

'Seventeen ... You hurried back.'

'There was an ocean between us.'

'Really? And how long have you been back in England? At Oxford?'

He stared intently at the floor. 'Five years, I suppose.'

'Five years and not a word.'

'I've been here many times. You never were.'

Elaine stayed behind the counter, while he remained framed in the doorway. She dreaded to think how she looked to him. Her hair, her clothes. Her ... ample form. If his mother provided the model for the women in his life, and Millie in any way reflected his tastes ...

'Are you closing up here? Can I walk you home?'

'This is home. Upstairs.' She indicated a door behind her.

'A walk then. Away from home.'

She continued working for half a minute longer and then looked directly at him. 'OK.' Her hands wanted to check that her hair was in place and smooth the creases in her skirt and tights, but she refused to yield to their insecurity.

Charlie turned in the doorway and indicated the way outside with a sweeping gesture.

She locked up. 'There's a small park down this way,' she indicated in turn with a sweep of her arm.

As they walked away he slipped his arm into hers. 'Elaine ...'

Neither spoke further for some minutes.

The park was basic: two swings, a rusting roundabout, a seesaw. They sat on a bench in the late afternoon sun. She shaded her eyes with her hand. The air was heavy with pollen that challenged her sinuses. 'So what's with the waif?' she asked eventually.

And Charlie told her. Everything. His mother. The Daughter of Abraham. Sophia. Miriam/Millie.

During the telling, an occasional villager would pass by, nod in her direction and cast a suspicious eye over Charlie. 'Ev'nin'.'

During one such pause Charlie offered her a cigarette, which she declined.

'Anyway ...' he continued.

By the time he finished the sun had dipped below the cottage across the street and a slight chill descended.

'I don't know why I told you all that. It just seemed ...'

'What?'

'Necessary.'

'What on earth must Sophia think.' Elaine wrapped her arms around herself against the chill.

'I didn't tell her. She doesn't know ...'

'Charlie!'

'I know. I'm insane.'

'The insanity plea? I don't buy it.'

'Maybe Sophia and I ...'

She refused to meet his eyes, not wanting to see the end of that sentence in them. Not sure she wanted to know the beginning of the next.

They sat some distance apart, Charlie in his tight pants, with his legs stretched out before him. 'Anyway,' he said, 'I've been totally selfish. I've asked nothing about you.'

'It's getting late. I should head home.'

'Right.'

'I'll tell you my story next time.'

'And when will that be?'

'Another seventeen years?'

'How about tomorrow?'

Tomorrow was Saturday. She tried to recall if she had any plans. She would open the post office for half the day, and then ...

'We'll have a picnic tomorrow afternoon.' He seemed to read her mind.

'And who'll prepare the food?'

'Me. If by "prepare" you mean go to Bristol in the morning to buy stuff.'

'I'll—' No, she wouldn't. She would wait to see what he came up with. 'Where?'

He shrugged.

'I know the perfect spot. I'll come to the house at 1 pm. We can walk from there.'

'OK.'

'Tell me, who looks after the baby while you're out?'

'The ...? Oh, she's more or less housetrained. She scarcely eats, so food's rarely an issue. I've arranged for Mrs Pierce—your mother,' he suddenly realised '—to cook a meal for us two or three days a week, now that Tiggi's gone.'

'My mother's your cook? Is she your maid too? And who's Tiggi?'

'Just a friend. She's been babysitting Miriam for a couple of weeks or so.'

'A friend?'

'Yes.' He studied her for a moment. 'I'm glad you've resisted the fashion for short hair.'

'Are you saying I'm old fashioned?'

'In a nice way. The very best of ways.'

'Salt.'

'What?'

'The day we first met, I told you your mother was vanilla ice-cream and my father was a pork pie, and you asked what I thought you were. It was salt. That's what I thought then.'

'Salt? I don't remember.'

'Now I'm not so sure.' It was her turn to study him. Then she rose suddenly. 'Walk me home.'

'Tomorrow, then,' he said at the door, offering a slight, perhaps mocking, bow.

From the open doorway she watched the red taillights of his car—which she hadn't noticed earlier—sketch a path through the deepening dusk.

CHAPTER TWENTY-THREE

MILLIE DIDN'T LIKE THIS TURN OF EVENTS. NO, NOT AT ALL.

The woman with the nest of hair and shabby clothes had been waiting outside the house. Millie watched from her bedroom window on the first floor. The woman sat on the low wall fronting the road, glancing back occasionally at the front door. When the door opened, Millie saw it: the slight smile and the lowering of the eyes. The woman stood as Charlie approached carrying a picnic basket and a knapsack. He held out his arm for her and, after a brief hesitation, she slipped her arm through his and they walked off together down the road.

No, she didn't like this at all.

She rushed down the stairs and out the front door, and followed them down the road, ducking behind trees and buildings as they presented themselves.

It had been a tough few days. Tiggi had left, as she had threatened to do. And Millie's supply of dope had run out. She had no means of transport, and no idea where to go anyway. There was also the slight problem that she had very little money.

Since Tiggi's departure, Charlie had been taciturn, put out, no doubt, by the words exchanged with Tiggi, none of which Millie had heard, but many of which she could imagine. But yesterday evening at dinner time he had returned home in an ebullient mood. Millie had been unable to determine the cause. Until now.

Charlie and Post Office Woman were about fifty feet ahead of her, dawdling along arm in arm. If they were talking, they were doing so undemonstratively. She struggled not to catch up with them. They showed no inclination to look back, but when a car approached from the other direction, Millie ducked among the trees that lined the road.

At breakfast, the morning after Tiggi left, Charlie had sought to hold a conversation. He explained how he had arranged for Mrs Pierce to cook for them three or four times a week, but that at other times they would have to prepare their own meals.

'If you don't mind baked beans on toast,' she grumbled.

'I'm also going to see if I can help out around the farm a bit.' He hesitated. 'I wondered if you—'

'You're kidding, right?'

'Well, you have to do *something* with your time, don't you? What would you like to do?'

'Eat baked beans on toast.'

She had never liked to think about what she was going to *do*.

The car slowed down as it approached Charlie—and was it 'Elaine'?—and then stopped when it drew alongside. Millie peered through the foliage.

Elaine detached herself from Charlie and leaned towards the driver's-side window. Words were clearly exchanged, and Elaine shook her head vigorously. She then turned from the car and walked on, leaving Charlie in her wake.

Interesting.

Millie had not been sleeping well. Partly this was due to her lack of dope but also, she admitted to herself, because of concern for the future. She worried less under the influence. The future. The day was warm even under the shade of the trees, but still she shivered.

The car pulled away and picked up speed, but then slowed again as it approached her position. She knew nothing about cars, but this one looked surprisingly shiny and in good condition. She didn't associate shiny new cars with this part of the world. It halted directly opposite her hiding place and the driver looked straight at her.

'Don't normally see your type here away. What are you about, hiding there?'

Without any thought for the couple further down the road she stepped out from under cover. 'My type? And what type might that be?'

'You're a long way from Muller Road.'

She had no idea where that was, but she understood the implications well enough.

The man was darkly handsome in his way. Brooding. Probably mid thirties/early forties. The car suggested he had money, but he was not dressed to match: no jacket or tie; a threadbare collar on his shirt. Her eye was drawn to his bald spot.

'My fiancé would not appreciate your tone,' she said in her best BBC.

'Your fiancé? And who might that be when he's at home?'

'Lord Charles Kollock, the owner of Chetwood Farm.' She indicated down the road with a jerk of her head.

'"Lord" he's fashioning himself now, is he? First I've heard of his lordship having a fiancée. Least of all one such as theeself. And scarcely out of nappies to boot.'

'Well, here I stand before you. And who might you be?'

'I suppose that explains why you were following his lordship and my sister just now. Has a wandering eye and hand does he, your "fiancé"? Can't say as I blame him.'

She was not unaware of his eyes wandering over her body.

So, he was Elaine's brother. *Interesting.*

'And your name is?' she asked.

'Jack.'

'Millie.' She held out her hand. He didn't take it. 'Such a gentleman.'

'Such a "lady",' he sneered. His eyes drifted again to the considerable expanse of thigh revealed above her knee. She resisted the urge to adjust her skirt and stood up straight.

'How long have they known each other, Charlie and … Elaine?'

'Nigh on twenty years, I reckon.' He laughed when she failed to disguise her surprise, but then continued, 'But they ant seen each other for twenty years neither, since just now.'

Childhood sweethearts? Tough nut to crack.

Jack was still talking. 'Now, spadger, we both of us know you're not afianced to his lordship, so what is it between you?'

'Why do you say that?'

'I reckon as someone like you would be flashing a big stone around.'

'It's not *official* yet.'

'Nor ever likely to be.'

'I spoase'—she mimicked his accent—'you'd quite like a *lord* in the family, and lots of little lordlings running about the farm.'

He looked as though he had sucked on a lemon. 'It won't happen if I have anything to do with it. Want nothing to do with his type.'

Very interesting indeed.

'Looks like you and me might have some common interests,' she said, leaning into the open window.

He locked his eyes with hers and waited for her to say more.

'We'd both of us benefit if my fiancé and your sister had a falling out.'

He still said nothing.

'Fine.' She glanced down the road. Charlie and Elaine were out of sight around the bend. Was there any point in following them further? 'Suit yourself. I'll take care of it.' She began walking back towards the house.

'Wait. Hop in.'

'I don't think so.' She walked on, and the car began to move alongside her.

'What did you have in mind?'

It was her turn to ignore him.

'I was reckoning on me and a few mates roughing his lordship up a bit.'

This caught her attention. 'I don't want Charlie hurt.'

'So what's your plan, then?'

'Come to the house. We'll talk.'

He drove on ahead slowly and pulled off the road just past the house, out of sight from the road. By the time she reached the house he was waiting by the door. She led him through the house to the kitchen. She had no intention of making him too welcome. They sat on opposite sides of a sturdy wooden table.

Slate floors. Heavy black pots and utensils hanging from the ceiling. A similarly black oven to one side. Whether black by design or due to the accumulation of decades of grime she couldn't say. The sun was warm on the back of her head, and bluebottles *tip-tapped* against the glass or buzzed in futile circles on their backs.

'I don't care,' she said suddenly.

'Eh?'

'She can have him. I have to get out of here.'

'And where might you want to be?'

'Where do you live—' she hesitated '—Jack?'

'Leeds, for the most part.'

'I want to live in Leeds.'

'You're rampin!'

'What the fuck does that mean?'

He spun his index finger by his right temple. 'No one *wants* to live in Leeds.'

Her mind flashed back to her only trip to northern parts a few years earlier to visit her grandmother in Manchester.

'I'll go nuts if I stay here much longer.'

'What about his lordship?'

Then she thought about her brother. She hadn't thought about him for two or three years. 'Australia. That's where I should go.'

'I've better things to do than listen to your ramblings. I'll take care of his lordship myself.' He started to rise.

'Wait!' She stretched a hand towards him, but couldn't quite reach across the table. 'I need some dope to keep me sane if I have to stay here much longer. I reckon you might know the right people.'

'You do, do thee?'

'Am I wrong?'

'And have thee the means to pay?'

She hesitated, but not for long. 'Not with money.'

His upper lip curled slightly on the right, with a flash of greyish teeth. His eyes slipped to her cleavage. She leaned further over the table.

'You're disgusting,' he said.

'But …?'

His tongue briefly flicked across his lips.

She grew bolder. She stood and moved around the table. Jack froze, his hands palm down on the table in front of him. She watched his

Adam's apple bob up and down as he swallowed. She took his hand and slipped it between her thighs, just above the hem of her skirt. 'For one ounce.'

As his hand slipped upwards she thought, *It's worth it.*

'Upon delivery,' she added.

CHAPTER TWENTY-FOUR

CHARLIE REMEMBERED THE PLACE WELL, THOUGH WITH MIXED emotions. It was almost midday, and a haze of dust and probably pollen hung in the still air, lit by shafts of sunlight. He undid the buttons of his shirt sleeves and rolled them up.

They set down the blanket outside the circle of standing stones. There seemed something … irreverent about eating ham and pickles within their compass.

Rather than shop in Bristol that morning, Charlie had scoured the markets for local produce. Cider and cheddar cheese, of course, but also homemade chutney and relish, ham, smoked eels, ox tongue and black pudding. He had strived for what he hoped was authenticity.

'You know I left here to get away from food like this, don't you?' Elaine laughed as the spread unfolded before her. At his crestfallen look she added, 'But it's been a while, and it's a lovely gesture. I've actually missed some of this.'

'There is also this!' He whisked a bottle of champagne from the basket.

'Are we celebrating?'

'Always. We're still here.'

'Did you have reason to think we wouldn't be?'

'Sure. Didn't you? I still do.'

'What?'

'Wonder if we'll still be here next year, next week or tomorrow.'

'I don't like to think about it.'

'It's all I think about.'

'You sure know how to brighten a girl's day.'

'Sorry. Let's eat.'

They did so in silence for a while.

'It's not just the big things, you know.' He held up his glass, watching the sunlight through the bubbles.

'What do you mean?'

'It's not just about war and the "eve of destruction" and all that. It's the little things that can strike us down.'

'Like what?'

'Well, think about Millie—I told you what happened to her parents.'

'Yeah.'

'Just a completely random, ridiculous occurrence that …' He shrugged. 'But it's not even just one thing. It's all the little things that chip away at us.'

'What's chipping away at you, Charlie?'

'Oh, I don't know. Nothing really, I suppose.'

Elaine lay back on the blanket and closed her eyes. Charlie found himself watching her face. The way her eyes moved behind her eyelids. Her mouth slightly open. The sun caught a feathery down on her cheeks. She wore too many clothes, and he couldn't really get a sense of her body.

But he wanted to.

This was ridiculous. He was engaged to Sophia. Or, at least, he thought he still was. Maybe. She wasn't the Daughter of Abraham. No one was. But he had more or less kidnapped Miriam—Millie—because … And he had dragged Tiggi into his madness. And now Elaine …

He needed no one else to point out that somewhere along the way he had …

'I'm just a postmistress in an insignificant village. I find it hard to get my head around such things.'

'But you *know* things, don't you? You just *know* things. Like your mother and father. They *know* things too.'

She shrugged slightly and shook her head.

'It's not the way I know things, by reading about them in books,' he continued. 'You …' He struggled to find different words.

'*Know* them.' She laughed lightly. 'I get it. But I don't really.'

'That's because you know it like the air you breathe or the ground beneath you. You know it unconsciously. And unselfconsciously. I'm just clever. Well read.'

'You're a romantic fool, Charlie.' But she said it with a smile.

He bent over and placed his lips gently against hers. She gasped but offered no resistance. But when he placed his hand on her hip she said softly, 'No, Charlie.'

'Ellie …'

She opened her eyes. 'You haven't called me that before.'

'It's what your father calls you, isn't it? He's very proud of his little "Ellie", who got college edicated and all.'

'You've talked about me?'

'Mostly about the farm and its future.'

'And where do you see yourself fitting into that future?'

'You'll just think I'm a fool. You already do.'

'No.'

'You said as much. What was it? A "romantic fool".'

'I was just teasing.'

'Well … I want to feel … connected.'

'To …?'

'Something. Anything. I would watch my mother gardening, and it was as if she was … she was … And I see your father around the farm …'

He lay down and closed his eyes, letting the sounds invade him, feeling the heat of the sun in patches on his body. Something crawled across his hand and he let it. Feeling it.

'I'm not sure I understand.' Elaine's voice was close to his ear. Almost, he thought, he felt her breath.

'No.' Then he sat up again. 'Listen to this.' His eyes remained closed as he recited:

In every cry of every man,
*   In every infant's cry of fear,*
In every voice, in every ban,
*   The mind-forged manacles I hear.*

'I want to create a short circuit between the world and my experience of it, bypassing my rational mind.' *I want to make love to you without my mind intervening.*

'I don't know what that means.'

'Nor do I, really.' He laughed lightly. 'I suppose I want to experience a closer, more immediate connection to people and things. I think I could do that here, on the farm.'

'And how do you plan to make money, My Lord? Or is that something only us humbler folk have to worry about?'

'Oh, there's no plan, really. I don't think Sophia and her family—or my father—are too happy about that.'

'But you have something in mind.'

'Not really. Only vague, foolish ideas. Maybe a community of some kind … I did read about a place in the Cotswolds. Maybe you'd like to come with me to take a look sometime.'

'What kind of community?'

He shrugged. 'Maybe we might try to become self-sufficient.'

'We?'

'Maybe encourage artists, musicians … Somewhere to come to, to retreat from the world for a while.' He shrugged again, embarrassed at how this must sound. 'I would write.'

Elaine's silence was eloquent.

'There's the matter of your Millie,' she said eventually.

'What about her?'

'What on earth are your plans for her? Or are there no plans there, either? She really can't stay there, Charlie. The two of you …'

'There's nothing between us.'

'You've said that before, but you don't "rescue" someone and live with them over "nothing".'

'Yes, yes, there's something of course, but nothing …'

'What is it, Charlie, and where's it going?'

'She has a brother. In Australia, I think. Over the last couple of weeks I've made some enquiries. No luck so far, but I do have another idea. As for the future … I've had a couple of thoughts. My grandmother is all alone now in Fernlea. When mother comes over just before Christmas we're going to try to persuade grandmother to come and live here. We would sell Fernlea—'

'Really?'

'Yes. We could then invest the money here, into the farm and into some additional cottages.'

'Do you know if Millie even wants to go back to Australia?'

'I doubt if Millie knows what Millie wants! In fact …'

'Yes?'

'Well, I was wondering if maybe you …'

'Me?'

'Yes. Could you talk to her, get to know her? Befriend her.'

'Oh Charlie, really! Why would she want to be my friend? She's obviously in love with you and would surely see me as a rival.'

This revelation surprised him at several levels. He took a moment to sift through it.

This is what settled to the bottom: 'And are you? Are you her rival?'

Elaine would not meet his eyes. 'Whether I am or not, she'll think I am.'

'But Millie doesn't …'

'Oh, Charlie, you can be such a noggerhead sometimes.'

When he stopped laughing she continued, 'So you see why the two of you can't live there alone together, right? Sooner or later … And what about Sophia?'

Right. Sophia.

'What have you done …? What are you doing to her? You can't leave it like that.'

'Can I kiss you again?'

She caught his eye, shook her head and took a deep breath. On the exhalation of that breath she may have said, 'Oh, all right!' That was what he chose to hear.

Unlike the first kiss—which he had managed to bestow on Elaine while she lay with her eyes closed—this kiss required serious choreography and became awkward and ungainly. Heads needed to be placed at appropriate angles, movements forward coordinated and the clashing of teeth avoided. When they finally succeeded in making contact, Elaine exploded into laughter.

'Sorry,' she spluttered, covering her mouth with a hand.

'Not very good for a chap's ego, Ellie dear.'

'Sorry,' she repeated, and then seized his head between her hands and guided him towards her lips.

The kiss lingered and deepened, but when his hand drifted towards her breast she pushed it away and broke the connection.

'I should get back to the cottage,' she asserted. 'I'm staying with Mum and Dad tonight. I promised to help Mum with some baking. Would you like to come to Sunday lunch tomorrow?'

'I would love to … If you're sure your parents won't mind.'

'I won't let them.'

As they packed away the picnic things he laid a hand upon her arm. 'The door's always open,' he said. 'My room's the first on the right at the top of the stairs.'

He thought she blushed as she turned away.

CHAPTER TWENTY-FIVE

CHARLIE REALISED THAT ELAINE WOULD NOT COME TO HIS ROOM THAT night but couldn't entirely suppress the tingle of excitement that arose at the thought. He made sure not only that the front door was unlocked—it generally was—but also that the door to his own room was slightly ajar.

He indulged in a couple of glasses of scotch to ease his nerves and make it easier to sleep.

Sleep he did, but his dreams were a riot of incoherent images, many of them erotic. There were vivid scenes that seemed to make sense but, upon waking, never would, and would be difficult to retain in the memory. It was not unusual for alcohol to trigger these in him, particularly if he consumed it just before sleeping.

He sensed his erection and began moving rhythmically, still within the dream. There was no reason to ask questions.

But he gradually became aware of a naked figure lying beside him, and that the hand caressing his penis was real. He reached down and touched the hand that touched him. It had freed his penis from the boxer shorts he habitually wore to bed. At the contact, the body next to him shifted, rose above him. She straddled him and guided his penis inside. He shuddered as he felt himself enclosed in warm, slippery wetness.

The figure began to gyrate and move up and down.

Feeling himself on the brink he gasped, croaked, grunted a single word: 'Elaine.'

Even as he came, he felt the stinging slap across his cheek. 'Don't say that bitch's name,' said the voice.

The voice of Miriam. Millie.

Millie! Oh my God, what have I done?

His erection quickly wilted.

'Shit,' she said.

She slipped off and used her hand to try to revive his erection, but he pushed her away and sat on the side of the bed, his back to her.

'What have you done?'

'We. *We.*'

'Fuck.'

'We just did.' She laughed. 'Well, mostly. Come back here. Touch me. I'm not finished.'

'You have to leave. First thing in the morning.'

Millie didn't answer. Her fingers lightly traced the ridge of his spine, and he felt himself becoming aroused again, despite himself.

He stood, gathered up the clothes he had thrown in the corner, and hastily dressed. He left the room and descended the stairs without a word, picked up his keys from the Demilune table by the front door and drove away.

It was already after one o'clock and there was no sign of Charlie.

'I'll go and see what's holding him up.' Elaine glanced at her mother, crouching in front of the oven. 'I thought Jack was coming too,' she added before leaving.

'Aah well ... I've given up trying to work out the comings and goings of your brother.'

Her mother struggled to rise after checking the dinner, placing her hands in the middle of her back. A glance around the kitchen revealed that little had changed since Elaine's childhood. A more modern, much smaller radio had replaced the ancient thing they used to listen to while baking; there was a new refrigerator in the corner. But the curtains were the same; the old paint on the wall only a little more stained. The ancient, wood-burning stove still crouched on its four legs, like some ungainly animal hiding in the shadows.

But her mother had changed, she realised. Collapsed in upon herself somehow. Charlie was right. Her mother and father wouldn't be able to run the farm for much longer.

'Be back in a minute. Hopefully with Charlie in tow.'

As she walked around to the main house she reflected that it wasn't like Charlie to be late. But then she caught herself. *What do I know about him, really? I knew him for a few weeks as a boy, and now for no more than a day or two as a man.* Perhaps he was late all the time. Perhaps it was his habit not to meet commitments.

She knocked on the door.

And again.

When still no one answered she tried the door. It was unlocked, so she opened it and called, 'Charlie!'

She hadn't been inside the big house since she was a small child. Here, too, little had changed. To the left, the sitting room. Rising along the wall to the right, the stairway. The image of the young Charlie bouncing down the stairs flashed through her mind and she shivered.

'Charlie!'

'What do you want?' Millie emerged from the kitchen, dressed in a bathrobe.

'Is Charlie here?'

'No. Haven't seen him since he left this morning.'

'Where did he go? Do you know?'

'No clue. He left in a hurry.'

Elaine took a deep breath. 'Look, Millie, can you ease up on the hostility just little?'

When Millie pulled the belt of her robe tighter but said nothing, Elaine said, 'Perhaps a cup of tea?'

Millie turned her back and returned to the kitchen, which Elaine chose to interpret as a 'yes'.

But in the kitchen, Millie sat at the large table, an empty cup and saucer in front of her.

'I'll help myself then, shall I?'

After she had done so she sat across the table from Millie. 'Look, Millie, there's no need for us to be enemies.'

'Or friends.'

'We're both friends of Charlie.'

'Is that what we are? His *friends*?'

'Aren't we?'

'Charlie was a little more than *friendly* last night.'

Elaine's warm tea was not enough to combat the cold sweat that swept over her. She lowered the cup to hide the tremor in her hand.

'Ha. See?' Millie pursued relentlessly. 'You're no more just his friend than I am.'

'What happened between you?' Elaine asked in a quiet voice.

'Oh, it doesn't matter.' Millie dismissed the issue with a wave of her hand. 'He's a man. Just like all men.'

'I know what happened to you, Millie. Before, anyway. Before you disappeared. I know about your parents. But what happened afterwards?'

'What's it to you?'

'Why are you like this?'

'Like this. Like this. Like *what* exactly?'

'A fucking, vindictive bitch!' Elaine's own vehemence shocked her. She clenched her hands together beneath the table, afraid of what they might do otherwise.

'Well, well. Miss Prim-and-Proper has a temper.'

There was a long silence. Elaine wasn't quite sure why she stayed.

After a while, Millie echoed her thoughts. 'Why are you still here?'

Unable to think of a reason, Elaine stood to leave, but almost bumped into her brother Jack as he entered.

'Jack!'

'Ellie!'

They spoke at the same time.

'Jack, what are you doing here?'

He glanced over her shoulder at Millie, who said, 'Is that Charlie's package?'

'What?' He glanced down at a plastic bag in his left hand. 'Yes. Yes, it's Charlie's. Is his lordship here?'

'Charlie's what?' Elaine stepped to the side so that she could see both Millie and Jack.

'Charlie needed some dope,' Millie said coolly. 'Jack has been kind enough to supply it.' She winked in Jack's direction.

Elaine pushed passed her brother. Once outside she headed for the courtyard behind the small house, retrieved her bicycle and returned to the village. She had completely forgotten about lunch.

-168-

PART FIVE

CHAPTER TWENTY-SIX

CHARLIE DROVE THROUGH THE NIGHT ALL THE WAY TO OXFORD, WITH no real plan in mind. His encounter with Millie left him badly shaken. *The recovering alcoholic*, he thought, *doesn't keep alcohol in the home and staunchly resist temptation. He keeps alcohol out, so that temptation doesn't arise.* How foolish he'd been, leading himself into temptation. What had he been thinking? Elaine had been right.

Elaine!

Tiggi had probably understood too. Yes, Tiggi. He would talk to her.

He had no idea what the time was. He'd left his watch on the bedside table in his haste. He didn't know what time he'd left. But the sky still looked totally dark. No hint of dawn yet.

He stopped the car in a village on the outskirts of Oxford. In the nearby market square some stallholders were already setting up, and a clock in the church tower read 4.55 am.

He sat watching for a while from a bench, but it was a little cold so early, this late in summer, and he wasn't really dressed for it. He did a circuit of the town, taking inventory of his life.

He had practically abandoned Sophia. His reasons for doing so were a little fuzzy now.

He had virtually kidnapped Miriam. His reasons for doing so …

He had abandoned his studies. There were no even fuzzy reasons for this. In fact, until this moment he hadn't realised he'd done it. His thesis—'The Influence of Pre-Socratic Philosophy on the Philosophical Writings of Alfred North Whitehead'—had once been a virtual obsession. Determining what, precisely, had been the influence of pre-Socratic philosophy on the philosophical writings of Alfred North Whitehead had been a matter of the utmost importance. But who would care? His supervisor probably wouldn't. The academic community probably wouldn't. He wasn't sure even he cared anymore.

He had virtually burned the bridges between himself and his father. The safe, secure path was cut off.

His mother would no doubt offer some profoundly ridiculous advice. Tiggi might offer something more practical.

So Tiggi it was.

He had known Tiggi for about five or six years now. They'd met at a bar in Oxford, he drinking on one side, Tiggi serving on the other. She was from a modestly well-off family in Cheltenham, but she was determined to be as independent as possible.

They had briefly become lovers, but then settled down into a solid friendship. Through Tiggi, he had met her cousin Anthony; and through Anthony he had met most of his other friends.

'It's understandable that you would want to come home from the colonies,' Anthony had said upon meeting him. 'The prodigal son, and all that.'

Charlie pulled up outside Tiggi's Oxford flat, the sky just beginning to lighten. She was not an early riser, which meant she would be angry at him if he roused her before about 10 am. He couldn't wait that long. He might as well incur her wrath at 6 am as 9 am.

A response to his persistent knocking was a long time coming.

'Who the fuck is it?'

'It's me, Charlie.'

'What the fuck do you want at this time of the morning? You'd better be dead or dying!'

'I wish I were.' He sounded pathetic even to his own ears. 'Bugger it, Tiggi, can I come in?'

The door opened. Tiggi pulled the robe tightly around her. Her normally short, neat hair was strangely sculpted on one side where her head had lain on the pillow. She wore no make-up. She stood aside and gestured impatiently for him to come in.

'Coffee,' she said. It was neither a question nor an offer. Nevertheless, she returned with coffee for herself and tea for him. 'So what's going on? Have you made a mess of things again?'

He explained what had happened with Millie.

'Here, chill out for a bit.' She lit up a joint, which they shared.

'I need something to eat,' he said afterwards.

'Let me get washed and dressed. We can go out somewhere for breakfast.'

'I didn't bring anything with me … razor, clean clothes.'

'Thinking ahead as always. The most I can offer you here is toast … and more tea or coffee.'

'That will do for now.'

'Help yourself. I'll be back in a minute.'

He pottered around. He knew where most things were, but the butter was hiding somewhere in the fridge. He checked behind … He couldn't really say what that was. What Tiggi regarded as food remained largely a mystery to him, as did her organising principles.

'The butter …' he began when she returned in a bathrobe with her hair wrapped in a towel.

She reached past him.

'Ah.' It had been in a Tupperware container marked … 'Butter'. *Sneaky trick!*

Tiggi left and returned again after dressing. 'So …' she began. But instead of continuing she made herself some toast and another cup of coffee. She wore a frown and paused occasionally in what she was doing, biting her bottom lip. Charlie knew well enough to let her work through whatever was on her mind. Eventually she sat at the table with the makings of breakfast and lit another cigarette.

'You're a fool, Charlie. Something has to be done about Millie. You can't keep her there. At least not while you're there too.'

'I know.'

'Her brother?'

'I haven't been able to find him, but I have an idea. I need to go to Scotland Yard. And,' he added, rather sheepishly, 'I should probably see Sophia.'

'Yes, you probably should, but first we'd better get you cleaned up and in some fresh clothes.'

When he returned from the bathroom he found a pair of slacks, a man's shirt, underwear and socks laid out on the couch. They were a good fit, although not precisely his style.

'Anthony's?'

She offered no explanation.

Charlie suppressed an irrational twinge of jealousy.

It was cold and raining when Tiggi and Charlie returned to the farm three days later.

Tiggi had followed in her own car. She had no intention of becoming stranded. Sophia, much to Charlie's surprise, was with him.

The house was empty.

Miriam Levinson—as he'd hoped—was still registered as a missing person with Scotland Yard. From there word had finally filtered through to Sgt Plod, who constituted the entire police contingent in the village of Coxton Sudbury. He should be pedalling their way at any moment to confirm that Millie Lewis was, indeed, Miriam Levinson, and that she was alive and well. Word would then be sent to her brother in Australia, whose contact details were still on record.

Only, the house was empty.

Beds were unmade upstairs. A woman's underwear was scattered on the first-floor landing.

'I don't suppose you recognise those?' Tiggi asked with a wry grin.

Sophia was not amused.

'I never—'

'Hallo?' It was Sgt Plod calling from below. He stood in the entryway, shaking the water from his standard-issue waterproof cape.

The man's name wasn't actually 'Sgt Plod'. He may not even have been a sergeant. But Charlie was damned if he could remember his actual name and rank.

'Up here, Sergeant …'

'Righto, sir. What have we here, then?' He heaved his sizeable frame halfway up the stairs. 'Would you be this Chollock fella?'

'Charlie Kollock.' He extended a hand, which the sergeant used to heave himself further up the stairs. Charlie barely kept his balance.

'I understand you want to report someone missing, a Miriam—'

'No no, Sergeant. I want to report someone … someone found.'

'Someone found.' He stared at Charlie quizzically.

'I'm Tiggi—Tigraine—Spencer.' She held out her hand, which the sergeant touched briefly. 'And this is Sophia.'

Sophia went out of her way not to pay attention. Yes, she was here, but Charlie couldn't claim that their reunion had been an unqualified success.

'And what's your … all of your … connection with the missing … with the girl—' he glanced again at his notebook '—Miriam Levinson?'

'No connection really. An acquaintance,' Tiggi responded.

Sophia said nothing.

'And your connection with Mr … Krodduck here?'

'A friend. Sophia's his … fiancée?'

Sophia snorted.

'A friend.' He added the word to a clean page of his notebook. 'Tig … Tig …'

'Tigraine—T.I.G.R.A.I.N.E.—Spencer—S.P …'

'Thank you, Miss Spencer. Got that. And Sophia …?'

'Sophia Abramovna Batiashvili.'

'S.O.F.—'

'*P.H.*I.A.'

He waited. 'Malabova?' he asked hopefully.

She strode towards him, snatched his pad and pencil and wrote it out for him. When she had finished she returned both into his hands, which remained frozen in place.

'Right then.'

He glanced down at the underwear on the landing, perhaps puzzling over the pink bow that adorned the front of the sheer panties. The colour rose to his cheeks as his mind discerned the pattern in his field of vision and gave it an identity.

'Righto.' He coughed. 'So where is this Miss'—another glance at the notebook—'Levinson.'

'She's not … She doesn't seem to be here.' Charlie felt the colour rising in his own cheeks.

'Not here. So where is she then?'

'I … I don't know.'

'The missing girl … the found missing girl is not here.'

'It seems not.'

'The found missing girl is … missing.'

'Well, no … I don't know. Mrs Pierce might know where she is. I'm sure she'll know. She's been cooking for Millie.'

'Millie?'

'Miriam. She's been calling herself Millie. Millie Lewis. I'm sure it's—'

A surprisingly sharp look from the policeman's extraordinarily blunt face halted Charlie's flow of words. 'P'haps we should go have a chat to Mrs Pierce then, shall we?'

The rain had eased. The sergeant's bicycle leaned against the pillar holding up the portico. Charlie glanced at the vast girth before him, and then back at the bicycle with some sympathy. It was a difficult mating to visualise.

'Mrs Pierce!' The sergeant rapped on the smaller cottage's kitchen door.

'Walter, is that you?' Mrs Pierce wiped her hands on her apron.

'Aarr, Nellie.'

'Come in, Walter. What can I do for thee?' When Charlie and Tiggi hesitated on the threshold she added, 'And Mr Kollock. I'm sure thee'd love a cuppa. And …'

'Tiggi, Mrs Pierce.' She held out her hand, which Mrs Pierce took after wiping her own again on the apron.

Charlie glanced back towards the house. Sophia hadn't followed them. She wasn't going to make this easy for him.

'And it's Charlie, please, Mrs Pierce. I won't tell thee again.'

'Now don't be mocking our ways … Charlie. And it's Nellie.'

In her direct gaze he saw something of Elaine, which he hadn't noticed before.

As she filled the kettle and set it on the range she repeated, 'What can I do for thee, Walter?'

From his speech patterns it was clear that the sergeant—Walter— was not a local, but he had clearly been around long enough to become well known by those who were.

'Just a few questions about the young woman who's been staying in the big house … Miriam. Or Millie, it seems.'

'Oh aarr?'

'It seems she was reported missing a couple of years back … If this Millie and Miriam are the same filly, at least. Now she seems to have gone missing again. When did you last see her, Nellie?'

'It would've been two days back, now. Took her a meal. I went back yesterday, but there were no one there. The front door was open and the kitchen were a right mess. I cleaned it up. Didn't go upstairs, mind.'

'Any idea where she might've gone.'

'None at all.'

'Well then—'

Throat clearing from the back door drew everyone's attention.

'Excuse me. Sorry to interrupt.'

'What is it, Pete?'

The de facto farm manager stood hat in hand, stooping below the lintel, although there was room to spare.

'Pardon me, Nellie … Mrs Pierce—and all—but I couldn't help overhearing. About the young miss.'

'Come on in, Pete. There's plenty in the kettle.'

'What can you tell us, Pete?' The sergeant licked the tip of his pencil.

'Well, I was driving the tractor by on Tuesday night, two nights back, when I saw a car pulling away from the main house. I didden recognise the car, but I could see the driver and his passenger well enough. The passenger was the young lady.' He paused and looked at Mrs Pierce. 'I be sorry, Nellie, but the driver were your Jack.'

'Jack?'

'Aarr.'

'You're certain, Pete?' asked the sergeant.

'Right enough.'

'Nellie, do you know where Jack's staying?'

'I only know it were somewhere in Bristol. But I thought he'd be gone back up north by now. Our Elaine might know.'

'Elaine. Righto. Well, I have to pass the post office on the way back to the station, so I'll pop in and see her. But this is not something we'll be spending much time on.' He shot a warning glance towards Charlie.

CHAPTER TWENTY-SEVEN

ELAINE DECIDED SHE HATED HER ROOMS ABOVE THE POST OFFICE.

It was really just one room, a bedroom cum living room with a small kitchenette. The bathroom and toilet were a short way down the hall, but they didn't quite feel as though they belonged to her.

She'd opened the post office, but then retreated upstairs. What was the point? There were never any customers. The occasional rambler might stumble in later for a postcard. Mrs Tremethyk might pop in this afternoon with some scones. Wednesday was baking day, she said. Yesterday Celia Penprase had requested a postal order to send to her emigrant son in Australia.

She could hear the bell just as clearly upstairs.

But the room was dark and cloistered. She wasn't present. There was nothing here to mark her presence, aside from her body.

She recalled the last time she'd felt like this.

Maurice. It was that evening when Maurice said what he had to say. There were words. She was sure they had meanings of one kind or another.

It was then that she realised she couldn't let Charlie do the same to Sophia.

And it was then that the bell rang downstairs.

A distraction perhaps.

'Coming!'

The local policeman—she'd seen him around, of course, but never been formerly introduced—took up a large proportion of the doorway.

'Officer, what can I do for you?'

'Miss Pierce?'

'Elaine.'

'Elaine, I'm trying to locate your brother, and I wondered if you happened to know where he's been staying … in Bristol, I believe.'

'Is he in trouble? What's he been up to?'

'No no, not at all as far as I'm aware. It's just that we believe he might have with him a young woman who was reported missing some years ago. We wish to confirm that it is indeed her and that she is well.'

'Millie?'

Millie was with Jack? Why? Maybe she already knew why. Jack probably *was* in trouble, even if the police didn't know it yet.

'Miriam Levinson, currently known as Millie Lewis, it seems.'

'I don't know where he was staying. Not in a hotel. With a work contact I think. But I expect him to be gone back north by now.'

'Right. Back north. To where exactly?'

'Leeds. I have an address somewhere. Not sure if it's current, though.' She looked through her address book.

'That's all right, Miss. If he's gone to Leeds I won't be pursuing him. It seems to me that this Millie—if she's with him—may not want to be found anyway. And can probably look after herself.'

'Can I at least have the address of Miriam's brother?'

Charlie's voice surprised Elaine. He must have been waiting outside. He and another woman came in. Charlie and his women.

Why did it bother her? Why did any of it bother her? As far as she knew, Charlie was still engaged to Sophia. What right did she have to be jealous of him? If that's what she actually was, jealous. And why should she be surprised, anyway? If he was prepared to cheat on Sophia with her, why not cheat on her with Millie? And whoever this new woman was … Maybe this was Sophia. Although she looked nothing like she had imagined.

During her moment of confusion she caught Charlie's eye.

What did she know, anyway? It was Millie who had said—implied—that she and Charlie had made love. Not the most reliable witness. Even if it was true, Charlie probably wouldn't know that she knew.

The ground didn't feel altogether steady beneath her feet.

'Are you all right, Miss?'

'What? Yes … Yes.' She was leaning forward on the counter. Suddenly everyone was closer and wearing concerned looks.

'I'll fetch some water.' Charlie began casting around.

'Don't worry.' There was a jug of water and some glasses on her side of the counter, which they couldn't see.

She poured half a glass and took a sip. It tasted stale. How was water supposed to help anyway?

'I'm fine. It's just stuffy in here of an afternoon.'

'Elaine—'

The woman interrupted Charlie. 'I'm Tiggi. Why don't you sit down for a while?'

'I'm fine, really.'

'Well, Mr Kollock, sir, I don't think there's much more I can do. Just let me know if this Millie turns up again.'

'Sergeant, her brother's address?'

He thought for a moment. 'It's a bit irregular, sir …'

'It would save you from having to concern yourself with the matter any further.'

'Very well, Mr Kollock, but I don't have the address here. It's at the station just up the road a way.'

'You go with the sergeant, Charlie. I'll wait here with Elaine. Any chance of a cup of coffee, Elaine?'

There was a small fireplace in Elaine's room. On the mantel was a trophy. She had been very proud of that trophy. She won it for a nationwide writing competition when she was in her final year at primary school. It was the only thing she'd ever won.

Now she was embarrassed by it, her room, and all it contained as Tiggi took a seat on the threadbare couch.

'I don't have coffee, I'm afraid, only tea and hot chocolate.'

'Tea will be fine. Black, no sugar.'

It seemed very warm. She opened the window, which looked out over the street below. Charlie and the police officer were still walking towards the station, the sergeant wheeling his bicycle. Laurel and Hardy, minus the hats. She laughed despite herself.

'He's complicated,' she observed, turning her attention to the tea preparation.

'Yes, dear, he is.'

The 'dear' irritated her a little. She was at least Tiggi's age, perhaps older, but Tiggi assumed a superior, condescending air.

'As a child he seemed to be struggling to form an identity. I wonder if he has yet.' It didn't hurt to remind Tiggi that she had known Charlie back then.

'I don't think it's been required of him yet, but I imagine when he's cut loose from his father's purse strings he'll actually have to become someone.'

'Do you think we all love him because we think we can mould him into shape?' She carried the tea, with some tea cake made by her mother the day before, and set it on the coffee table. She sat in one of the armchairs opposite Tiggi. None of the furnishings matched.

'"We all"?'

'There are at least four of us that I know of. Probably more.'

'I'm not sure Millie is quite capable of love … yet.'

'And Charlie?'

'Ah, well …'

Tiggi had a squarish face, almost Slavic in appearance. Her hair was cut in a short bob reminiscent of the twenties or thirties. Elaine detected some western textures in her speech.

'I don't mean I *love* love him,' she insisted. But she wasn't really sure what that meant anymore. She'd thought she loved Maurice, and that he'd loved her.

'Let me tell you a story that happened not long after I met Charlie.' Tiggi slipped off her shoes and tucked her feet under her legs. 'Charlie was walking me home after my shift at the pub—I was working behind the bar in those days. There was nothing between us at that stage beyond friendship, but there were hints of possibilities. For me at least.' She paused to take a sip of her tea. 'There was a light mist rising from the river and settling over the town, but it wasn't particularly cold. There were haloes around the streetlamps, you know? We paused briefly beneath one of them and he said, "Have you ever listened to the sound of silence? Really listened?" This was at least two years before that song came out. You know the one? Then he said, "They say, 'Silence is golden,' but it's more akin to darkness, don't you think?" He sounded very sad. So I kissed him. And that was the first time I took him back to my room.'

Elaine waited a moment before asking, 'And why did it end?'

'Well … There were too many times when I thought he wasn't there in the room—or the bed—with me. Just not *really* there. There's always a bit of him that's off somewhere else. I still love him very deeply, you know … As a friend. But …'

Elaine waited again.

'Back then I thought how very deep he was. Now I'm not so sure. Not deep, so much as …'—she shook her head and Elaine thought she saw a tear form—'… empty.

'When I first heard that song a few years later,' she added, steadying her voice, 'it sent a shiver down my spine. I reminded Charlie of that night and said how weird it was that the words of the song echoed what he'd said. He smiled and nodded, but I knew …'

'Knew what?' Elaine prompted.

'He didn't remember. I just knew he didn't even remember.'

Charlie took that moment to call out from downstairs. 'Hello?'

Elaine stepped out the door. 'Up here, Charlie.'

'Don't lose yourself in him, Elaine; whether in his depths or in his emptiness.' Her words were very quiet, and Elaine may have misheard them.

CHAPTER TWENTY-EIGHT

THEY DIDN'T GO TO LEEDS.

Millie and Jack spent a few days in Jack's room in Bristol, smoking dope and fucking, and then drove northwest into Wales.

'I know a place,' he said.

Millie had nothing better to do or any other place to be.

Jack was an arsehole. She knew that. But so was she. He was a ride for a while.

He drove to a small village called Llanfairfuchinell. Or maybe not. Something like that. There was an empty house on the edge of the village.

'Belongs to a mate,' he said.

Conversation was not a big part of their arrangement.

'What the fuck are we doing here?'

'Lying low for a while.'

Had she fallen into a gangster movie?

After three days she was bored and wanted to start a fight. So she did.

'I didn't leave that shithole of a farm to come and live in this shithole on the edge of nowhere.'

'Leave then.'

Later, after she threw a chair through the window and Jack knocked her to the ground with the back of his hand, she thought she probably should. Leave, that is. She'd outstayed her welcome.

But where to go and how to get there?

During the night she snuck out with nothing but the clothes on her back. She had not shared Jack's room that night. It wasn't that she thought he would prevent her from leaving, but she was going for dramatic effect.

It was a warm night and the sky was slightly overcast. A crescent moon occasionally peeked through. They were some distance from the next house. There were no streetlamps this far out from the village and no lights shone from any windows that she could see. The moonlight was her only guide.

The next house was a two-storey white Georgian which stood out ghostly in the night. She opened the low-set gate, which triggered the barking of dogs. She hoped they were confined somewhere at the rear of the house.

The door was as white as the house, with no knocker that she could see. She rapped it with her knuckles. The barking became more frenzied, but no other sound emerged from within. She took off her shoe and banged the door with the heel. She hoped the occupant wouldn't notice where it chipped the paint, at least until after she was long gone.

Eventually a light came on upstairs and a curtain moved. A voice called down from the open window. A thin, high-pitched voice. 'Who is it at this hour?'

'Help me. Please help me!'

'What is it, child? Look at you now.'

'Help me. This man … He took me away and … and … I've just got away, but I need …'

'Get down there Gareth and let the child in. I'll call the *heddlu*.'

Millie guessed that 'haydler' was probably 'police'. She hadn't set out with any great plan in mind, but one began to form as she waited for Gareth. Yes, calling the police would be fine.

The man who answered the door was at least a hundred years old. He was so bent over that he was shorter than her. His head thrust upward and forward. Whiskers, unreached by any razor, hid in the deep crevices of his face.

'Help me,' she said. 'He hurt me.'

She no doubt looked the part: thin, pale and with a fresh bruise across her right cheek and eye. Her lip was slightly cut.

The ancient man eyed her up and down, perhaps assessing whether she constituted a threat. In truth, she could probably have blown him over with a single breath. He wasn't on her hit list, however.

'Come in, child. Missus will put the kettle on.'

Millie had never liked old people. Gareth smelt of piss. She followed him down a passageway towards the kitchen at the back of the house. On the way they passed an open door. In the room beyond, 'Missus' was on the phone. She waved at Millie, urging her in.

'Are you all right, child? Do you need a doctor, like? Let me look at you now.' She held her hand over the mouthpiece of the phone while she looked closely at her.

'I don't want no doctor.'

'Are you sure, now?'

She just nodded.

'She says not, Bill … Righto … We will. I'll get David over here … Righto … Hwyl fawr.

'They can't send anyone over right away, pet,' she continued to Millie, 'but first thing in the morning.'

Again she nodded.

'I'm Bethan, dear, but you can call me Betty.'

'Millie.'

'Nice to meet you, Millie. Let's pop into the kitchen and have a nice cuppa. And maybe some soup. You'll like my cawl, you will.'

Unlike her husband, Betty smelt of soap. There were other contrasts too. The skin—on her face at least—was smooth. Her eyes were sharp and bright. She stood up straight but was still tiny—barely five feet tall. Her gaze seemed to know too much.

Millie drank the tea and ate a little of the soup. It was delicious. She explained to them—keeping it vague—that Jack had taken her from the farm. She had thought, she said, that he was taking her to—she had to think on her feet—to a doctor in Bristol, because she had been unwell.

'He's the son', she said, 'of the farmer at Chetwood Farm, where I'd been staying. I … He …'

She knew she wouldn't be able to cry. She tried not to overplay the role.

'He just kept driving. We got here three nights ago. And …'

'It's all right, dear.'

'He said if I didn't … he would … he would …'

Millie let Betty hug her.

'We'll sort it out in the morning. I'm sure things will look different by the light of day.'

A sharp rap on the back door startled all of them. 'It's me, it is, David.' He pronounced it 'Dahffid'. He didn't wait for an answer before coming in.

'David—this is our eldest, David,' she addressed to Millie. 'I explained the situation to him. He'll stay over the night, won't you, son. For assurance, like.'

'Aye, that I will.'

He was huge. At least twice the combined size of Gareth and Betty. It was inconceivable that he could have sprung from their loins. His height barely surpassed his width, and his height caused him to duck as he came through the door. Millie had a momentary thought that almost brought a smile to her face. For a moment she wished that Jack would burst through the door and try to take her away, so that she could see 'Dahffid' flatten him like a steamroller.

'Thank you, David,' she said, as meekly as possible. 'Thank you, Betty.'

'Let's get you up to bed now, and we'll see how things look by the light of the morning.'

Millie wondered if there was something in her tone and glance to suggest that she wasn't completely convinced by Millie's story. She was probably being paranoid.

Later that night, as she lay on the edge of sleep in a wonderfully comfortable bed, a pretty woman with bright red lipstick leaned towards her and said, 'It came out of nowhere, you see.' A briny, fishy smell was on her breath. She didn't want to see the images that flashed before her. The bile rose into her throat and she fought back the urge to vomit. It was only then that she realised why her hosts' Welsh accents disturbed her.

After a sumptuous breakfast, Sergeant Someone-Or-Other arrived to interview Millie. David must have eaten half a pig's worth of bacon and at least a dozen eggs at breakfast. Millie managed a decent portion herself, though it made her feel ill.

She told the sergeant the same story she had told last night. He went to check on the house where she and Jack had been staying, but found it empty. She wasn't surprised. He did find the window broken and plenty of evidence of recent occupation.

'Turns out this Jack is wanted on another matter,' he said, without being specific. 'Any idea where he might have gone?'

'He lives up north,' she said. 'That's all I know. There's his family at the farm, of course.'

'Right. You sure you don't want a medical examination, Miss?'

'No. No, I'm just glad it's over.'

'Is there anyone we can get in touch with, to pick you up like? We will need to be in touch again when we apprehend this fellow. Where will we reach you?'

'I don't have …' She hadn't really thought this through, but where else could she go? 'I've been living at Chetwood Farm in Somerset, near … near …' She tried to remember the name of the village where Elaine ran the post office. Cockhole Suckberry came to mind. What was it? 'Cock … Coxton … Suddlebury?'

'A phone number?'

There was no phone in the large house and if there was one in the cottage she didn't know the number.

'No.'

'We might have contact details for his parents at the station. There are maps there too. Perhaps you'd like to come back with me to Llandeilo and we can check it out.'

'All right.'

'Do you have anything back in the house that you might like to collect?'

She was suddenly worried about what he might have seen. The presence of her suitcase might punch a hole in her story about a doctor's visit.

'No—'

'Not a small blue suitcase, then, or any of the girly things lying around the bathroom and bedroom?'

Shit. The walls closed in and she felt like vomiting.

'Look, girlie, I don't know what the full story is, but the fact is we might be a bit closer to getting this fellow now. He can't have gone too far. What you were doing with him I don't want to know. But you can move on now. What do you say?'

Millie glanced at Betty, who had been sitting in on the conversation. She didn't look surprised. In fact, a smile tugged at the corners of her mouth.

Millie nodded.

'Good. Let's get your things then.'

As they rose to leave she took a step towards the old, elf-like woman. 'I …'

'Don't you worry now, girl. The truth is, we saw you and that fellow arrive the other day, we did. Don't get much excitement around here. I didn't much like the look of him, but you didn't look like you was there against your will. I was glad to see you last night, though prattle a bunch of nonsense you did.'

She didn't know what to say, but tentatively returned her hug.

'Now, be off with you and get yourself sorted!'

'Thank you, Betty. I … Maybe I will.'

Maybe she would.

CHAPTER TWENTY-NINE

'I'M HAVING A BABY,' SOPHIA SAID, 'AND I'D LIKE TO SCRATCH YOUR eyes out.'

It seemed to Charlie that quite a few people would have liked to do that. Elaine, certainly. Sophia's parents, had they been there. Tiggi probably only wanted to punch him. Or cut his balls off.

It was not as if he couldn't understand their point of view.

Sophia shared this news with him after coming out of the bathroom. He had heard her retching.

'A baby?'

'Yeah. You know what that is, right?'

For the past week or so, Sophia, Tiggi and Charlie had been living together in the house. Separate rooms. Tense conversations and non-conversations.

'Well,' he said, 'that's great.' He hadn't had time to figure out if it was yet, but it seemed like the right thing to say. He tried to inject the appropriate amount of enthusiasm into the words. After a pause he added, 'I still want to marry you, Sophia. I still love you.'

It was all very strange, saying words without really knowing whether he meant them. He wasn't lying. He just honestly wasn't sure any longer what words actually meant, or what the experiences some words apparently referred to were actually like. What was the difference between loving Sophia and not loving her? He had no idea.

He thought he knew how to act the part. If he did, perhaps the appropriate feelings would follow.

They moved downstairs to the sitting room, where Tiggi was reading the newspaper. 'Did you see what your people are doing in Vietnam?' She thrust the paper towards him.

'They're not my people.' It was a story describing the burning of an entire village in South Vietnam by US marines. As shocking as it was, Charlie had more immediate concerns. He tossed the paper aside.

'Well?' he addressed Sophia.

'Well, Charlie, if you don't marry me now, my father will probably shoot you.' She sat, picked up the discarded paper and scanned the story. 'I just have to decide whether to scratch your eyes out before or after the wedding. What do you think, Tiggi?'

'After, I would think. You don't want to draw too much sympathy or attention his way on the day.'

'True enough.'

He supposed he should have been relieved. Perhaps even pleased.

And yet he thought of the last time he had spoken to Elaine.

They hadn't stayed long at the post office once he had the contact details for Miriam's brother. He had struggled over what to tell Sam, now that his sister was missing again. What should he tell him about Jack? At least he could inform Sam that Miriam was alive and well. He assumed she would be okay with Jack, but he knew nothing about him. What kind of man was he, that he would go off with a sixteen-year-old? He had no choice but to talk to Elaine.

Over the last few visits to the farm he had set his hand to repairing an old bicycle that lay rusting in one of the sheds. He was now confident that it was ready for the longer trip to the post office. It was going to be a hot, late-August day, but it was cool in the morning, and the trees along the route offered plenty of shade. Dahlias, verbenas and chicory lined the sunnier side of the road. As the morning grew warmer, bees set frantically to work in preparation for the winter.

He pulled up outside the post office and took a deep breath.

Inside, Elaine was finishing up with two customers. Not locals. Ramblers, by the look of it. *A walk through the countryside. I'd like to do that with Elaine.*

She smiled and nodded, exchanged a few words with them. Her accent was much broader than usual. She had become part of the tourist experience. Her eyes avoided his.

After more nodding and smiling the visitors left and she glanced in his direction: past him; beyond him.

'What can I do for you, Charlie?'

'I'm trying to write a letter to Miriam's brother Sam … in Australia.'

'Yes?'

'And … well, I'm not sure what to tell him about Jack.'

'What about him?'

'Well, if she's gone with him, I want to be able to assure him she's safe. She is safe with Jack, isn't she? I'd also like to be able to say where she is. Perhaps Jack's address …'

'You'd better come through.'

A door behind the counter led to a room that served as both an office and a kitchen. She sat at a laminated table and indicated for him to sit on the other side.

'Millie told me you slept with her, Charlie.'

This wasn't the conversation he had expected. His hesitation in denying it was all she required as confirmation.

'It wasn't like …'

But what was it like? She wouldn't believe he was an unwilling participant in the event. He had enough doubts about that himself.

'Right. So you're engaged to Sophia, you sleep with Millie … So what is it you want with *me*, Charlie?'

Before he could respond she stood and slammed her fist down on the table. Cups jumped. Spoons rattled.

'I won't be fucked over again, Charlie, not by you or any other man.'

'I love you, Elaine.' And, at that moment, he was sure of it.

'Oh right. You love me.' She began to stride back and forth. 'I don't think you love anyone, Charlie. I think you love the *idea* of me. I don't think you see real people around you, Charlie; just your idea of people. Your idea of Sophia, Millie … me.' She paused and leaned towards him, her hands on the table. The pressure of her fingers made the nails turn white at the tips.

She didn't wear nail polish. She rarely wore make-up of any kind. Her naked colours sent a frisson of excitement through him.

He held his tongue.

She sat.

'What do you want to know about Jack?'

'I want to be able to assure Sam that Miriam is safe. Is she safe with Jack?'

'It seems Millie has a habit of being swept away by older men. What is it about her, do you think?'

'Is she safe?'

She stood and began to pace again. 'I scarcely know Jack these days. Don't know what he gets up to. I don't think she'll hold his interest for long. Or he hers.' She paused before adding, 'If she pisses him off he might not be gentle. She pisses people off, does our Millie.'

'Do you have his address?'

'I have *an* address. He's married, you know, though I'm not sure if he still lives with her. I've never met her. None of us have ever met her.'

'So you have no idea where they might be?'

'None at all.' She sat again momentarily. The energy seemed to drain out of her. 'I'll make a cup of tea.'

He left after a while, not really sure what any of their conversation had meant. The ride back to the house was long and hot. That afternoon he composed the best letter he could, but drove over to Chewton Mendip to mail it.

'So the wedding should be sooner rather than later, don't you think?' Sophia was suggesting.

'What? Yes, right. Mother wrote to say she's coming over in October, so maybe November?'

'I thought we might get married in New York, Charlie, otherwise everyone will have to come over here.'

'But your father will be here anyway, right?'

'I guess so.'

'The only other person I would want to invite from back home would be my brother. I suppose my father would have to come, but honestly … Maybe we could have the wedding right here on the farm.'

He could hear himself talking as if this all meant something.

Then came the knock on the door.

CHAPTER THIRTY

'THANK YOU, OFFICER.' THE NEW MILLIE WANTED TO PRACTISE politeness. She was sixteen now. She could do this. She could grow up.

The drive down from Wales had passed largely in silence. They had collected her few things from the house, the sergeant had driven her to the station and taken a formal statement, and then a junior officer had driven her back to the farm. He had told her his name, but she forgot almost at once. She sat in the back.

She'd probably had a narrow escape with Jack. She'd been in dodgy situations before, but this was the first time she'd actually felt frightened. Maybe being frightened was also part of growing up.

She was also a little scared of knocking on the door. She could hear voices inside.

But she knocked, and entered without waiting for an answer. Fuck fear! 'What's for lunch?'

She was almost slightly half pleased to see Tiggi. And Charlie, of course. But Sophia? She hadn't expected that.

'Miriam?'

Charlie's surprise was pleasing. But she had to decide now: Was she Millie or Miriam?

She would go with Miriam for a while.

'I could kill for some fish and chips. I missed lunch.'

She sat on the end of the couch furthest from Sophia and threw her leg over the arm.

'It's only four o'clock.' Charlie seemed to be having some difficulty pulling the strands together. 'Where have you been? How …?'

'Here and there. No fish and chips then? What is there?' She strode into the kitchen. Charlie followed.

'We were worried …'

'We?'

'Well, then, *I* was worried.'

'Were you, Charlie? *Really?* I thought you'd be glad to see the back of me.'

'No.'

'Can't imagine Sonja's so delighted I'm back.'

'Sonja?'

'The fiancée.'

'Sophia.'

'Whatever.' She searched through the fridge and cupboards. Cornflakes seemed the best bet. And some toast.

Charlie sat at the table. The other two women stood at the open door. She hadn't heard them follow.

She looked from one to the other, slowly, deliberately. 'Well?'

'Were you with Jack … Elaine's brother?'

'Yeah. For a while.'

The toast was ready. She found some fresh strawberries and sliced them into her cornflakes. 'Tea, coffee anyone? No?'

She sat opposite Charlie. 'So, what's been happening?'

'I've written to your brother in Australia to let him know you're OK.'

That threw her.

'Sammy …'

'We haven't heard back yet, but …'

She'd lost her appetite. She hadn't seen Sammy in years. She had adored him once, but who would he be now? Who was she now?

'You had no right to do that.'

'Don't you want to see him?"

She stood and undertook a circuit of the kitchen. Tiggi had taken another seat at the kitchen table. Sophia leaned back against the sink. It wasn't a large room around which to make a circuit, although a circuit was appropriate, as an island of benchtops—above which hung ancient black pots and pans—stood at the centre. Around that island she moved, her journey taking her past cupboards from which the paint was flaking, a large, black cast-iron range, and a white—and discordantly modern—

refrigerator. When her circuit brought her around to the sink she paused in front of Sophia.

'So what—'

The sting of Sophia's open palm against her cheek caused more surprise than pain, although the cut inside her mouth, caused by her teeth, promised to hurt. And bleed profusely.

'That's for sleeping with my fiancé.'

'He told you?' It took considerable effort not to retaliate. See? She was growing up.

'No. But now I know for sure.'

'Anyone in this room Charlie hasn't slept with? A show of hands? Preferably not against my face.'

'Well, there's me.'

'Elaine!' Charlie rose to his feet.

'I knocked, but you were all obviously pre-occupied. How's my brother, Millie, or Miriam, or whatever you want to call yourself now?'

'Your brother's a first-rate arsehole!'

'And are you Bonnie to his Clyde?'

'Who?'

Laughter broke out for some reason. It made Millie—Miriam—angry. 'Oh, there you all go again, being oh so much smarter than me.'

After the laughter had settled, at least the atmosphere seemed more relaxed. Maybe no one felt like hitting her now.

'Perhaps it's time we all sat down together for a chat,' suggested Elaine.

Maybe one of them could manage the whole 'grown-up' thing.

'This is cosy!'

'Shut up, Miriam!' Four voices in unison—well, almost in unison; she thought Tiggi may have called her Millie—went some way towards persuading her that she should.

They had adjourned to the sitting room, where they all … sat. Charlie, Elaine and Sophia shared the couch. Tiggi and Miriam snagged an armchair each.

Elaine seemed to have taken charge of matters.

'What exactly is going on here? Millie?'

'Miriam.'

'Right, of course. Now it's Miriam. Well?'

'Why did you come here?'

'What?'

'Just now. Why did you come here? It wasn't to do this. What was it?'

'Actually I did come here to do this. Or something like it. I was at Mum's, and I saw you arrive—'

'But why? What's it to you?'

'Stop avoiding the issue.'

'I don't think I'm the one avoiding the issue. At least, not the only one.'

Miriam was quite proud of herself. She had Elaine on the back foot. She pressed her advantage.

'You're in love with Charlie.'

'So are you!'

'Wait a minute here.' Sophia couldn't remain seated.

'I'm not.' Tiggi gave a tentative wave from the armchair.

'Really?' Elaine turned on her. 'Yet here you are. Again.'

'Can I say something?' asked Charlie.

'No!' they shouted, in unison.

At the look on his face they—the girls—burst into spontaneous laughter. It didn't last, though. Sophia began to cry.

Oh shit!

In her mind, Millie saw Charlie stand and take her in his arms. A powerful weapon, tears.

A beat passed. Charlie remained seated. Another beat, and he stood. Too slow. Too late.

Something closed in Sophia's face. Without a word she marched from the room and out of the house. They heard a car engine start up, and the crunch of gravel as the car pulled away.

'My car!'

Charlie rushed to the open door. 'Sophia!' he called.

If Sophia had heard, Miriam didn't think she would have been impressed. Like the other women, she would have probably concluded that his main concern was for the car.

Being a grown-up wasn't going well for Miriam yet. She sat down again. The others—who had drifted towards the door—gradually joined her.

There was a long silence.

'Thank you, Charlie, for contacting my brother.'

Charlie was startled out of his reverie.

'Really?'

He seemed to be grasping after the idea that he may have done *something* right.

'Yes, Charlie.'

Miriam had never been the kind of person to be moved by the sight of a big-eyed puppy, or a cute baby ocelot. She was just as likely to kick a kitten out of the way as pick it up. So she struggled to understand her next impulse.

She knelt beside Charlie and hugged him.

He was unsure what to do with his hands, but she didn't mind. After a moment she returned to her seat.

'Don't know about anyone else, but I could use a joint.'

'Why not?' said Tiggi. 'What do you have?'

'This stuff's not bad, that Jack got me the other day.'

'He got it for you?' asked Elaine.

'Yeah …' Miriam paused, thinking back to the last time she had seen Elaine. 'Yeah, sorry about that. It was for me, not Charlie. Want some, Elaine? Charlie?'

'Not for me, thanks,' Elaine said stiffly.

'No …' Charlie waved a hand vaguely.

'Share?' she asked Tiggi. 'It's pretty potent.'

'Sure.'

The silence continued for a while longer. Everyone was absorbed in their own thoughts. Elaine wore a frown, Charlie gazed past everything and Tiggi sat back with her eyes closed. So that she and Tiggi could share the joint, Miriam positioned herself on the floor, with a cushion for padding, leaning back against the side of the chair.

The silence, which at first seemed like the pin-dropping variety, gradually assumed a greater complexity. Leather creaked as people shifted their positions. The house groaned and clicked in the warmth of the late-afternoon sun. Bird and animal sounds drifted in through the open windows, most of which Miriam could not identify beyond that broad classification. She became aware of Tiggi's breathing, above and behind her.

She could easily have fallen asleep, but made an effort not to, easing up on her intake.

'Charlie, Charlie, Charlie,' she said. How loudly she spoke she wasn't sure. Perhaps they were only her thoughts, because neither Charlie nor anyone else reacted.

Charlie and Elaine sat at opposite ends of the couch. Miriam tried to understand the distance between them. Were they close, or were they far apart? They were as far apart as they could be on the couch. Yet they shared the couch. They shared the room.

They shared the room. What was it that held them together?

'Sophia was never really part of this, was she Charlie? Not really.'

'Part of what?' Irritation and hope played in waves across his face.

'This. Us.' Miriam opened her arms to embrace the room.

'Shut up, Miriam. You're stoned.' Elaine's frown remained unchanged.

'You'd understand if you were too.'

'Where's my brother Jack now?'

'I don't know. He left. I think the pigs are after him for something he did in Bristol.'

'What?'

'I don't know. Maybe assault, or something.'

'Shit!'

'Yeah, but, think about it. How Charlie and me first met. And then how he found me again. Spooky.'

'It's not spooky.' Elaine remained taciturn.

'Yeah. It kind of is, though,' piped in Tiggi. Miriam had thought she was asleep.

'You're stoned too!'

Charlie didn't dismiss the idea completely. 'I've always thought …'

'What?'

'Well, that … that there was some kind of … I don't know. Destiny, maybe.'

'Yeah, that's it.' Miriam leapt on the concept. 'Destiny.' She felt compelled to touch her knee, and struggled not to laugh.

'I mean it.' Charlie remained very serious. And that's when he filled Miriam in about the 'Daughter of Abraham'. She thought it was a load of shit, but held that thought lest the dope speak through her.

'No, no, that's not it,' Miriam insisted. 'It's fish and chips. It's something to do with fish and chips. Fish. And chips. I was eating them when we met, and I want to eat them now. Is it time for dinner yet?'

Again Miriam struggled not to laugh. Tiggi didn't struggle.

Miriam gave up. Even Elaine's mouth twitched. Charlie pouted. That was the only way to describe it. But then he surrendered to a wry grin.

'Do you have any more of that? Maybe I'll see the funny side.'

SOMEONE HAD TO, SO ELAINE TOOK CHARGE. MILLIE—MIRIAM—could have her old room in the cottage. Her mum wouldn't mind. Well, she would. Elaine doubted she would want a teenage girl under her feet. But she could persuade her, if only by pointing out the impropriety of her staying with Charlie in the big house.

There was still Tiggi. She would leave the next day, she said.

'I'll be stranded!'

'I can take you back to Oxford.'

Charlie thought about it for a moment. 'No, I'll stay here. Out of the way. I need time to think.'

In Elaine's opinion, he had already done far too much of that.

And now, three weeks later, she had the letter from Australia. It was easy to spot amongst the morning's mail delivery. She took it out while sorting the mail, before Bill collected it for delivery. She would deliver this one herself.

She and Charlie had one long conversation during those three weeks. It was after a Sunday lunch. Her mother had taken to inviting him to join them on Sundays. Now that they were over his being 'his lordship, and all' they seemed almost ready to adopt him as a third son.

He asked Elaine to take a walk with him.

'How have you been, Elaine?' he began.

'I'm fine.' She had begun to think that Charlie was concerned mainly with Charlie. If he began with this conversational gambit, it was only for the sake of politeness. He would soon return to his main area of interest.

'Once again, I want to apologise about this business with Miriam.'

'It's none of my concern.'

'I wish it were.'

'What do you mean?'

'Nothing. Nothing.' He paused to gather his thoughts. His brow creased. 'I'd like to have another picnic with you at some stage. You never really had the chance to tell me your story.'

'There's not much to tell.'

'I'm sure there is.'

She let it pass.

'My mother's coming over in a few weeks. I'm sure she'd love to see you again.'

'That would be nice.'

'Hopefully we'll hear from Miriam's brother soon.'

'Yes. And if not?'

He waved this away.

'I have to talk to Sophia, too.'

'Good luck with that. What do you intend to do?'

'I'll take responsibility for the baby, of course, but I'll never marry her. If she'd even have me.'

They had walked away from the house, towards the village. Elaine could see her old school not very far away, and the church spire beyond it. Some of the leaves were starting to turn. Autumn was not far away. The sun was hot, though. She wished she'd worn a hat. She moved to the side of the road and stood under the shade of the trees.

'We should head back soon,' she suggested.

He offered a silent nod.

'Do you enjoy your job here? Your life here?' He took in the countryside with a sweeping gesture.

'My job … It's OK. Here though?' She drew in a deep breath. 'It's beautiful. Rather here than the city.'

'I think I could love it here too.'

'I'm not sure I exactly "love" it. I love my parents.'

'I …'

He reached out towards her.

She stepped back.

'You have a leaf …'

'Oh, right. Autumn's on the way.' She felt around until she found it.

'Why did you do that?'

'What?'

'Back away like that.'

She wasn't sure how to answer.

'We should get back.' He put the matter behind him, and began to walk away.

For a moment she didn't follow. He paused a few feet away and looked back. 'Are you coming?'

After a while he said, 'Things will get better, Elaine. I don't mean only for us. I mean for the world. They have to, don't they?'

She wasn't sure they did.

'I'll get better,' he continued. 'I'm learning, slowly, how to do this.'

'What?'

'Live.'

She wasn't so sure of that, either.

'Most of us just do it, Charlie. Like that bee over there, or those sheep in the field. Maybe if you asked a few less questions and just got on with it.'

'It comes naturally to you, I guess. It doesn't to me. I have to work at it.'

'Why?'

Instead of answering, he asked, 'How do you know what to do, from moment to moment?'

'I rarely think about it.'

'Exactly.'

'It doesn't always work out, Charlie. I've made some huge mistakes over the years.'

'Like what?'

'When I was in Birmingham …' Did she really want to talk about this?

'Go on.'

'There was a man, Maurice. I fell in love with him, or thought I did. Thought he loved me too. Turns out I was wrong … on both counts.'

'But you believed at the time that you loved him.'

'Yes.'

'So did you? I mean, are you only now thinking it couldn't have been love?'

'You see, this is what I don't do. I don't overthink things.'

'But if you believed you were in love, and it turned out not to be the case, how could you trust such a belief in future? Or if you really *were* in love, and this was the result, how could you ever allow it to happen again?'

'Overthinking, overthinking, overthinking.' Her voice began to rise.

'But this is it, you see. I mean, I find myself completely paralysed, not knowing what to believe, what to do. Should I turn left or should I turn right? Should I take the next step or should I stop right now?'

'You can never know, Charlie. No matter how much you think and plan beforehand. You can never know.'

'And that's terrifying.'

'You just do it and face the consequences.'

Charlie plunged his hands into his pockets and shivered.

'I wasn't always like this,' he said. 'Once I thought I knew what to do. I thought I had a "destiny".'

'The Daughter of Abraham.'

He nodded. 'Now, there's nothing.'

'There's eating, there's sleeping. There's Miriam and Sophia.'

'There's you.'

Something sucked the breath out of her lungs.

And now she had the letter from Australia to deliver.

The door was unlocked. It was always unlocked. She pushed it open when there was no answer to her knocking.

'Charlie?'

She could smell cigarette smoke and followed the trail down the hallway, into the kitchen and out through the back door. The wings of the house formed a courtyard. The fourth wall was formed by an unruly hedge, with a small gate leading through to the barns and stables beyond.

Charlie was sitting on the edge of the small fountain, looking away from the house. He was humming a tune she didn't recognise. Either it was a tune she didn't know, or he was humming it badly.

'Charlie.'

As he turned, his surprise was replaced with a broad smile. She could see the young boy who had been driven away almost twenty years before.

'You've taken some sun,' she remarked. 'You're not quite as pale and ghostly as you were.'

'The country life suits me. What brings you here?' He patted the low wall beside him.

As she sat, spray from the fountain occasionally brushed her as the breeze shifted. It was refreshing.

'This arrived this morning. Thought I would bring it in person.'

'Ah!'

He wasted no time in opening and reading it.

'Uh … I don't think he likes me. Or believes me.'

'What? Why?'

'Well, I think he thought I had something to do with Miriam's disappearance. You remember I told you …'

'Oh yes. Awkward.'

'So, he says, if I do now know where Miriam is, it's because I knew all along.'

'Hmm.'

He glanced again at the head of the letter. 'There's a phone number.'

'So you could phone him!'

'Or Miriam could.'

'Great idea! If she will. You can use the phone at the post office.'

'We should ask her.'

'What's she been doing with her time?'

'You'll never believe it. I caught her helping your mother with the baking yesterday. And one of the days last week, I saw her collecting the eggs. She's turning into you.'

'And how have *you* been spending your time?'

'Well, I do actually have a thesis to complete. I have my notes, but at some stage I'll need to go back to the Bod. There are some texts I need to check.'

'The Bod?'

'The Bodleian Library at Oxford.'

'So you're still set on finishing? I had the impression you'd lost interest.'

'Oh, well, I've come this far …'

'Good for you.'

'We should show Miriam this letter.'

They did.

'Shit, he doesn't like you, does he?'

Elaine glanced at her mother, who was again making tea. There was only the smallest flicker of an eyebrow when Miriam swore. No doubt she'd heard worse.

'You can phone him, Miriam,' Elaine said. 'Let him know you're OK.'

She didn't have a smart response to this.

'He won't want to hear from me,' she said after a while.

'Of course he will, dear.' Her mother set the tea things out, adding a plate of home-baked shortbreads and some apple cake.

'Thanks, Mum.'

'Our Miriam here helped make these, didn't you love.'

'Our Miriam' actually blushed.

'So, tomorrow morning,' Elaine suggested, 'why don't you come to the post office and make that call. There's about an eight or nine hours' time difference, so eleven in the morning should be about seven or eight in the evening there.'

'He won't want to talk to me, after all …'

Were they actual tears forming in her eyes?

'Miriam, dear'—Elaine took her hand—'my brother, as you rightly pointed out, is an arsehole.' She glanced apologetically at her mother. 'But I still love him.'

And so, at eleven the next morning, Charlie, Miriam and Elaine gathered at the post office. Charlie had borrowed Pete's car.

They placed the call.

'Sammy?'

The others could hear only half of the conversation.

It looked as though Miriam was going to cry. She fought back the tears and said instead, 'Charlie kidnapped me and has been holding me prisoner for the last two years.'

Even from the other side of the counter Elaine could hear Sammy's squeaky voice, raised in anger.

Miriam laughed. 'No, no, Sammy. I'm just kidding. Honestly, I'm just kidding … Calm down. No, really, I'm fine. Charlie found me a few weeks ago and brought me to the farm here. He … They've all been very kind.'

Then she did cry. 'I've been … I've been …' But she couldn't continue.

Charlie took the receiver. 'Mr Levinson … Sammy … It's Charlie here, Charlie Kollock … Of course … No, no … Yes, yes. Please do. Please do … Well, I don't know. Here, she's calmed down a little.'

He handed the phone back to Miriam. 'Yes?' She listened for a while. 'I don't … I don't … Maybe … Oh yes, yes! … OK. Charlie, do you need to say anything else to Sammy?' He shook his head. 'OK. OK, bye Sammy. Yes, I … I love … you too.'

Sammy would fly out as soon as possible, and, if she wanted to, Miriam would go back to Australia to live with him and his wife.

'And do you want to?' asked Charlie.

'Not sure I have too many options. We'll see. Maybe I'll go into hiding with Jack. Maybe you can whisk me away to Marrakesh.'

'Do you even know where that is?' Elaine asked with a wry grin.

'Does it matter?'

'Well, whether you decide to go or not, we should start on your paperwork. These things can take a while,' said Charlie.

He looked pleased with himself.

PART SIX

CHAPTER THIRTY-TWO

THE MONTHS OF SEPTEMBER, OCTOBER AND NOVEMBER BARRELLED towards Elaine and threatened to bowl her over.

On the last Friday in August, Charlie called on her at the post office.

'I've arranged to have the phone put on at the house,' he began. 'In the meantime, I spoke to Tiggi yesterday from the public phone. I've asked her to look in on Sophia.'

'Right.'

'Sophia has a phone, but I thought she probably wouldn't talk to me.'

'OK.'

'So I thought Tiggi could be a kind of intermediary.'

'Is there a point to this, Charlie?'

'I'd like your advice. Are you closing up soon?' He glanced at his watch. 'I thought we might have dinner at the pub.'

'I doubt that I can give you any advice.'

'Still …'

'I need another half hour here, then about the same to freshen up.'

'I'll meet you there, then, outside.'

'Fine.'

The sun was still above the rooftops to the west when Elaine joined Charlie. They manoeuvred a shade umbrella into place. He was nursing a beer. He ordered her a lemon squash.

'Have you ever been to Paris?' he asked

'I've never been further than Sussex.'

'Went there with Sophia last year. She was playing with the orchestra at the *Conservatoire*. Wonderful city.' His eyes looked far away, before abruptly focussing back on her. 'What are your plans for life, Elaine? Where do you see yourself in—say—ten years' time?'

'Probably not Paris. I don't know. Married, I guess, with a couple of children.'

'How will you ever find anyone to marry around here?'

'I'm not exactly looking.' She was annoyed by Charlie's questions and attitude. He was fidgeting, and his voice was edged with cynicism. He wouldn't look her in the eye. 'What's bothering you, Charlie?'

He released a long sigh. 'Well, decisions, you know? You make some decisions, and before you know it you're off down a path that you can't remember choosing; and you can't go back because the path disappears behind you.'

'So you keep going forward.'

'Yes, except there are too many paths forward; a new fork in the road every few steps.'

'I don't see so many choices ahead of me. Maybe you're the lucky one.'

'So what do I do about Sophia?'

'You say that as if it was all up to you.'

'What do you mean?'

'Sophia will determine Sophia's future.'

'I didn't mean … But I still should talk to her, right?'

'Maybe listen to her instead.'

Charlie gazed into his almost-empty glass. 'You're very wise, Elaine Pierce.'

'Hmph.'

'Will you come with me?'

'Where?'

'To talk to Sophia.'

Elaine struggled to keep her drink down. 'I thought if anyone would go with you it would be Tiggi.'

'I'd rather it was you.'

'No.'

'No?'

'In any language you like. It's time you grew up, Charles Kollock,' she added.

'You don't like me very much, do you?'

She couldn't help but be moved by the depth of sadness in his eyes. She took his hand across the table. 'It's not that, Charlie. I *do* like you. But you can be a bit draining at times. It's all just so … *intense*.'

'You should feel it from my side!' He managed a laugh, which decayed into a wry smile. 'OK,' he continued, with some attempt at resolution. 'I'll go and see Sophia … And listen to her. I'll be gone a few days, I imagine. Want to catch up with a few friends, as well as some papers in the library and my supervisor. He'll be wondering what's become of me. I hope to come back with my own car. Or a new one.'

They ordered dinner.

Charlie had been gone for almost two weeks when another letter arrived from Australia, this time addressed to Miriam. Elaine would play postman again. She was going to dinner at the farm that evening anyway.

Miriam had been very quiet during her last few visits. Her feistiness flashed briefly on occasions, only to be swallowed by a slight frown that creased her forehead. After dinner—after she had helped with the washing up—Elaine took her aside.

'Can we go to my—your room for a minute? I have a letter here from your brother.'

Elaine's room hadn't changed much over the years. Miriam had, so far, failed to leave her mark upon it. Except that the skimpy underwear on the floor would not have been there in Elaine's day. Nor would it have been so skimpy.

She wrinkled her nose at the smell. 'Don't smoke that in my parents' house, in *my* room.'

'I didn't. I don't. Well, maybe a couple of times …'

'No more!'

Elaine sometimes felt like a giant next to Miriam's slight form. She sat on the old leather armchair in the corner to reduce her size. Miriam sat on the bed and tucked her legs beneath her.

'I don't have anything to open it with.' She fluttered the aerogram towards her.

Elaine never went anywhere without a letter opener in her handbag. She handed it to Miriam, who looked at it and the letter for a moment. Moved it towards an edge. Glanced up at Elaine.

'I, er … I don't know where, how …'

'Give it to me.'

Elaine slit open the aerogram and handed it back.

'He's going to be here in October. Wants to take me back with him.'

'And is that what you want?'

'What choice …?' And she burst into tears.

Elaine was beginning to feel like a mother to these two dysfunctional children, Charlie and Miriam.

'Oh, for Pete's sake, what's wrong?'

'I think … I think … that I'm, you know …'

'No. What?'

'Having a baby.'

'Oh great! Whose is it?'

'Not sure. Probably your brother's. Chances are. But I'm not sure. Could be Charlie's.'

'But you're sure you're pregnant?'

'No, but … you know.'

'Well, we should get that checked out first.'

'OK.'

'But, whether you are or not …'

Miriam's sobs had ceased. Her face remained streaked with mascara. Elaine handed her a tissue from her purse as she continued to sniffle. She blew her nose with considerable gusto.

'But whether you are or not,' Elaine resumed, 'don't you think you'd be better off with family?'

'Sammy won't want anything to do with me now.'

'Surely that's not true!'

'I'll only be a burden.'

Elaine refrained from pointing out that she would be a burden with or without a baby in tow.

'Do you know if you have any nieces or nephews?' She deflected the conversation.

'Sammy has a two-year-old daughter and a new baby.'

'There you are, then! Instant friends for …' She waved vaguely in Miriam's direction.

'He called his daughter "Miriam".'

This led to more tears.

'So he thinks of you,' Elaine suggested.

'I guess. But …'

A few days later she took Miriam to see the local doctor to confirm the pregnancy. Elaine didn't have a car and didn't drive, so actually Pete took them in the car.

Elaine's brother Ed, in Canada, had two children. She and her parents had never seen them. Now, in all likelihood, she was going to be an aunt again. She reflected that she would probably never see this one either.

For the moment she refrained from informing her parents that they were—probably—going to have another grandchild.

Of course, there was also the problem of whether to tell Charlie. The child probably wasn't his. Nevertheless, he was likely to overreact to the news. So, when he returned to Chetwood later in the week, Elaine said nothing and advised Miriam to do the same.

Besides, the matter was largely pushed out of her mind by the telegram.

CHAPTER THIRTY-THREE

WHEN CHARLIE WAS IN HIS LATE TEENS HE WENT TO COLLEGE IN Pennsylvania. While there he became reacquainted with a childhood friend, Gillie. Gillie was the first girl he ever slept with. They squeezed into his narrow single bed in his room at the college dorm, when his roommate was out. He always knew when to go out.

He and Gillie would make love tirelessly and talk about their parents. They wouldn't make the mistakes they had made, they affirmed.

'We'll make new ones,' they would say, without great originality.

As Charlie climbed the stairs towards Sophia's apartment, he wondered how original his mistakes were.

Tiggi had phoned ahead on his behalf. Somehow she had persuaded Sophia to see him. Tiggi was waiting in the car, ready to come up and scrape his remains off the floor if need be.

His hand rose. His knuckles hovered, poised before the door. He remembered to breathe. He could do it. One more breath. The sound of a cello. He knew this one. Bach.

Knocking seemed like an act of violence, but he did it anyway. The sound reverberated throughout the hallway. The music died.

The door opened a crack, revealing Sophia's pale face. Thinner somehow, but with contrasting red patches at her cheek bones. Descriptions of consumptive heroines in nineteenth-century novels sprang to mind. There was something of that feverish intensity in her eyes. He put it down to her playing.

'May I—'

'Come in, Charlie.'

'How are you?'

'Fine. Tea?'

'Sure.'

He was not sure what to do. At one time he almost lived here. Spent many hours and days here. Should he sit and make himself at home? Should he follow her into the tiny kitchen? Scarcely room, really. He sat in one of the threadbare armchairs.

She knew how he took his tea. No need to ask. Was he a guest now? He was not sure how to act like a guest here.

'So …' She set out the tea service with some slices of cake. Yes, he was a guest. 'You wanted to talk.'

Some of his things were still here. In the bathroom. In the bedroom. At least he assumed they were still here. She may have tossed them out. Wasn't that what women did? The books. Were some of them his? And the LPs? The Dylan was his.

'I should take my stuff,' he suggested.

'Oh Charlie! Is that why you're here? Your stuff? My life is ruined and you're thinking about your stuff!'

'What do you mean—'

'My career. My life. How can I do that with a baby hanging off of my boobs?'

He'd told Elaine he would never marry Sophia now. He'd told himself that. Yet he said, 'If we get married—'

'And what? You'll hang the baby off of *your* boobs?'

'I don't know. Nannies and stuff … I always had a nanny.'

'And look how well you turned out.'

'We could do it, Sophia.'

'And you'll go work in your family business?'

His hesitation was once again eloquent.

'Right. That's it then.'

Sophia stood and paced back and forth between the sofa and the kitchen door. The tea and cake had been forgotten.

'Take your fucking things then,' she said at last. 'I packed them in some cartons.' She waved a hand towards the bedroom.

'You know, Charlie,' she continued suddenly. The way she said 'Chawlie' choked him up. Whatever she was going to say caught in her throat too.

He stood and moved towards her but she held her hand out to stop him and stepped back, bumping into her cello which rested in its cradle next to her stool. It fell to the floor and cried out in pain. She crouched down next to it. 'No, no.' She picked it up and held it to her breast like a child.

'I'm sorry—'

'Don't say that! Don't you *dare* say that!'

For a moment she held the cello by the neck and pointed the spike towards him. Had anyone ever been stabbed by a cello? Was he to be the first?

He was spared, he was sure, by her concern for the cello, not her concern for him. She drew it back to her breast.

'Go!'

He did so, unaccompanied by any boxes. He could always purchase another copy of Dylan.

'How did it go?' Tiggi was leaning against the side of her car, smoking.

'My car!' he suddenly remembered. There was no sign of it on the street. He didn't have the keys anyway. 'I can't go back up.'

'It went that well, huh?'

'I don't know what I was thinking.' He chose to ignore the shift of Tiggi's eyes heavenward.

She sighed. 'Shall I talk to her?'

'No. Leave her be. I guess I can buy a new car as well as a new Dylan.'

'What?'

'Never mind.'

'Don't be a complete arsehole, Charlie. You can't buy a new car just because you're too much of a coward to face Sophia again.'

'I'm not ...' But Tiggi strode towards the entrance of Sophia's building.

A few moments later she re-emerged carrying two boxes. 'Give me a hand with these. They're bloody heavy.'

They loaded them in the boot of her car and she dangled keys in front of his face. 'It's parked around the corner in Orsett Terrace. I'll drop you there.'

'How did she seem?'

'Upset. Angry. What do you expect?'

'How can I fix this?'

'Give her time.'

When they found his car there was a scratch extending the length of the passenger side. He hoped it had been inflicted by a stranger.

He spent a few days in Oxford on thesis-related matters. Although he was somewhat distracted, the academic world had its attractions. Dusty bookshelves. Dusty ideas. There was something unthreatening, even comforting, about them. It was easy to believe in ghosts within the shadowy nooks of the library. There were moments when he thought he might be one himself, wandering around, not realising he had been dead for decades, if not centuries.

The sense that he was haunting the world did not diminish after he returned to the farm. He had frightened away all the occupants.

He could still be surprised, though, as he was on the Monday morning after he returned.

He shaved, washed and dressed, and headed downstairs for some breakfast. As he passed the door to the sitting room he sensed movement. Perhaps nothing more than a shift in the light, but enough to make him pause and glance inside.

'Mother!'

She slumped in an armchair, her eyes closed, her hands clasped together in her lap.

'Mother,' he repeated, 'what are you doing here? You didn't … I wasn't expecting you for another couple of months.'

She opened her eyes, but they remained unfocused for a moment. He sat on the sofa opposite. 'Are you OK?'

'Ah, what a question. Am I OK? I think so, yes. Come here.'

He bent down and hugged her, and then sat on the edge of the coffee table, holding her hands. She held his eyes with one of those penetrating gazes. Gone was the lack of focus, the moment of confusion.

'When did you get here? Why didn't you let me know you were coming?'

'Just now. It was a … spur of the moment thing.'

He shouldn't have been surprised. She was a master of the unexpected and the non sequitur.

'I'm going to get some breakfast. Would you like something?'

'No. I really couldn't eat a thing.' She laughed unexpectedly.

'Tea, though, I'll make some tea. Just a moment.'

They talked for almost two hours. It had been a while since they had spent so much time alone together. Not that they talked all the time. There were long moments of silence. She didn't touch her tea.

Charlie talked more than he had for years. He brought her up to date on the situation—the situations—with Sophia and Miriam. Perhaps she was the one person who could truly understand. Perhaps they shared a little of that necessary insanity.

'I've not been a good mother,' she said at one point. She didn't add, 'But I did my best.' Nor did he offer her that superficial comfort.

'I've never been entirely sure that I was human. Or even alive,' she added later.

He knew the feeling.

Their silence was interrupted by a knock at the door.

'Excuse me.'

He opened the door to Elaine.

'Elaine. Come in. You'll never guess—'

'Charlie, it's—'

'It's Mother—'

'You know?'

'I don't think you two have seen each other since that summer when we were kids, have you? Come in. She'll be so pleased to see you.'

'What do you mean?'

'I was totally surprised, but she just turned up out of the blue.'

'Who did?'

'Mother.'

'But Charlie …'

She burst into tears. Charlie had no idea why. 'Come in. What's wrong? Have some tea.'

She didn't move. 'Charlie, I wanted to tell you in person, because this … This is just so impersonal.' She waved a piece of paper.

'What is it? A telegram?'

'Yes. I'm so sorry, Charlie.'

'What's happened?'

He reached for the paper and she yielded it up to him reluctantly. He read it, but it made no sense.


```
Regret  to  report  your  mother's  death  Vehicle
accident Please come home asap Funeral Friday

Charles Kollock Snr
```


'But … But … This is nonsense. Some kind of joke. A sick joke, Elaine.' He rushed into the sitting room, laughing. 'Mother, reports of your death are—'

But the sitting room was empty.

Elaine was confused. What was Charlie talking about?

She followed him into the sitting room, but he rushed past her into the kitchen.

'Mother? She must have gone outside.'

When that yielded no results he rushed past her again and up the stairs. 'Mother!'

Elaine followed slowly.

There were six bedrooms upstairs. Only two doors were open, the one on the right closest to the stairs, and the one on the left at the end of the corridor.

The room on the right was obviously Charlie's: bed unmade, clothes on the floor. Elaine headed towards the other door.

Charlie looked up from where he was sitting on the bed. 'I don't understand where she could have gone.'

'Charlie …'

'It can't be true, Elaine. She was *here*.'

She sat next to him on the bed. 'I don't know what to say. Why would your father lie? And where is she *now*?'

A sob caught in Charlie's throat.

She held him.

The tears flowed. She felt the dampness on her blouse. The weight of his head on her breast.

She stroked his back. His hair.

He lifted his head a little and kissed her neck. At the side. At her throat. Just above her breast.

She held her breath.

Her hand stopped moving, resting on his head.

His hand moved to her top button. Undid it. And another. His kisses moved lower.

She was frozen.

Another button, and another. Soon her blouse fell open.

She didn't resist as he pushed the blouse off her shoulders, or as he moved aside the top of her bra to place kisses there, on the newly exposed flesh.

For the next thirty minutes or so, she offered no resistance at all.

Sometime later, Charlie phoned his father, when it was a decent time on the east coast. He seemed to have accepted the truth of his father's telegram, and the phone call confirmed it. He wept inconsolably.

Elaine had stayed with him, preparing food that went uneaten and cups of tea that were ignored. It seemed unwise to leave him alone.

She stayed the night.

She shared his bed.

The regrets would come later.

He left for America on the Wednesday.

CHAPTER THIRTY-FOUR

AT THE END OF THE DAY ELAINE CYCLED OUT TO THE FARM TO GIVE Miriam the news. Her brother Sammy was booked on a flight and would be arriving in London in the last week of October.

'I hate this fucking baby,' she said. 'I'm throwing up every morning.'

But she had put on weight and was looking healthier than Elaine had ever seen her.

'He'll be here in about six weeks, Miriam,' she reiterated.

'Do I have to go to London to meet him? Is he coming here?'

'He'll come here. Stay a few days. You need to get to know each other again, right?'

'When's Charlie getting back?'

'I'm not sure. Maybe a week or two. He didn't say. The funeral's Friday.'

'I want to see him before I go. What if he decides to stay longer? Or not come back at all!'

'Of course he's coming back. He'll be home in plenty of time. You're brother won't be here for weeks yet.' The thought of Charlie *not* coming back almost stopped her heart.

'You've definitely decided to go back to Australia, then?' she added, to settle herself.

'I suppose so.'

That was about as definite as Miriam would ever get.

Elaine was staying in the house while Charlie was away. At first, when Charlie had asked her, she was a little nervous. Charlie had described in great detail the conversation he'd had with his mother the day she died. He had been quite convincing. Elaine didn't want to bump into her or anyone else's ghost during the middle of the night.

Fortunately, her sleep was undisturbed until she heard the front door open late one night. A light came on downstairs. She didn't imagine that spectres required artificial lighting.

She had heard nothing from Charlie. No word about when he planned to return. She was beginning to realise that this was typical of him. He lived in a world of his own, often only vaguely aware of the other world, and people, around him.

She slipped into a dressing gown and crept to the bedroom door. 'Charlie?'

'Elaine.'

She wondered what time it was. Late.

She moved to the top of the stairs and met his eyes as he stood in the doorway of the sitting room.

'Elaine,' he said again.

She heard tears and weariness in his voice.

'How …?' *How do you ask something like this*. 'How was it?'

'Oh, Elaine, it was *awful*.'

She moved down the stairs and embraced him.

'My father … They say there's no reason she should have been driving there on that road, at that time of night. My father …'

She pulled him closer. His head rested on her shoulder. His breath brushed against her ear. She was aroused. And ashamed that she was aroused.

'My father says she took her own life. Suicide.'

'Come to bed, darling.'

Had she just called him darling?

And she led this little boy to bed and took him as far inside her as she could.

And she was both thrilled and ashamed.

And still the days and weeks barrelled towards her and threatened to bowl her over.

In the middle of October Charlie received a phone call from Tiggi. Elaine was no longer staying at the house, but he came by the post office to tell her.

'What's happening, Elaine? The world's caving in. What's happening?'

'Charlie, what is it?'

'It's Sophia. And the baby. Tiggi rang to say that Sophia lost the baby.'

'Oh Charlie, I'm so sorry.'

'Yes. But no. It wasn't an accident. Sophia got rid of it. She rang Tiggi a day or two later. She wasn't well. She was bleeding. Tiggi called our friend Dickie, and they managed to get Sophia into hospital for a couple of nights.'

Once again Elaine found herself hugging Charlie, but she was horrified. Speechless.

'Is Sophia OK?' she asked eventually.

'Yes. Well, I don't know. Physically, yes. Tiggi and Dickie want to bring her out to the farm for a few days. They don't think she should be alone. And maybe the peace and quiet …'

'When?'

'Later today.'

'Do you want me there?'

'Could you?'

How could she be in the same town, let alone room, as Sophia now? But yes, she said, she could.

She'd been wanting to talk to Charlie about something else, but it wasn't the right time to tell him that her own monthlies were late.

Doctor Richard Hawkins—Dickie—was the first homosexual man Elaine had ever met. At least as far as she knew. There were plenty to tell her later that she was incredibly naïve. All she thought at the time was, *Oh my God, someone else in love with Charlie!*

Her brother Jack would have called him a fag. He was, indeed, foppish. But she found him fun and surprisingly flirtatious. He flirted with Charlie and her—and anyone else in the room—with equal—not to say 'gay'—abandon.

But Sophia was immune to his flirtation and flamboyance. Untouchable, it seemed. She had locked herself away somewhere.

Elaine found herself playing hostess.

'Tiggi, lovely to see you again.'

'Here, Sophia, can I take your coat?'

'Milk, Doctor Hawkins? Yes, all right: "Dickie".'

'Please help yourselves to the bickies. Mum and I baked them yesterday.'

'Charlie, it's getting a bit chilly. Could you start the fire?'

Charlie hovered in the background. It seemed a good idea to give him something to do.

Sophia was yet another of Charlie's thin, pale women. Elaine wondered where on earth she herself fit into that schema. Sophia had always been pale, with her red hair and fair colouring, but now her freckles stood out on her face like the inverse of constellations. Every so often she shivered.

'Tiggi, could you fetch a blanket from upstairs please. The cupboard just back from the stairs. Yes, of course, you already know that.

'Sophia.' Elaine sat beside her on the couch and took her hand. It was thin, cold and dry. Sophia whispered something to her that she struggled to hear. She leaned in closer, trying not to react to her bad breath.

'I had to do it. You know that, right? He knows that? I couldn't … I couldn't … My music.'

'No one's judging you, dear.' Sometimes you just say what needs to be said.

Sophia didn't cry. Her eyes seemed to burn with a dry heat.

'I'll organise some food. Who's staying? Tiggi? Dickie? OK, then. I could use a hand.'

For the next few days Elaine played 'mother'. She didn't share a bed with Charlie while the others were there. Especially Sophia.

'Physically she's just fine,' Dickie assured them. He was making another house call on the weekend.

'Did you bring her cello? No? Really? She needs it. She loves it more than the baby. More than she ever loved you,' Elaine said to Charlie.

'I'll get it,' Tiggi offered. 'I have the key to her apartment. I'll go now and be back in the morning.'

That cello probably saved her life. Over the next week or two she had to be coaxed into playing it, but gradually she did. Gradually someone emerged.

Yet it wasn't quite Sophia. Elaine didn't know her well enough to say, but Charlie could tell.

'Something's gone, Elaine.'

Elaine didn't have a great deal of sympathy for her. She was more certain, now, that she was pregnant herself. The soreness of her breasts; some morning nausea. She could never do what Sophia had done. Of course something had gone.

'It will take time,' was all she said.

But it was precisely time that seemed to be barrelling towards Elaine, only to be lost somewhere behind her.

CHAPTER THIRTY-FIVE

MIRIAM DIDN'T LIKE BEING IGNORED. THAT'S WHAT IT FELT LIKE, WITH all the fuss about Sophia at the big house. She thought maybe she should do the same thing, but had no idea how to go about it. Maybe she should just barge in there and announce her pregnancy to all and sundry. All and sundry seemed to be there at the moment. But she wasn't.

Then again, her brother would be here in a day or two.

She wanted to run away.

'Here are the eggs, Mrs Pierce.'

'Miriam, dear—I'm sure I've told you already—it's about time you called me Nellie.'

'Oh, I don't think I could really. How about … How about Auntie Nellie?'

'That would be lovely.'

The first time Miriam had collected the eggs—'gone aggy'—she had just about vomited. The smell of the coop. Those beady eyes staring at her. Heads jerking about. One of the fucking things pecked her! What was that on the eggs? She broke two that first day.

Only one the next day. And she clucked right back at that bitch of a chook that tried to peck her again.

She hadn't broken any eggs now for some weeks. She felt ridiculously proud of herself.

Mrs Pierce—Auntie Nellie—had been trying to talk her into milking a cow. No fucking way!

She wondered if she was slowly turning into Elaine.

'Sit thee down, love, and get the weight off your feet.'

'I'm fine.'

'Now, there baint much of you, and in your condition …'

'My condition?'

'Aah, I know the signs well enough.' Mrs Pierce sat opposite Miriam and held her eyes. The older woman's own eyes shimmered with doubt. 'Is it …? My boy Ed lives in Canada, and we've never set eyes on his two nippers. Jack's not given us any grandchildren. That we know of anyway. Unless …' Her eyes fell to Miriam's stomach.

'It's Jack's.'

'You're sure?'

'I'm sure.' She wasn't, entirely, but it seemed most likely. And it seemed like the right thing to say.

'Then …' Tears pooled in her eyes. 'You know …'

'What, Auntie Nellie?'

'Well, you're up and leaving us in a few days, likely enough.'

Shit. She's going to bloody cry!

'Not sure I have much choice, Auntie Nellie. Sammy's the only family I've got.'

'Well … If the baby's Jack's, I reckon that makes us your family too.'

'So, what are you saying?'

'You could stay here with us … for as long as you like.'

The table was made from a single slab of wood, as far as Miriam could tell. Scratches and stains had been polished in until they were part of the fabric. A work of art. Painted by the passage of years and lives. *What the fuck's wrong with me? All this emotional shit!* She was on the verge of tears herself.

'I don't know what to do.'

'Well, no need to decide yet. Let's wait for yer brother, first.' She patted Miriam's hand across the table.

Waiting was not something Miriam did well. She needed to find something to break.

Pete—Pete with too many teeth and who smelled like pigs—was an easy target. After lunch the next day she intercepted him on the way out in the truck.

'Can I get a lift?'

'Where too, miss?'

'Where are you going?'

'The feed store in Barrow Gurney, Miss. Can't see as you'd want to go there.'

'Let's play hooky for the afternoon. Let's go to that seaside place, West …'

'Weston-super-Mare, miss?'

'Yeah! Let's do the arcades and rides!'

'I don't think so, miss.'

'Do they have a real beach there? Not more of those damn pebbles.'

'It's a lovely beach, I reckon.'

'So, let's go.'

'I don't think so, miss.'

Miriam paused for a moment. Standing next to the driver's side door, she leaned towards the open window. 'If you take me there, I'll let you see my tits. You'd like to see my tits, wouldn't you, Pete?' She licked her lips. 'Maybe even touch them.'

Her tits had become significantly augmented over the weeks, although Miriam scarcely showed elsewhere.

'Miss, I'm sure your tits is lovely, but if I don't get to the feed store pronto, Mr Pierce will have my balls. And they mean more to me than your tits, miss.'

Miriam wanted to storm away in anger but, in fact, she laughed.

'Well, for that, here's a freebie.' She lifted her tee-shirt and exposed her breasts.

'Thanks, miss. I'll be on my way now, then.' She watched him pull away.

'You really should be wearing a bra, young lady!'

Miriam nearly jumped out of her skin. Mrs Pierce—Auntie Nellie—was standing at the kitchen window, tea towel over her shoulder.

For a moment, Miriam felt like responding as she might have responded to her mother, but that gave rise to many conflicting thoughts and emotions. A sarcastic response stuck in her throat. She tasted half-digested donuts.

When she vomited, it was easy to pass it off as morning sickness.

'Oh, come inside, dear. You really are puggle 'eaded sometimes.'

The train was late. Miriam couldn't quite believe that it would ever arrive. Or, if it did, that Sammy would be aboard. Or, if he was, that he would be pleased to see her.

The day had dawned grey and miserable. Drizzle came and went with sudden gusts of wind. The old rooster crowed. Today it sounded like a complaint.

Miriam's room—Elaine's room, in fact—was at the back of the cottage overlooking the courtyard—the small cottage forming one side, a wing of the main house forming another, and a row of wooden outbuildings forming the third. The fourth side transitioned gradually into woodland that lined much of the road into the village.

So, here it is.

The day that would decide her future.

She had slept very little, and been plagued by disturbing dreams when she did. In many of them she lay in a dark room on a dirty mattress. From the darkness a figure loomed before her. Sometimes it bore Charlie's features, sometimes Elaine's; sometimes Jack's, wearing a smile that bared his crooked teeth. Worse, though, was the faceless man. She knew intuitively it was her brother Sammy. The fact that she could not see his face brought her awake, trembling. Even awake, she struggled to remember his face. She struggled to recall her mother's face. Her father's. How had her past become so lost to her?

She was forced to admit she had done all she could during the last few years to bury it, dead or alive.

Now part of the past was returning to reclaim her.

Auntie Nellie was kind enough not to insist that Miriam get up early to carry out her usual duties, but at around 7.30 she popped her head around the door and offered to make breakfast.

Miriam's stomach churned, and she shook her head.

'Not even a little porridge, love?'

'Maybe a little.'

'And a nice cup of tea.'

When Mrs Pierce returned a few moments later, she sat on the bed at Miriam's side.

'Young Mr Kollock's downstairs.'

'What's he want?'

'He had a phone call a short time ago from your brother.' She paused while Miriam ate some porridge, head down, avoiding Mrs Pierce's eyes. 'He's coming in on the 10.10 to Bath.' Again she paused. 'You'll be wanting to go with him—with Mister Charlie—when he picks him up, I'm thinking.'

Miriam wasn't thinking that. Miriam was thinking two things. *One,* that she really needed to vomit up the porridge she had just eaten. *Two,* that Spain might be nice at this time of year. Or not. She had no idea. But she most definitely did *not* want to think about going to the railway station to meet her brother.

The need to vomit became urgent, and she threw off the bed clothes and ran down the hall towards the bathroom.

About half an hour later she came downstairs to find Charlie still sitting in the kitchen, chatting to Auntie Nellie.

'More tea, dear?' asked Mrs Pierce. Miriam hadn't touched the last cup. 'Sit down.'

'You have to protect me from your brother, Miriam,' Charlie said with a wry grin. 'Last time we met he flattened me.'

'Are you OK?' he asked.

Miriam recalled the ghostly face with the dark shadows under the eyes that had greeted her in the mirror a few moments ago. She had forgotten that Charlie didn't know about her pregnancy. She had grown used to the look.

'I'm fine,' she muttered. 'Just nervous.' Feeling some of her spirit return as she sipped the tea—Auntie Nellie had slipped in some honey—she added, 'You look like shit yourself.' Dried bird poo, actually. Charlie was never dark enough to look like a healthy pile of dog shit.

'We leave in about an hour, Miriam.'

And now, an hour an a half later, the train finally glided to a halt. Doors opened. Legs descended steps. Faces turned here and there, searching, eyes wide, mouths poised to greet. Announcements reverberated. Laughter exploded. Words shattered.

People began to close in around Miriam and Charlie, where they waited on the platform. Charlie bobbed up and down.

'You don't even know what he looks like,' Miriam muttered.

People were close enough to smell. They formed a wall around her. She would never be able to see Sammy. She couldn't remember what he looked like either. She would have made a break for it, had there been a breach in the human palisade that enclosed her.

She scanned the area, looking for a fracture, a weakness, through which she might escape. Charlie held her arm, as if sensing her desire. She pulled away. She would have run, too. She had run before. She could run again. But then a head bobbed up in front of her, behind a shoulder that didn't belong to it. A head with dark, curly hair and impenetrably brown eyes. Those eyes met hers.

'Jeez, Miriam, I'd forgotten how bloody tiny you were!'

He pushed through the palisade and dragged her into an embrace.

She had forgotten how tall and muscular he was.

'Jeez, are they feeding you? There's practically nothing of you.'

Miriam would have spoken, but he held her too tightly. That was good. She wasn't sure what would have come out of her mouth, otherwise.

'Mr Levinson? I'm Charlie. I don't know if …'

'Yeah, yeah, I remember you all right. What have you been doing to her? She looks like death warmed up.'

He eased his grip on Miriam and that's when they came out of her mouth. Words her mind had scarcely taken time to form.

'I'm going to have a baby,' she said.

'What?!' Two voices collided.
'I'll kill you, you fucker.'

CHAPTER THIRTY-SIX

'WHAT?!' SAID CHARLIE.

The look in Sam Levinson's eyes suggested to Charlie that this might be a good time to duck. 'I'll kill you, you fucker.'

'No, no, no. It's not his,' Miriam was saying.

Not mine.

Until that moment, Charlie hadn't really thought about the baby that Sophia had … lost. His concern had been for Sophia. But now it struck him that a child—his child—had been … erased. And now this child wasn't his.

He'd assumed he'd have children, one day. It hadn't yet become a high priority.

But suddenly he felt as if he had lost, not one, but two children.

And his mother had lost two grandchildren. What would she have thought about that?

Some part of his future had died.

'Charlie?' Miriam tugged the sleeve of his sweater.

'What? Yes. We should go. Let me help with your bags.'

Charlie felt somewhat insubstantial beside Miriam's brother. Sammy and Miriam looked nothing alike. Charlie might have been Miriam's brother, rather than Sammy. Sammy was tall, solidly built and dark of colouring, both his hair and his skin. Some of the darkness of his skin was surely due to the sun, but not all, Charlie suspected. There was something of the south of Italy or the Middle East about him.

During the drive, Sammy asked Miriam many questions, few of which she answered fully or eagerly. Charlie learned little more about her 'missing years'.

Sammy told her about his wife and children, about where they lived, and how much she would like it there. He pulled a photograph from his wallet and passed it from the back seat to Miriam. Her reaction was difficult to read, even when she said, 'Your wife has a big butt.'

That the photograph revealed nothing of the woman's posterior anatomy did nothing to temper her comment.

'It's like bloody Paddington Station in here,' she remarked when they reached the house.

Charlie had to admit the house was a little crowded today. Tiggi and Sophia were still staying there. Elaine was visiting, as were Anthony and Dickie, the last in a semi-official capacity, checking on his patient. With the arrival of himself, Sammy and Miriam, eight people had to find positions around the sitting room.

Miriam looked sullen. Sammy looked uncomfortable.

After brief introductions, Charlie suggested, 'I'll show you to your room. Miriam, why don't you come up with us.

'I imagine you'd like some time together,' he added in the room. 'But first, about the baby … And let's try to keep a calm head here! Are you sure?'

'Yeah, I'm sure.'

Charlie glanced nervously at Sammy. 'And it's … Jack's?'

'Yes. I think so. Yes, almost certainly.'

'Almost?' Sammy shot Charlie a threatening glance.

'Well yeah, sure.'

'But it could be his? You've touched my sister?'

'It wasn't like that.' Charlie wasn't at all sure that he could explain what it *was* like. He hoped Miriam would offer some kind of explanation.

'Sammy, it wasn't Charlie's fault. I seduced him. In the middle of the night. He didn't even know what was going on at first. And he thought it was …'

Sammy sneered.

Charlie was impressed with Miriam's honesty.

'I thought—hoped, actually—no offence, Miriam—I hoped it was Elaine.'

Sammy looked unconvinced. 'Is there anyone you haven't …?'

'I love Elaine.' And, once again, Charlie realised he meant it. *I love Elaine*.

'And if the baby *is* yours?'

'You *love* her?'

Sammy and Miriam spoke simultaneously, both confronting Charlie. Could he say—do—nothing right?

'Miriam,' he said, 'you're a sweet kid … Well, no you aren't really, are you? You're manipulative and I suspect you snack on kittens when no one's looking. But you *are* just a kid. I don't suppose we'll ever know for sure whose baby it is. I'll support you any way I can, either way. I'm sorry you have to deal with this. I think maybe—just maybe—you're going to be OK. That you'll turn into a lovely young woman—and even mother. But I don't love you. I love Elaine. I've probably loved her since I was about eight years old.'

Miriam looked at Charlie for an uncomfortably long time. Several expressions crossed her face, the landscape shifting subtly. Her eyes changed colour, from deep-ocean green to mint green, as different responses flitted through her mind.

'The baby's Jack's. I'm sure it is. It has to be.'

Those green eyes. Charlie couldn't help it. Thoughts of 'the Daughter of Abraham' resurfaced. And of his mother. What did it all mean? Did it mean anything? Could he make it mean something? *Why could you never speak plainly? Why did you have to go?*

'You must be there for the Daughter of Abraham when she needs you.'

He didn't know how. Was Miriam the Daughter of Abraham? Was the moment now? Had he fulfilled his mother's prophecy by returning Miriam to her brother?

'Thank you for clearing that up, Miriam. Thank you for being honest.' It seemed the safest thing to believe.

He needed to talk to Elaine.

The opportunity did not present itself for a few days. Anthony stayed on for a day or two and persuaded Charlie to go for a two-day hike through the Mendips, around Chew Valley Lake. The circuit they would follow was only about five miles, but they would take it slowly and camp overnight.

Although it was a little chilly, no rain was forecast, and the weather was not yet intolerable.

'You're idiots, the two of you,' Tiggi admonished them. 'Look at you. Anthony, when did you ever walk further than from the lecture theatre to the toilet?'

Charlie, however, was rather proud of the way he had toughened up during the past few months, working around the house and garden.

'I'll look after him, Tiggi. Don't you worry.'

Elaine did not show herself at the house for a day or two after they returned. Both of them had colds.

'Look at you!'

'I suppose your dear mother has some ancient concoction that will set us right in no time,' Anthony suggested with a smirk.

'Stop being a jerk, Anthony. Elaine'—Charlie led her aside into the hallway—'let's go outside for a moment. I want to talk.'

'It's much too cold outside, you numbskull. You should be inside in the warmth. Maybe even in bed.

'Not like that, silly.' She slapped his hand away from her waist as he tried to pull her towards him. 'I don't want your germs!'

'Let's go upstairs. Just to talk. Honestly.'

'All right. As a matter of fact … There's something *I* want to talk to *you* about.'

'What?'

'Not here.'

In Charlie's room they sat on the bed, but not too closely together.

'What did you want to say, Elaine?'

'You first.'

'No, you first. You came here to say something, obviously.'

'OK.' She took a deep breath and exhaled slowly. Even so, she did not speak immediately. Charlie looked at her again. What was it about her? Her hair, certainly. Her spirit was in her hair. To someone who did not know her, that would have sounded odd. She always dressed conservatively. She was not conventionally beautiful or even, perhaps, pretty. She seemed reserved. A librarian or … a postmistress. But such people would miss the point. Her spirit was in her hair. It was unruly. Untameable. Somehow it interacted with the world. It caught the wind. It caught the leaves of trees. It moved freely. With her hair—her spirit— Elaine painted her way through life.

She left streaks across his vision.

'OK,' she said again. 'Charlie, I'm having a baby.'

'OK,' Charlie repeated. What else could he say? What was the universe doing to him? *The universe taketh away, and the universe giveth.* Or something like that. He thought he might be going slightly crazy. Or that he was a character in some crazy person's novel.

'It's a lot to take in,' he said, as much to himself as to Elaine. 'All of it. All of the last few months. It's a lot to take in.'

'I know.'

They breathed. He felt his breath move in and out of his body. It was reassuringly real and ordinary. *OK.*

'But I'm glad, Elaine. You have to believe that.' He slid closer to her along the bed, held her face in his hands and turned it towards him. 'I was going to say to you—and please, believe me; this was what I planned to say, and it has nothing to do with this, with the baby—I love you, Elaine, and I want to marry you. I want to spend a lifetime with you here. Or wherever. Anywhere.'

'Oh, Charlie, yes, yes!'

They didn't tell anyone about their decision for a few days. There were too many other issues to consider. Sophia was on the improve, it seemed. She had even begun playing her cello with a little more energy. Mournful pieces, but it seemed an improvement.

There were still conversations Charlie felt he should have with her, before making any kind of public announcement. God only knew how she would take the news.

Then there was Miriam. It was difficult to fathom what was going on in her mind. Sammy had been very angry with Charlie, but more so with Jack. 'Who is this "Jack"? Where is the bastard? I'll murder him!' Miriam was unusually quiet, even in the face of her brother's anger.

Some of that anger was directed towards Miriam when she didn't demonstrate an immediate desire to return to Australia with him. Charlie also struggled to understand this, until Elaine had a word with him as they went for a walk together. The weather was turning cold, and most of the trees were bare.

'I thought we might go to Fernlea House soon. I worry about my grandmother all alone there.'

'Is there no one there with her?'

'There's a handful of servants. I think one of her friends stays there occasionally. We won't be able to keep the servants on, though, forever; and the house costs a fortune to run and maintain, even though very few rooms are actually used these days. And with winter coming …'

'You said before you might ask her to come and live here.'

'Would you be OK with that?'

'Yes, of course.'

'So once all the mess is sorted out here'—he waved vaguely back in the direction of the house—'let's pay Grandma a visit and raise the topic with her. I'm not sure how she'll respond. We may have to sell Fernlea. If we can find a buyer, these days.'

'Yes, about this "mess". I had a chat to Mum yesterday about Miriam.'

'I don't understand what's going on in her mind.'

'Apparently Mum has offered to let Miriam stay at the farm. She wants to help raise her grandchild. Miriam can't make up her mind. In some ways it would be easier for her here, but she doesn't want to upset her brother. Or lose him. Or so I gather. She doesn't say much to me.'

'What would you do in her place?'

'I think the last two or three years have built a wall between Miriam and her life before that. I think a lot of guilt's gone into building that wall. I think Sammy reminds her of everything she's lost. He doesn't really *know* her anymore. And I don't think she can ever go back to being the Miriam she was. His little sister. Here she can have a fresh start.'

'You're a wise woman, Elaine Pierce.'

'And, well, she's kind of *our* family now.'

'Even though she doesn't talk to you?'

'Oh, I think she'll come around.'

'You're a good woman, Elaine Pierce.'

'Stop it, silly.' She punched his arm and laughed.

On the Sunday, Miriam came knocking at the door. Earlier, Elaine had warned him that she would. She had sat down with Miriam and her mother for a little conference. Miriam had something to tell him, Elaine said. And to tell her brother. She wouldn't drop any hints, but Charlie thought he knew what she would say. Clearly, she had made a decision. He hoped she would stay. Elaine was right: in some strange way they had become family.

Charlie was upstairs when the knock came. Elaine called up to him. He had been having another conversation, this time with Sophia. A conversation that was long overdue.

Sophia's father would be back in England within a few days. He had an apartment in Cambridge. Sophia would go and stay with him for a while.

'I'm almost ready,' she had said. She was referring to her studies. Early in the new year she would face her final exams. Then …? Well, then she would move on. She was ready to move on, she said.

'I'm really sorry, Sophia. Sorry things didn't work out. I guess in the end we just want different things.'

Sophia didn't answer immediately. Perhaps he should have said nothing. Perhaps what had happened between them—happened to her—required more than 'sorry'. But what more, Charlie could not conceive. He had treated Sophia badly. No question about it. But what could he do? How do you fix the past? He could only hope that the future would be good to her—to them.

As Charlie thought about his future with Elaine and their child—their children—guilt rose in his throat. He didn't deserve such a future. He pictured himself on the farm with the children. In his mind he saw himself and Elaine as children all those years ago. His children would know the land, even if he himself could never quite manage it. He would write his books. Philosophical treatises. Popular interpretations. Perhaps even the odd novel or too. He had been reading more and more Tolstoy. He would never claim that mantle. Of course not. Still …

Sophia would be lead cellist with the New York Philharmonic, he assured himself. She would feature as a soloist, playing Mendelssohn and Shostakovich. All would be well.

Eventually, from somewhere, Sophia manufactured a smile. She even hugged him when he stood to answer Elaine's summons from downstairs.

From the top of the stairs he saw Miriam standing just inside the door. She avoided his eyes, but cast a half smile in Elaine's direction. Elaine stood near the sitting room door, saying something about lunch being nearly ready, and asking him to organise drinks.

Charlie caught a glimpse of Sammy in the sitting room, standing to see what was going on. Perhaps that was Tiggi behind him. Charlie felt a surge of warmth towards Tiggi. What a friend she was! Things were finally working out. He cast a glance over his shoulder at Sophia, who followed him down the stairs.

Things were finally working out.

CHAPTER THIRTY-SEVEN

IT HAD BEEN AT BREAKFAST ON THAT SUNDAY MORNING THAT MIRIAM finally opened up.

Only Miriam, Mrs Pierce and Elaine were at the table. Mr Pierce was already out and about on the farm. Nobody really thought to include him in the discussion or in the decision. He had accepted Miriam's presence among them with little comment. They expected him to do the same whatever her decision might be. Elaine thought he was secretly happy to have another 'daughter' around the house. He had always said, 'Girls never fly far from the nest,' as much in hope as anything.

Miriam initiated the conversation with her usual subtlety and tact.

'This place sucks,' she said, 'but it may suck a little less than living with my brother and his wife in Australia.

'He's my brother, and he's OK, and all that, but I think what I need now is not a brother, but a …' She looked embarrassed and continued so quietly that Elaine struggled to hear.

'A what, Miriam?' It was Mrs Pierce who asked.

'A mum and dad,' Miriam repeated with some irritation.

'Ah, well. We baint quite that, love. We can never replace your parents. But we'll love you and the baby. You can be sure of that.'

And Miriam cried. A lot. Very loudly. Very messily.

'Have you told Sammy yet?' asked Elaine.

'No. No one.'

'Why not come over for lunch. I plan to cook a big lunch today. Tiggi's leaving tomorrow.'

***

The food was almost ready when Miriam knocked on the door and let herself in. Elaine came out of the kitchen to greet her, wiping her hands on her apron.

She caught herself thinking of the house as *her* house, the kitchen as *her* kitchen. How had that happened so quickly? She felt herself taking ownership. Or, rather, felt that in some sense this had always been her home. Since the first time she had stepped inside all those years ago. She fingered the pendant that still hung around her neck. The pendant Charlie's mother had given her.

'Charlie,' she called up the stairs. 'Miriam, maybe you can give me a hand with something in the kitchen. Everyone, if you'd like to take a seat in the dining room, dinner will be served in just a moment.' When Charlie appeared at the top of the stairs, she added, 'Charlie, can you organise drinks for everyone?'

It felt good to be taking charge.

Elaine paused by the sitting room door as Charlie started down the stairs, Sophia just behind him. As he caught her eye he smiled broadly, and she blushed vividly and lowered her eyes. Then she glanced back from under her fringe and smiled shyly. From the corner of her eye she noticed that Miriam caught the exchange and smiled too. Perhaps they could be friends after all.

When she looked back towards Charlie, Sophia was looking at her. She had clearly seen the exchange too, between Elaine and Charlie, and then between Elaine and Miriam. Elaine's blush deepened. She tried to send a timid smile her way. Perhaps bridges could be built in that direction too.

But Sophia's eyes were cold. No, not cold. Blazing with heat. Knives. Snake's fangs. They plunged into Charlie's back. It was almost as if he felt it. He certainly saw something change in Elaine's face and began to turn. But, before he could, Sophia's hands thrust forward.

In the instant before he fell, Charlie caught Elaine's eyes again, and Elaine flashed back and forth in time. There was Charlie, the young boy as she had first seen him, running down the stairs at his mother's summons. And there he was now, overbalancing, almost airborne. His

hands sought purchase on the bannister, but failed. His body twisted and
…

It seemed to Elaine that there was a peculiar aura around him. He seemed to flicker in and out of existence. Or perhaps she was the one whose existence faltered. She blinked, and was overcome by a wave of dizziness.

Although they fell from very different heights, Elaine always remained convinced that she and Charlie hit the floor at the same time.

AND SO WE COME TO ME.

Some fifty-five years have passed since my grandfather plummeted to the bottom of those stairs, shattering his spine. Fifty-five years confined to a wheelchair. Much has happened during those fifty-five years, yet the leap from then to now seems natural and inevitable. The leap to Bermondsey Antiques Market.

Elaine has gone. Miriam eventually returned to Australia, but she never married. I last saw her a year or so ago, during a visit there. A small, slightly shrivelled woman.

Tiggi is in a nursing home near Stratford-upon-Avon. My grandfather and I had visited her just two days earlier. Her mind is sharp though her body is failing. I can see her still, despite the crevices in her face. I still observe traces of the young woman I have seen in photographs. And I still see her love for Grandpa, too. And his love for her. He loved them all, in one way or another. Of that I'm sure.

And Sophia? I have found no trace of her during my intermittent searching over the years. If she changed her name and chose to vanish, I would not blame her.

Friday at Bermondsey Antiques Market. Grandpa chuckled as he pointed out the 'antiques' that were common items to him at one time. 'My watch is an antique,' he said, raising his hand and waving it around. '*I* am an antique.

'That stove … there was one just like it in the old cottage.'

The old cottage remains, although the kitchen has long since been renovated—gutted—to satisfy modern exigencies.

'Look there! Your grandmother used to hit me over the head with a cast-iron skillet just like that!'

There was still the faintest trace of an American accent in Grandpa's voice.

Grandpa Charlie and Grandma Elaine had only the one child. A son—my father—Abraham. I think there was both humour in that naming, and perhaps a nod of nostalgia towards Emily Kollock, my namesake.

Emily Helen Kollock. Helen for my other grandmother, Nellie. People call me Em. It's fitting that I'm the one telling this story, because, somehow, they have made me its target; its denouement. I didn't know that, of course, until that day.

Perhaps prophecies don't predict the future. Perhaps they create it.

We had wandered towards a stall of paintings and rather trashy statues, me pushing Grandpa in his wheelchair, him providing an ongoing commentary.

'I suppose some of the paintings—'

I'll never know how that sentence would have ended. Neither will you, for Grandpa stopped abruptly and looked up. Tilted his head to one side, as if hearing something.

No one will believe what happened next, because it was impossible.

I didn't see the truck. Not at first. Not until afterwards. Only then did I realise that it was white, with some writing and a logo on its side. I wouldn't know what they were until I saw the news later that night.

I didn't see it, but I did hear it. Perhaps that was what Grandpa heard, although the sound of a truck did not, of itself, seem so unusual; or enough to provoke the rapt attention on his face, or the arrow-point focus of his eyes.

Perhaps it was the rising murmur in the crowd, that turned quickly to shouts, and then screams of terror.

I did not see the truck.

But I did see Grandpa push himself up in his chair, using his arms, and then—impossibly—launching himself towards me on legs that had been unable to move or bear his weight for decades.

As he pushed me aside I saw the smile on his face. The instant of clarity. *This is the moment*, he somehow conveyed to me.

I did not have time to process this, because, as his impossible movement sent me to the pavement, a white mass, moving very quickly, ploughed through him and the stall behind him.

The van missed me by millimetres.

No one else had seen my grandfather launch himself like an arrow towards me. An arrow fired some eighty-two years ago. Only the driver of the van might have witnessed this, but he would not live to tell the tale.

Perhaps I would weep later, but for the moment I shared Grandpa's moment of recognition and triumph.

He was there, when needed, for the Daughter of Abraham.

They say only about two percent of the population has green eyes.

This is Philip's sixth published novel. Also available:

Maybe they'll remember me (2012)
Angel's Harp (2013)
Life Drawings (2013)
Christian de Palma: Man of Letters (2016)
The Woman by the Urn (2018)